Consciousness gradually returned to him as the warmth of the afternoon sun bathed his aching body, eased his tired limbs, soothed his tormented brain. He realized that, although the roar was still sounding about and beneath him, the movement had ceased, only a gentle rocking motion now affecting his perch. He remembered dimly an interminable nightmare of deafening sound and plunging motion, of drenching spray and jarring shocks, of limbs aching with the strain of holding on and of a stomach heaving with the constant stirring of the movement. He remembered his desire only for it to end.

And now it seemed that, partially at any rate, it had. He looked about him, fearful of what new terror might confront his eyes. But there was only a gently waving blur of green, flecked with dancing spots of gold where the sun reflected off the water on to the flora of the river bank. There was only the great golden star of a celandine flower nodding smilingly above his head and a steady slithering sound as an earthworm disappeared with stately langour into a hole in the earthy slope beyond. There was only quiet sound and easy motion and friendly warmth.

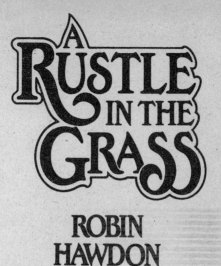

A RUSTLE IN THE GRASS

ROBIN HAWDON

TOR

A TOM DOHERTY ASSOCIATES BOOK
NEW YORK

Published by arrangement with Dodd, Mead & Company, Inc., 79 Madison
Avenue, New York, NY 10016

A TOR Book
Published by Tom Doherty Associates, Inc.
49 West 24 Street
New York, N.Y. 10010

Cover art by Allen Davis

ISBN: 0-812-50068-7   Can. ISBN: 0-812-50069-5

Library of Congress Catalog Card Number: 85-13780

First Tor edition: August 1989

Printed in the United States of America

0 9 8 7 6 5 4 3 2 1

For the three beautiful women who made the journey with me which led to this first modest destination: my wife and daughters

* 1 *

High up on a branch of a young larch tree a lone worker-ant was scurrying nervously about in the pale spring sunshine. He was a diminutive, somewhat undernourished creature, and he was investigating the corners and crevices of the bark surface with urgent intensity as if his task was a momentous one and he was unaccustomed to being entrusted with such responsibility. He was oblivious to the delicate glories of the erupting season which were manifesting themselves in a quivering display of green and silver all around. He was a part of that transformation; his energy was part of the universal energy; it was the natural way of things.

He was running along the outside ridge of a deep cranny which particularly seemed to interest him when he suddenly halted and stood with one foreleg frozen in mid-air, his feelers anxiously wavering this way and that. Yes— there it was again! The sensitive olfactory organs on his antennae had received the faintest waft of a strange, disturbing scent, borne on the frivolous breeze. He stayed,

motionless, only the tips of his antennae quivering. Then a
little jerk brought his head round, as his other senses too
picked up signals which helped to focus his attention: a
delicate vibration transmitted from the undergrowth far
beneath; a subtle alteration in the sound pattern of the
surrounding habitat. He peered anxiously down towards
the small, grass-covered mound that was his home, standing a little way off from the forest edge, near the bank of a
narrow stream. His limited vision could only just make out
the vague outline of the hump standing alongside the silver
glimmer and swirl of the running water, but as far as he
could tell nothing seemed to be amiss there. He waited in
an agony of expectancy, as if knowing that the cause of his
anxiety must reveal itself in a moment.

When it did so, it came with a terrifying positiveness.
The signals suddenly increased tenfold—as if whatever
was causing them had, at a sign, thrown caution to the
winds and was no longer trying to conceal its identity. The
ground trembled with the impact of running feet, the strange
scent pervaded the air in cloying wafts, the grasses shivered with the impact of powerful bodies. The little ant
peered down at the undergrowth's edge beneath him, as
from it, in their hundreds, broke wave after wave of huge,
reddish-coloured soldier-ants. With ferocious speed they
swept over the grassland towards the mound, crushing to
death with callous ease the few worker-ants caught out in
the open in the path. On reaching the mound they swept
over and into it in a merciless tide. The small community
stood no chance. In less time than it took the sun to pass
across one of the larch fronds above the watching ant's
head it was all over. The red horde, at ease now and
satiated, leisurely vacated the ravaged mound and disappeared back into the forest, bearing the spoils of victory
with them, and leaving no apparent sign of their coming
except for the strange, lingering scent, and the few forlorn,
stripped corpses scattered amongst the grass stems.

The chance survivor remained motionless, frozen into a
state of shocked paralysis, until the Lord of the Stars

spread his great wings across the face of the day, drawing the comfort and protection of his darkness over the scene. Then, slowly, dazedly, the ant turned and descended the tree, hesitated a moment at its base, and then turned his back on what was left of his home and set off along the river bank.

* 2 *

Winter had been, bringing with it the strange, numbed mystery of the Long Sleep—a sort of half sleep really, in which the mind floated trance-like, free from the semi-inert body, into previously unsuspected realms and dimensions. And with the Long Sleep had come his dreams—even more intense than those of his normal resting hours. As if knowing he could not escape, he met them, gave himself up to their embrace, relinquished his young soul to their whim for the duration of those long, frozen months. And this time they invariably took the same form. He was climbing. Climbing up the side of a gigantic hill. He knew not why, yet for some reason he had to reach the top. With fearful step and uncertain purpose he clung to the glowering rock, mounted the looming slope, braved the dizzying height— until at last, trembling and exhausted, he attained the summit and stood with the clouds sailing above his head and the world a distant, diminutive plateau beneath his feet.

And he called breathless into the wind: "I have come. I have arrived. I am here!"

And, as he had known it would, the Voice echoed back from the clouds: "I see you."

And he called again: "What then is your will? Why have I come? What is my purpose?"

And the Voice answered: "Your purpose? You wish to know your purpose?"

"Yes," he shouted, "what is my purpose?"

And the clouds foamed and swirled above him and the Voice murmured from their depth: "You will wander the world and find it full of mysteries: you will labour at your tasks and find them never completed; you will confront your enemies and find them not who you thought they were; you will laugh with your friends and find they are weeping; you will go on journeys and never come where you meant to come; you will seek your peace and find only more endeavours. And at the last, in the midst of the greatest endeavour of all, you may find your purpose."

The clouds rolled on and the Voice was silent. The dream faded—but only for a while.

* 3 *

Gradually, groggily, reluctantly Old Five Legs allowed himself to become aware of the subtle change in temperature and the increased activity taking place in the darkness all around him. After almost five months of comfortable semi-torpor neither his mind nor his body were willing to accept that once again reality had returned; that such things as light and darkness, hunger and thirst, warmth and cold still existed; that life was a positive, demanding thing which had to be actively challenged, not merely floated through on an undulating tide of half-consciousness. With all the caution and leisureliness of age he waited until he felt the moment was right, Then, gingerly, he stretched his rheumaticky limbs, staggered painfully to his feet, congratulated himself with his habitual surprise at having survived yet another Long Sleep, and tottered in a drunken fashion towards the Great Outside.

As he eased his large bulk somewhat irritably up the passage amongst scurrying hordes of younger worker-ants, he realized that the great colony had been coming to life for some time and that the initial eager burst of early springtime activity was in full flood. He was jostled and buffeted in the narrow tunnel, and several times exclaimed: "Watch where you're going! Out of my way!" kicking out tetchily with one or other of his five remaining limbs. This usually had the desired effect, at least temporarily, and the urgent stream of insects would hold back for a moment out of respect but then the general excitement would take hold again and he was swept along with the tide, onwards and upwards through the darkness.

Then, gradually at first, a pale light filtered through from ahead, illuminating the bobbing heads and hurrying bodies around him. It grew brighter and brighter, cruelly assaulting his unaccustomed eyes, while at the same time quickening his sense of anticipation—until suddenly he rounded a bend and it flared with direct, dazzling power all around. The floor of the passageway levelled out and broadened, the walls fell away, and Five Legs emerged, breathless and blinded, into the astonishing blaze of the morning sunshine.

He stood there at the threshold of the tunnel for a few moments, his senses readjusting themselves, his eyes peering painfully into the magical light, his antennae exploring the air for the myriad passing clues to the conditions and circumstances of the familiar surroundings.

He had emerged perhaps two-thirds of the way up the flank of the big mound, which stood in tranquil isolation beneath the overhanging branches of a beech tree, near the edge of a secluded forest clearing. Beneath him, on the well-trodden runs down the grassy sides of the mound and across the open country of the clearing, steady streams of insects were radiating out in exploratory lines. The lean, winter-deprived bodies of his own worker caste contrasted with the more powerful, scattered figures of soldier-ants, who strode about with a leisurely, authoritative gait as they organized operations and issued directions, all the time keeping a wary lookout for danger.

As Five Legs stood by his tunnel mouth, absolved by

reason of his age and authority from the general urgency, many of the passing ants recognized him, touching feelers by way of greeting, or calling out as they went: "Salutations, Five Legs," or "Greetings, old one—glad to see you're still with us!" to which he would reply with a nod of the head or a wry chuckle. Even many of the soldiers acknowledged him and moderated their normally superior demeanour as they passed.

Then another voice addressed him from behind in more familiar tones. "Come on, move yourself, you lazy brute—you can't stand there sunning yourself all day."

Five Legs felt a thrill of happy recognition and turned, extending his feelers to a wiry little ant, perhaps four summers old, who was approaching. He chuckled as their antennae embraced. "Well, well, Never-Rest, trust you to be up and about already."

"I've been out since sun-up," replied the other. "Scouted about a bit, having a look at things, pretending to be busy."

"Only pretending?" twinkled Five Legs.

"Well, I did help to bring in a moth carcass that one of the foraging parties had found." With a hint of wry sufferance he added, "They've taken it for the Royal Quarters, of course. How are you, old friend?"

"Still here, still here. And not so bad either." Five Legs resumed his gaze round the broad grassy space that was the colony's main territory. His hazy vision took in the mighty shadow of the forest edge on the far side, a short march away, rested for a moment on the familiar mass of the gorse clump to one side nearby, and moved on to the silvery green movement of the stream behind, which formed a boundary round one-third of the clearing. His reattuned senses told him that, miraculously, here too everything appeared to have survived the dark months unchanged and was trembling with newly awakened life. The enchantment of the spot touched his ancient heart once again, its spell as potent as ever.

"Wonderful," he murmured, "to see the sun again. The old place doesn't seem too much the worse for wear."

"No," said Never-Rest, "not too much damage. A few new rain gullies around, one or two branches down and a couple of trails blocked. And one of the early scouting parties has reported an oak tree fallen on the sundown side, which should provide some interesting foraging. Otherwise all much the same."

"Good, good," replied Five Legs. His antennae quivered in the breeze. "And the scent of spring in the air. It's almost enough to make one feel young again."

"Well, make the most of it while you can," said the other with a hint of sourness. "I'm told more worker-ants than usual have failed to survive the Long Sleep this time. It was a cold one. We'll have a lot of organizing to do to get everything ready before the new brood appears." He nodded back towards the face of the mound behind him. "And no doubt we'll be expected to have it all done in double-quick time, so we can then embark on some grandiose new design or other the Council dreamt up."

Five Legs declined to comment. He merely nodded and paused for a moment longer before gathering himself to make the steep descent down the hard-beaten earth of the run, which dropped beneath them through the grass stems. But just as he was about to join the busy stream of insects on the path he hesitated, with Never-Rest at his side. A strange murmuring had reached them, welling up from inside the mound. It grew and swelled, carried by the ants who were emerging from the many tunnel mouths; it spread like a ripple, a whispering, muttering, wailing tide, passed on from ant to ant: "Thunderer is dead! Thunderer is dead!"

Down the runs and along the trails radiating out across the surrounding land ran the murmur: "Thunderer is dead! Thunderer is dead!"

Along the river bank and into the forest; up the tree-trunks and through the undergrowth it travelled, until the very wind itself seemed to carry the whisper and the clouds unrolled themselves in awe at the stupendous news: "Thunderer is dead!"

Five Legs stood in numbed disbelief. Was it possible? Dead? The great leader of the colony; the mighty figure-head who commanded such unquestioning respect; who, through sheer breadth of vision and force of personality, had held his position of unchallenged supremacy for as long as any ant could remember? His still half-awakened brain could not quite grasp the enormity of the news.

At his side Never-Rest was standing rooted to the spot, uttering, "I can't believe it. I can't believe it," over and over again in an idiotic trance-like repetition. And indeed it was hard to accept. Thunderer had been the guiding-star of the colony's lifestyle, had dominated the Council's decisions, had loomed like some all-seeing parent figure, intimidating yet comforting, over the existence of every ant for so long that it seemd impossible that his gigantic energy could have been quelled forever. It should not have been really surprising of course. He was older than anyone except the Queen of Queens could conceive, and to pass quietly through the Long Sleep into the ultimate mystery of the Final Sleep was a fitting way for that great character to go. Somehow, however, he had appeared inviolate in his autocratic authority, immortal in his stern wisdom, and without him it seemed illogically as if the entire organization of the community's social structure might crumble into anarchy and disarray.

Five Legs pulled himself together and looked around him. On all sides and far below on the flat grassland the ants everywhere had frozen into a tableau of shocked disbelief at the terrible news. Then, gradually, they began to come to life again, to wander about in a state of dazed uncertainty, to mingle together in small whispering groups. Without any fixed sense of what he was going to do, Five Legs turned vaguely back towards the tunnel's entrance. At that moment however, a thin, wizened old ant emerged and came bustling up to them with a great air of urgency and agitation.

"Five Legs, there you are! I've been looking all over for you. Have you heard the news? It's true, you know. They've only just passed it up from the Council's quarters. He never awoke from the Long Sleep. The Queen of Queens has been told and the Council is gathering now to decide what to do. Word has gone out to find Black Sting and inform him. He's out there scouting somewhere." He waved an antenna towards the forest. His pointed, beady-eyed head was bobbing up and down, his feet shuffling to and fro, and his feelers shaking frantically with the excitement of it all. "We must meet too. We must get all the old ones together. We must send a deputation to the Council meeting. We'll really have to fight for ourselves now; the whole system could change!" On he rattled in breathless near panic as Five Legs nodded with calm toleration.

"Yes, Wind-Blow, we'll meet. Calm down or you'll have a seizure. Call everyone together." And he turned away and looked up to where the sun had now risen high up over the forest edge and was shining down, unchanging, unmoved, implacable.

"You see?" it seemed to be saying. "Nothing remains the same, except me. There is no permanence upon the earth. Only the need to start afresh—again, and again, and again."

Five Legs turned about and went below.

* 4 *

Dreamer was almost the last member of the entire colony to hear the news. He had been dispatched on a lonely mission: one of a number of single ants sent scouting far afield to discover whether any dramatic events or changes in the terrain had taken place during the winter months. It was a solitary task, and not without its dangers: a lone ant at this eager, avaricious time of year could fall prey to all sorts of perils, especially during the daytime. Ants prefer to travel at night because of their poor eyesight and keen antennae, and it is the time when the Lord of the Stars holds sway over the earth—the twinkling points of light in the heavens being his thousand watchful eyes—before he allows the sun and the keen-eyed predators to have their necessary moment. However, Dreamer was glad to be travelling in the increasing warmth of daytime. To be wandering free and self-reliant across the waking land was a miraculous experience after the dark, hallucinatory months of the Long Sleep. He strode out with a lithe, eager step, antennae alert for every tremor, every scent, every minute sound from the surrounding habitat.

He was not a particular distinctive figure as ants go. He was of modest size for a soldier, and his relatively youthful age—this was only his second spring—and low ranking gave him no great air of authority. His slender body was evidently built for speed rather than robustness, and there was nothing remarkable about the size of either mandibles or sting to mark him out as an adversary to beware of. The one distinguishing feature was his antennae. Unusually long and supple, they explored the air with a positive, curving grace which indicated a high degree of sensitivity and precision in function. Indeed the main characteristic of Dreamer's whole personality was awareness; an eager, slightly uncertain curiosity and consciousness about everything that went on around him. It contrasted oddly with a certain reserve in his make-up, a caution, almost an aloofness which kept him apart from the majority of his associates; a background figure, a watcher, a waiter. On the whole they mistrusted him for it, or at least were wary of him, for detachment is not a quality ants are at ease with. And this mistrust was, if anything, increased by another idiosyncracy which only manifested itself when he was asleep, when his whisperings, shivers and tiny spasms were an outward indication of the workings of his subconscious mind. It was this further strange and secret mental activity which had earned him, from his curious and sometimes amused fellows, his otherwise somewhat inappropriate name.

He was now some half-morning's journey from the base mound, heading upstream, following the faint insect trail which threaded its way through the stems of the narrow strip of grassland between water and forest. He had left shortly after dawn, in the midst of the earlier burst of waking activity, and had only been able to fill his crop with a few dried seeds and scraps from the almost exhausted winter food stores, so his long-fasted body was now feeling compulsive hunger pangs. It was animal protein in particular that he craved, and his scent organs were alert for evidence of a source. He knew it should not take him long to find one: the earth was busy with newly aroused life in all its forms; the grasses resounded with the scurrying of insect feet, the air hummed with the beat of diaphanous wings. For the most part such individuals abroad paid little attention to each other, beyond keeping a cautious distance apart—they were mostly concerned with avoiding hunters of a larger and feathered kind—but now and then a sudden fierce rustle amongst the vegetation, or the silver flash of dew on a shaking web of silent threads suspended above his head, told Dreamer that other creatures beside himself had a long period of starvation to make up for.

Suddenly he stopped, his feelers quivering. He had caught a whiff of one of the scents he had been seeking. He crept cautiously off the track to one side, and threaded his way with delicate step through the grass stalks. Now he could hear sounds which confirmed his suspicions: a nervous scrabbling and the patter of falling earth particles. He emerged from behind the cover of a dandelion plant, and there in front of him a little ground beetle was frantically covering her new-laid batch of eggs in their hiding place in the soft soil. So engrossed with her task was she that she was quite unaware of his approach, and he carefully scanned the surrounding scent for other sources of danger, before warning her of his presence. This he did by simply moving round until he came within her field of vision, which also, coincidentally, brought him upwind of her, his scent reaching her at the same time. She stopped her activity instantly, stared in his direction and chattered at him angrily. He moved slowly towards her, his sting curved warningly forward underneath his body. She redoubled her irate chatter, waving her puny mandibles in his direction in a futile show of aggression, but then, when she saw that he was not to be deterred, she slowly backed away from the half-covered nest of eggs. He slipped forward and seized one of the soft, succulent globes between his mandibles.

Watching the furious ground beetle warily, he swallowed the egg whole, gulping it down to his food crop as a future source of nourishment. Then he took another, and this time clutching it in his jaws, backed away from the nest leaving the indignant mother to return and hurriedly complete her tasks of concealment, all the while continuing her stream of outraged invective at the thief.

Dreamer backed off amongst the grasses once more and found himself a secluded spot under a clover leaf where he consumed the second egg at leisure. It was the first fresh food he had tasted in over four months and he savoured the experience, biting leisurely into the nutritious texture, swallowing it with indulgent relish. When he had finished the last morsel he cleaned off his mandibles and antennae with his hair-covered forelegs, paused a moment to enjoy the sensation of a full stomach and renewed energy, and then made his way back towards the trail.

Reaching the path, he was about to step out on to it from the protective cover of the grasses when something made him withdraw. He had caught the sound of a creature approaching from ahead up the track. He slid behind a thicket of stems and waited, his body crouched low on the ground to withhold his scent from the ubiquitous air currents. The sounds grew nearer. Whatever was making them was a smallish being, judging by the vibration strength of its footfalls, yet it seemed strangely incautious, hurrying along with erratic steps and nervous panting breath. Dreamer stayed motionless until he caught a waft of the other's scent, which came before any visual glimpse. It told him several things. The creature was an ant—of his own species but not from his colony. All members of the same colony have a distinctive scent, produced by the particular Queen from whom they are descended, which ensures instant identification. There is also a subtle difference between the scent of the various castes, caused by the varying maturation periods of the young ants in their larval stages. Worker-ants, for instance, are hatched out before the winter comes, or just after it is over, whereas the larvae of future soldier-ants are left to mature and develop throughout the winter and spring and to hatch in the more plentiful time of year. The approaching ant was a worker.

Dreamer waited until he caught a glimpse through the grass stems, and then he stepped out on to the path in front of him. The other, a small, bedraggled creature in an evident state of exhaustion and distress, halted and shied back in terror. Then, realizing that Dreamer was not a foe, he gasped with relief and approached urgently. Dreamer surveyed his tottering stance and mud-spattered body and spoke gently.

"Where are you from? What is the trouble?"

The ant answered in a breathless, disjointed gabble: "It was red ants . . . killers . . . hundreds of them! Came out of the forest . . . overran the whole colony . . . killed everyone . . . including our Queen . . . stole all the larvae . . . ransacked everywhere!" His antennae were waving frantically in his agitation. "I saw it all . . . I was up a tree, scouting for a new spring pasture for our aphid-bug herd . . . none of them bothered to go that high . . . but I saw everything . . . they just appeared . . . hundreds of them . . . soldiers, every one . . . very big . . . and they just killed . . . and killed and killed!" On and on he chattered in a compulsive stream of half-completed phrases. It was as if the trauma of the experience had lain and fermented inside him throughout his night of sleepless journeying, until now at last, when he had met someone to whom he could unburden himself of his awful tale, it came pouring out in an unstoppable, near hysterical flood.

Dreamer listened in silence. He did not question, he did not interrupt, he did not move. He had never heard such a harrowing description, first-hand, in all his relatively short life. He was used of course to witnessing conflict and death. He had been educated and trained in the violent and ruthless ways of Nature—such processes were accepted as an inevitable and necessary part of any insect's life—but he had never before encountered such an example of wanton, indiscriminate slaughter, such a vivid incidence of ruthless aggression. He was able to picture the scene with distressing clarity, for he was familiar with the location of the massacre. The colony was a small, single-Queen settlement about a night's march from his own home. It was one of a number of lesser satellite mounds situated on the fringe of the major colony's territory, a night's march being the maximum distance any ant will usually venture from his base, thus necessitating never more than a night and day's absence. The presence of these mounds was permitted by tacit agreement, providing, as it did, mutual benefits for all: the smaller colonies acting as lookout posts and warning systems for the central mound, whilst receiving a degree of protection in return. And now this harmless, unpretentious little community was no more.

Dreamer stood motionless, but inside he was a mass of unfamiliar emotions. It was as if he had had a revelation; as if the disclosure that there was naked, apparently purposeless Evil in the universe had come as a new realization to his innocent, hitherto trusting self. The world had seemed a basically benign place—fierce, yes; competitive, hazardous—but only out of necessity, only as an essential condition of the system of existence. Now, suddenly, he was aware that there were elements at work other than mere natural forces; that somewhere within the Lord of the Stars' domain differing codes were in operation, a moral debate existed. It was a momentous discovery.

He waited until the little worker-ant had talked himself out and was standing in silence, drained and exhausted; then he touched the other's feelers reassuringly with his own and said gently, "All right. We must go and warn my colony. We must inform the leaders. Follow me." And he turned and led the way back at as good a pace as the smaller ant could manage.

∗ 5 ∗

"Here comes Black Sting! Black Sting is returning!"
The relieved whisper rippled around the clearing and up
into the mound, where life was gradually coming back to
normal and work had commenced again, albeit with some
reluctance and lack of purpose.

Out of the trees and across the grassland, followed by
his two habitual attendants, came running the most magnificent of ants. Powerfully built, yet with the long legs
and sinewy thorax that indicated great speed and agility;
fiercely curving mandibles carried high on a sternly arrogant head; and behind, the long, lethal, darkly coloured
sting that gave him his name—the commander of the
soldiers was indeed a formidable looking individual. It was
not merely that he was a splendid physical specimen; there
was too a certain grandeur about his personality—a directness and an authority which seemed to say that destiny,
however awesome it might appear, whatever terrors it
might present, would never intimidate him.

Behind, his two lieutenants were as easily recognizable

as himself. One was a huge, squat creature, lumbering on thick, short legs, which at this moment were having considerable difficulty in enabling him to keep up. There was an expression of ironic complacency on his massive head, which advertised that he had nothing to fear from any source, and no one to answer to. Named Dew-Lover, on account of his fondness for honey-dew—that great opiate of ants everywhere—he was perhaps the most feared personality in the colony, because of his gigantic strength and his lack of qualms about using it, though none would deny that this entitled him to his rank: in the ant world, might is irrefutable right.

The other was Snake's Tongue. An extraordinarily long, lean insect, he was named not only for his lighting speed and reactions in battle but also for his habit of maintaining an enigmatic silence in company and then suddenly breaking it with a quietly delivered observation which went to the heart of the matter with a directness that some found uncomfortable.

This impressive threesome had been located on their scouting trip off in the forest somewhere, and, having been informed of the death of Thunderer, were returning urgently for the emergency meeting of the Council that would inevitably follow. Worker- and soldier-ants on their path stood aside respectfully to let them pass, and as he came Black Sting took careful note of their apprehensive expressions.

We shall have to move fast, he observed to himself, or the colony's morale will fall to pieces. The thought was a disturbing one for him. It was not just that he possessed the good soldier's practical regard for the well-being of those in his command. Behind Black Sting's forbidding exterior there lay a real concern; he cared with a fierce patriotism for the welfare of the community with whose protection he was entrusted. In his proud and autocratic way he was an intensely moral being.

The three had reached the mound and were now ascending the lower slopes. On their way up they passed a group of older worker-ants gathering together, nodding and muttering amongst themselves. They were centered around Old Five Legs, whose gnarled frame bulked solidly in their midst, a focal point of calm imperturbability. Black Sting took note of those present as he drew level.

The worker-ants' leaders getting together to discuss the situation, he thought. Doubtless they'll want a say at the Council meeting. We must be prepared for that. He nodded briefly to Five Legs as he passed, receiving a deferential wave of the antennae in return. At least we can rely on him to keep his head, he reflected.

A moment later Dew-Lover's harsh, growling voice made him stop and turn. The huge ant had turned aside to the gathering of workers and was accosting them in his usual gruffly intimidating manner: "All right, let's get back to work shall we? There's no need to stand around all day talking about it. Leave that to the Council."

He waved his ponderous feelers at them imperiously and the little group began to break up with glowering, resentful glances.

"It's all right, Dew-Lover," said Black Sting quietly. "These are special circumstances. I think we can allow some discussion."

The big ant lumbered over to him, and growled, "We don't want to let them do too much discussing. They might start getting ideas."

Black Sting glanced at the group, who were hesitating uncertainly. "Better they should do it in the open than in secret," he said. "After all, they are bound to have their feelings about the occasion."

"That's what worries me," muttered the other.

Snake's Tongue was standing, impassively observing the situation. He offered no comment. Black Sting looked at Dew-Lover with a hint of amusement.

"Who knows," he said. "They might have some useful suggestions to make." He turned away. "Come, I want to address the office before going on to the Council meeting. They too will no doubt be having their feelings." And he

continued on up the slope, forcing the other two to follow
and leave the old workers to resume their meeting.

They soon reached one of the tunnel mouths, where a
milling crowd of ants fell back to let them pass. The little
group entered the darkness of the passageway where, with
the effectiveness of the keenest eyesight, their antennae
took over full responsibility for guiding them. They sped
down the well-trodden route, threading their way through
the busy throng, past the openings to ventilation and drainage shafts, dwelling and storage chambers and the mouths
of other linking tunnels, until a subtle change in temperature and in the texture of the earthen walls told them that
they were below the outside ground level. Here the angle
of the tunnel was not so steep but the maze of intercon-
necting passages and chambers was even more complex.
The thoroughfares were not so crowded now, for these
were regions where only the most illustrious and privileged
denizens came with regularity, and the traffic consisted
mostly of senior citizens, Council members and high-
ranking soldiers, almost all moving in the same downhill
direction.

The three soldiers came to a major junction of tunnels,
where Black Sting turned off from the main stream of ants,
travelled a little way further and then entered a wide
chamber. Here, as in many of the larger communal chambers, a direct ventilation shaft admitted a very faint light,
and by this he could see that most of his officers were
already gathered, conversing together in groups, the sound
of their tense discussion filling the air. At the entrance of
the three this talk rapidly ceased, a hush fell over the
assembly and a space was automatically cleared in the
centre of the floor. Black Sting strode into the space, his
antennae held aloft, his eyes firmly scanning the gathering
in a deliberate show of resolute confidence. He spoke with
brisk authority.

"You have all heard the news. Great Thunderer is no
longer with us." He paused momentarily and looked steadily round the chamber. Not a limb moved, not a breath

was heard. "His reign has given us a long period of stability and prosperity. But inevitably his passing leaves us with an alarming gap in the chain of authority. I have often pressed for a delegation of power to prepare us for this very eventuality, but such was Thunderer's domain in the Council that it never came about, and so now we are caught at the end of this Long Sleep in a state of dangerous vulnerability." Once more he looked around at the assembled ants. "The responsibility is with us soldiers to maintain the discipline and security of the whole colony until such time as the succession has been decided. I want you all to be on your guard. I want you to listen for any signs of discontent. I want you to watch for hints of insurrection from any direction. We must preserve the traditions and the strength of our community at all costs. I know I can count on your loyalty."

He finished speaking and there was a moment's pensive silence in the chamber. Then an ant in the front of the throng spoke up. "Will Great Head now take over the leadership of the Council?"

Black Sting nodded. "For the moment. But he is old now also, and his energy is fading. I know he will not want to take all the responsibility of power on his back for long."

"Who then is there to take his place?" asked another voice.

"That is what has to be decided," replied Black Sting. "It may be that we have to evolve a new system of command now that Thunderer is no longer here. It may be that a new figurehead will arise. Who knows." A fleeting sparkle of amusement crossed his features. "No doubt there will be a lot of hot wind and thunder before it is decided."

"I think you should be the one to take command, leader," said a third member of the ranks, and at this there was a general murmur of agreement and nodding of heads, as if all had been thinking the same thing but none had agreed to say it.

Black Sting paused a moment before answering. "Thank you, but I am a soldier, not a debater. I prefer the battles of the forest to those of the Council chamber. However, we shall see. Are there any more questions?"

There was silence. He looked once more round the chamber, then turned and strode out, with Dew-Lover and Snake's Tongue following.

The Council chamber was the largest single space in the whole complex network that made up the colony. It was a splendid domed cavity carved out of the solid earth, with passageways entering at intervals all round and in the roof, the openings to a series of ventilation shafts, which permitted a continuous circulation of fresh air as well as admitting a dim illumination. The chamber was capable of accommodating perhaps two hundred ants, but was rarely used to full capacity. The Inner Council consisted of about thirty of the most distinguished elders, but on important occasions, when the consultation of a larger circle was required, there would be perhaps twice that number present. At rare times, such as today, when the life of the whole settlement was affected, every ant with any influence or prestige at all, from whatever class of society, was present. Whatever class, that is, except the highest. The Queen of Queens and her progeny, the young Queens, never interfered directly in affairs of government. She, however, expected to be kept fully informed of any developments or decisions and everyone was aware that she possessed the ultimate right of veto over any ruling the Council might make. Consequently her all-wise, all-knowing regal influence was always a powerfully felt entity in the chamber.

The other body which was never directly represented at normal Council meetings was that of the common worker-ants—the most lowly and the most numerous caste of all, consisting as they did of perhaps two-thirds of the entire population of the colony—and it was only on very rare, extraordinary occasions such as this that they were grudgingly permitted to send a deputation to the proceedings.

As Black Sting and his two subordinates approached this great meeting place they could hear the murmur of many voices and catch the mingled scents which indicated that the majority were already assembled. At the entrance to the chamber, two of the Royal Guard, distinguished by the pale colour and distinctive scent caused by their constant underground life, stood guard. At Black Sting's approach they saluted by withdrawing their antennae and stood aside. Black Sting acknowledged them with a cursory nod and strode into the chamber. Dew-Lover sneered disdainfully at them as he passed and Snake's Tongue followed close behind.

Black Sting paused on the threshold and took in the tense, expectant atmosphere, the bobbing heads, the nervous buzz of lowered voices. The packed throng was massed around the walls, leaving a space free in the centre of the floor. He could make out the various figures of the most venerable elders in the front ranks surrounding the space. On the far side a group of officers of the Royal Guard were centered around the tall, virile form of their captain, Noble, Black Sting's opposite number in that elite body. The latter caught Black Sting's eye at that moment and nodded his recogniton. Black Sting curled his antennae in a return salute and then made his way to the front rank on his side, followed by his two companions. There was a slight lowering of the general hum of conversation as the assembly became aware of his entrance, and then the talk picked up again and Black Sting himself was soon engaged in discussion by a group of elders at the edge of the floor. The proceedings had not yet begun and there was a powerful feeling of apprehension within the chamber.

Then there came a sudden hush in the babble of talk, as two of the Royal Guards entered from one of the passageways and cleared a path through the crowd. Behind them, at the slow pace of the very aged, came the three ants who had been the Thunderer's closest associates and advisors. First was Great Head, now the community's oldest and most high-ranking Council member and immediately recognizable by his enormous skull supported precariously and somewhat incongruously on a rickety, fragile body. It was said that Great Head was at least six summers old, though none knew for sure, and his vast knowledge of the world had been of invaluable help to Thunderer during his period of supremacy. Behind him shuffled One Feeler, who in his distant youth had lost an antennae in a battle with a rove beetle; and Mutterer, so-called on account of his somewhat senile habit of muttering aloud to himself when agitated. The three came to the forefront of the expectant gathering, murmured for a brief moment with some of the other elders there, and then Great Head detached himself and waddled slowly into the centre of the chamber floor. The silence was almost tangible as the crowded ranks waited for him to speak. After gazing slowly and steadily round the chamber, he did so, his quivering old voice suffused with a sadness that affected every ant who heard it.

"Friends. Thunderer is gone. His great heart is stilled. His mighty voice will be heard no more in this chamber. His implacable will can guide us no longer through the obstacles and dangers of the world outside. He was not perhaps the most lovable of ants—his enormous energies left him no time for the pursuit of such trivialities as the affection of others. Yet I for one feel a greater sadness to his passing than if I had lost my dearest friend or closest blood relatives. For with him has passed away a whole era in our colony's history. With him has gone a great part of the moral substance that has bound our community together. We have come to rely on his strength over the summers more than is perhaps healthy for a society such as ours that is so vulnerable to dangers from without. Our task now is to find a replacement for that strength. It will not be easy." Great Head paused and again looked slowly round the assembly.

"For the present I shall continue to preside over the Inner Council, and together we shall carry on the process of rule. But it is not in my nature to take the ultimate

responsibility of leadership—quite apart from the fact that
I am now too old and too tired—so therefore, before long,
there will have to emerge a new leader, and if necessary a
new system, to replace those which have served us so well
for so long.'' There was a gentle buzz of conversation,
quickly silenced as he continued. ''Our Great Mother, the
Queen of Queens, has asked me to convey her grief at our
loss, which she perhaps feels more keenly than any of us,
and to assure you of her faith in us all to surmount this
crisis. I now leave the floor free for anyone who wishes to
speak.''

As Great Head shuffled slowly back to his place there
was a hushed moment of expectancy. Then a low murmur
of discussion again broke out around the chamber. At first
it seemed that no one was eager to take up the old ant's
invitation. Many were looking expectantly in Black Sting's
direction, but for the moment he seemed quite content to
stay where he was. On the opposite side the captain of the
Royal Guard, Noble, also seemed unwilling to be the first
to take the floor. Then there came a lull once more, caused
by a movement amongst the ants at the rear, behind where
Black Sting was standing. Someone was pushing his way to
the front, but whoever it was was evidently having difficulty in getting through, for his progress was slow and
laborious, accompanied by a certain amount of jostling and
explaining as it seemed that the ants in his path were not
willingly making way for him. Eventually, however, he
reached the front and broke through to the centre of the
floor. It was only then that Black Sting realized with
surprise that it was Old Five Legs.

Out of the company of his fellow worker-ants, and in
the midst of so many larger-built leaders and soldiers, the
old ant did not seem nearly such a dominant figure. Indeed, he appeared distinctly insignificant and fragile as,
puffing somewhat from his exertions at getting through the
crowd, he limped slowly to the centre of the floor. The
silence was one of astonished curiosity as he peered awkwardly round at the assembly. Rarely in living memory

has a member of the worker caste dared to take the Council floor at all, let alone be the first to do so after the leader. When he spoke there was a certain diffidence mingled with the usual bluff directness in his voice.

"It is perhaps not my place to speak first after Great Head, if indeed to speak at all." He cleared his throat gruffly to cover his embarrassment at being stared at by so many curious, and often openly disapproving faces. "I am but a common worker-ant and this is only the third time in my life that I have been admitted to this great chamber. However . . ."—he paused for a moment as if to determine how best to express what he wanted to say—"However, that life has been a good bit longer than that of some here at this moment and I do represent the feelings of many of my fellow worker-ants, who after all make up the majority of the citizens of this colony—humble though we may be—so I would like to get in what I have to say before the floor is taken over by more illustrious speakers than myself." There was the faintest glimmer of amusement in his eyes as he added, "And before I lose my nerve at being the centre of attention of so many distinguished personages." This little jest appeared to give him confidence, for he raised his head now and continued with more of his usual directness.

"My name—with which a few of you may be unfamiliar— is Five Legs. It is so for a fairly obvious reason. My name before I lost my sixth leg—crushed under a falling stone during the building of the new brood chambers two summers ago—was Blunt, also for an obvious reason. And if you will permit me, I wish to be blunt with you now. I and my fellow workers were as shocked as any of you here at the death of Great Thunderer. He was in all ways a remarkable ant. However, in our case the general reaction to the news was, despite ourselves, somewhat mixed. There is no doubt that Thunderer's rule has given the colony a long period of stability and, for some, prosperity. But it is also true that under him we worker-ants experienced a certain amount of hardship, and, in some ways, deprivation.''

A buzz of indignant reaction went round the chamber at this. Five Legs, however, continued as if he hadn't heard.

"It is we who have had to carry out the heavy labour entailed in his far-seeing plans for the extension of the colony's boundaries; it is we who have had to do the construction work on the enlargement of the base mound and the quarters beneath; it is we who have had to keep supplied the splendid, but numerous force of soldiers and of Royal Guard that he insisted be maintained; it is we who have served the large Royal Staff that is only fitting the Queens of such an illustrious colony should retain. All this of course is right and proper. It is for such duties that we exist. Just at it is right and proper that it should be we who dwell in the quarters most vulnerable to the extremes of heat and cold, frost and rain; it should be we who go without when food runs short, it should be we who are most exposed to the dangers of predators during our daily routines. Yet . . ."—he paused momentarily—"despite all this, we have no say in the Council, no right to express our desires through that body to the Queen of Queens, no influence in any way over the decisions that condition our own lives.''

Once more he paused and looked around the now silent gathering.

"I assure you that in no way do we wish to challenge the existing order, nor to threaten the security of the colony as a whole. We are very conscious that we *are* only humble workers, and that it is such security which provides us with our livelihood. We are only asking that in the new order we may have a voice in the decisions which affect that livelihood. In other words . . ."—he hesitated, as if knowing the effect his next statement would produce—"for a small representation within the Council itself. Thank you for your attention." And he was limping back to his place in the crowd before the reaction could commence.

When it did come it was like a thunderclap—an explo-

sion of protest and outrage. Worker-ant representation on
the Council! Never before had such a proposition been
voiced anywhere in public, let alone within this hallowed
place itself. An indignant babble of talk reverberated round
the chamber, no one being quite sure how to react.

Black Sting too felt the general indignation. It was not
that he considered the suggestion morally indefensible;
merely that it was irresponsible to challenge the existing
order of things at such a delicate moment; that the scheme
of things had been ordained with a specific purpose in
mind, and one tampered with it at one's peril. He stepped
into the open space and the tumult gradually died away.
He spoke with quiet deliberation.

"There was a time when such a demand as we have just
heard would have been punished by instant death." He
waited to let the ripple of agreement die away. "However,
we live in more tolerant times now. I do not wish to
pre-empt the Council's judgement on this matter by discussing it at length here. I say only this: the Council exists
solely to fulfill the needs and desires of our great Queen of
Queens and of her present and future progeny, for it is
upon them that the whole future of our colony depends.
For the same reasons, the workers exist solely to fulfill the
needs and desires of the Council. It is not . . ."—and he
paused deliberately to add significance to his words—"the
other way round."

A loud murmur of agreement and applause ran round the
chamber. Black Sting glanced round to the spot from
which Old Five Legs had made his appearance, but there
was no sign of him or any other of the small group of
workers who had accompanied him, merely a little ripple
of movement fading out by one of the tunnel entrances.
Their mission having been accomplished, they had evidently slipped quietly away without waiting to hear the
response. Black Sting put the incident out of his mind for
the moment and turned back to speak of other matters.

"I wish now to mention a proposal of my own for the
Council's consideration. Now that the major work of the

last few years on the development and extension of our
colony has been completed, I am of the opinion that my
force of soldiers, splendid fighters that they are, is not
sufficient for the protection of such a major and extensive
habitation. I would like to suggest to the Council that they
make request to Our Great Mother to designate a larger
than usual portion of this year's brood for development
and training as soldiers, for my force." He paused briefly,
then added significantly. "From the last speaker's remarks
it might appear that there is now an even greater necessity
for such reinforcements." And he strode back to his place
to a general murmur of agreement and nodding of heads.

Immediately, however, this was stilled as the tall, pale,
aristocratic figure of Noble stepped to the centre of the
floor. The captain of the Royal Guard spoke with a cool,
almost languid tone. "In the light of Black Sting's suggestion, may I remind the Council that it was always Thunderer's policy, fully endorsed by Our Great Mother, that
the forces of the ordinary soldiers should at all times be
balanced as exactly as possible by those of the Royal
Guard. I do not need to explain to any of you the very
prudent reasoning behind this policy." And, with a non-
chalant glance at Black Sting, he returned to his place.

There was a further mutter of discussion around the
chamber. It was evident that battle lines were already
being drawn up in the contest for power. The Council
prepared itself for a long debate, and various of the more
elderly members settled themselves to snooze.

* 6 *

Dreamer and the little worker-ant from the riverside colony had reached the mound and were now descending one of the tunnels inside. They had learned of the death of Thunderer as they approached. It had come as a shock to Dreamer, but one in which the element of surprise was strangely lacking. He felt grief, yes, at the passing of a great one. A sense of gratitude too that the Lord of the Stars had endowed the earth with so splendid a life, and had only now chosen to take it back when its finest purposes were completed. And perhaps some apprehension—for what was now to take its place? But no surprise. Rather an expectancy, an anticipation, as he had known that such a momentous event was due, that life could not indefinitely have continued its calm route as it had done before, and that, now the disruption had occurred, the pattern was free to unfold itself once more; and that furthermore he himself had a part to play in that pattern.

Now he was hurrying towards the Council chamber bringing news of still further gravity. He was apprehensive as he reached the passages below ground level, the little ant scurrying nervous and weary behind him. Dreamer had never before entered the Council chamber; rarely even descended to these regions, which were now relatively empty as so many of their habitants were at the meeting. But he knew that it was his duty to convey such tidings to the Council immediately.

He could sense the distant noise and activity emanating from the chamber as he descended towards it, and his apprehension was tempered by his curiosity concerning that great meeting place. His general sense of excitement increased as the tunnel widened out in front of him and the faint light from the chamber filtered through, silhouetting the two Royal Guards standing at the entrance. He beckoned with his antennae to the little worker-ant to stay close behind him and marched with as much confidence as he could muster up to the two sentries, who instantly barred his way with raised mandibles.

"I have a messenger with urgent news for the Council," said Dreamer. "It is vital they hear it immediately."

The two Royal Guards flickered their antennae cautiously towards Dreamer and his companion, seeking for alien scents or suspicious nervous secretions but, finding nothing ominous in such an insignificant pair, they drew back and allowed them to pass. For the first time in his life Dreamer entered the legendary place where the debates and decisions that governed the whole existence of the colony took place.

At that particular moment, the ancient Mutterer was holding the centre of the floor with a long, rambling, disconnected reflection concerning some moral point or other. Most of his listeners were showing distinct signs of restlessness as Dreamer pushed his way apologetically through the crowd, followed by the diminutive worker, who was by now in a state of dazed stupefaction at the momentousness of all that was happening to him. As they reached the open floor, and Dreamer led the way round the edge to where he could see Black Sting standing, there was quickening of interest and a craning of heads at the untoward intrusion. Old Mutterer continued his discourse, apparently unaware that he had by now totally lost the attention of his listeners.

Dreamer went straight up to his commander, with whom, in his brief life, he had previously had but little direct communication. He withdrew his antennae in the customary salute as Black Sting stared at him with quizzical curiosity.

"I'm sorry to intrude upon the Council meeting, sir. I was out on a scouting mission and I met this worker from the riverside mound. His colony was overrun by alien ants yesterday. He says all except himself have been killed. I thought the Council should be informed."

Black Sting gazed at him steadily. Then he looked towards the bemused little ant at Dreamer's side. Dreamer could sense him assessing the implications of the statement.

"Follow me," said Black Sting in a calm voice, and led the way across the floor to where Great Head stood with One Feeler at his side. All eyes were upon them, and even Mutterer finally became aware that something was happening and faltered to a stop in mid-sentence.

"I apologize for interrupting the debate, Great Head," said Black Sting, "but one of my soldiers has brought in a messenger with news that I think the whole Council should hear. May I ask him to relate it to you?"

Great Head inclined his huge cranium in consent. Black Sting turned to the little ant.

"Tell the elders your story," he said in gentle tones.

The poor creature stared at him, as if struck dumb at the immensity of the request. Black Sting waved him forward with his antennae towards Great Head. "Come, don't be nervous."

The worker-ant stumbled a few steps forward and began to mumble incoherently. Great Head stopped him and said, "Speak up. There is nothing to be afraid of. We all want to hear."

The other looked around, petrified at being the object of

so many inquisitive stares. Finally he began to speak in a breathless gabble, telling the story he had related to Dreamer. There was not a sound in the chamber as all strained to catch his tumbling, confused words. And, when finally he had finished and his voice had trailed away, the hush continued as imagination recreated the details of the events he had described.

Black Sting was the first to make a move. With characteristic decisiveness he turned to Great Head and requested his permission to ask some questions. The old ant nodded his consent. Black Sting turned to Dreamer.

"Dreamer, isn't it?" he enquired in a low voice, and then asked about the circumstances of Dreamer's meeting with the other ant. Then he turned to the worker himself and questioned him closely about the attack; requesting specific details concerning the red ants, their approach, physical characteristics and numbers. All this was done in low, gentle tones, so that only Dreamer and the immediate elders were able to hear the conversation. Then Black Sting turned once more to Great Head, held a brief, whispered discussion with him and finally wheeled around, signalled to Dreamer to follow him and, beckoning to Dew-Lover and Snake's Tongue, crossed the chamber towards one of the entrances.

The four ants entered the darkness of the tunnel as a babble of discussion broke out in the chamber behind them. They travelled only a few paces, enough to be out of the hearing of the Royal Guards at the entrance, when Black Sting stopped and waited for the other three to catch up. He addressed Dreamer first.

"Well done, Dreamer," he said. "You were right to come straight to the Council." Then he turned abruptly to his two lieutenants.

"Let us speak here, for I don't wish to leave the Council chamber for long," he said in a low voice. "I don't have to tell you that this is a serious matter. If the red ants have reached the river mound, it must mean that their own base cannot be too far beyond it. And if they are openly attacking other colonies, it means that they are intent on extending their domain. Which in turn means that eventually they will come to us.''

He paused to let the full significance sink in. Dreamer had the impression that he had been forgotten. He waited awkwardly, not knowing whether he had been dismissed or was expected to stay, but he was caught between the Council chamber to his rear and the three officers in the front and so had little alternative but to stand and listen. Black Sting continued.

''No member of this colony has ever explored far beyond the riverside mound, and although ants from that base itself have gone further, none has yet come across the red ants' own base. It is presumably, therefore, somewhat further than a night's march beyond, and its members either travel very fast or are prepared to camp out on their expeditions. It's essential that we discover how far off, and how large their colony is. Also something about their habits. The fact that they carried off the larvae from the other colony may either mean that they want them for food or that they intend to use them for slave-breeding purposes. Neither possibility bodes well for us here.'' He turned to Snake's Tongue.

''I have a mission for you, Snake's Tongue. I select you because of all my soldiers, you stand the best chance of succeeding. But it involves great danger, and is one from which you may perhaps never return.'' He paused. Snake's Tongue showed no sign, merely stood waiting. ''I want you to select two soldiers to accompany you. Choose them with care, because your safety will depend on their skill and courage as much as on your own. I want the three of you to fill your food crops to capacity—since you can't be certain of finding easy food where the red ants have been— and then I want you to set off with all speed to the riverside mound, and from there to follow the red ants' trail, day and night for as long as you have to, until you find their base. I want you to discover how large their base is, how numerous its population, how strong its force of

soldiers and how much territory it already controls. I want
you to study their foraging habits, their fighting methods,
their system of command—anything you think it may be
useful for us to know. And then I want you to return as
fast as you can with your information.''

Black Sting paused again. "It may be that you have to
sacrifice one or more of your members in order that the
last member may get back, in which case you must do so
without hesitation. Nothing is more important than that the
knowledge you acquire reaches us and enables us to prepare for whatever danger is threatening. Do you understand?''

"Yes," said Snake's Tongue simply.

"Good," said Black Sting. "Do you know who you
wish to take with you? You may choose whoever you
wish.''

There was a brief pause as Snake's Tongue pondered the
matter, and in that moment Dreamer made the rashest
move he had ever made in his life. He did not know what
prompted him, except that somewhere deep in his innermost being he knew that his impulse was right; that his
heart approved of the challenge responded to. He stepped
forward and spoke in a firm voice.

"I would like to go with Snake's Tongue, sir.''

A silence greeted his words. He could sense the three
powerful ants considering their startled reactions to his
impetuous statement. Dew-Lover was the first to break the
silence with a snort of amusement.

"Like to go too, would he? That'll put the wind up the
red ants all right!''

Black Sting spoke quietly. "I'd forgotten you were
there, Dreamer. Why do you wish to go?''

"I feel I could be of use," said Dreamer simply.

Again Dew-Lover roared his amusement. "You can't
dream your way there, you know," he guffawed. "It's
going to mean real soldier's work.''

"I know," replied Dreamer in a low voice.

Again a pause. Dreamer could almost feel both Black

Sting and Snake's Tongue summing him up through the darkness.

"I am told you are a good soldier," said Black Sting.

Dreamer was surprised that the most respected fighting ant in the whole community should have even heard of his merits. Black Sting was continuing: "They say you have unusually keen senses."

"I was lucky to have been born with long feelers," answered Dreamer humbly.

"Long feelers can't help you in a fight," growled Dew-Lover.

"I hope that fighting will be the least of the expedition's activities," replied Black Sting. "Otherwise I would have put you in charge, Dew-Lover." He turned to Snake's Tongue. "Well, Snake's Tongue? The decision must be yours."

Snake's Tongue had not uttered a word throughout the entire conversation and still there was no sign from him. Only his scent betrayed that he was there at all in the darkness. Then Dreamer sensed a tiny movement in the black. He did not know what it was—a delicate air-tremor, the faintest of sounds—but his instinct warned him of something approaching and he automatically crouched down into the angle between the wall and the floor. Something flashed by almost touching his head, and suddenly Snake's Tongue's scent was much closer. The latter's voice came from just above his head, and feelers gently touched his own. "Yes, his senses are very quick. I would have taken most ants by surprise then." Snake's Tongue stepped back. "And your dreams," he said in his low voice. "What of them?"

"I don't understand," said Dreamer, puzzled.

"Dreams can be either a scent trail or a mist on the path. Which are yours?"

Dreamer spoke hesitantly. "I don't really understand my dreams," he said. "But they are no mist. I know that."

Another moment's pause, then: "Very well. You shall come."

Dreamer felt a surge of excitement, a long-awaited sense of anticipation. He realized for the first time how unconsciously frustrated he had been by the calm and ordered nature of his life up till now; how passionate had been his desire to stretch his faculties, test his courage, expose himself to the winds.

Black Sting was speaking. "Good. Make your other choice, Snake's Tongue, then I suggest that you feed and rest well before you leave. You must replenish yourselves after the Long Sleep. Leave at high-sun tomorrow, then you can aim to be at the riverside mound by sundown. From there you can travel in the new regions in darkness. I wish you luck and when I inform our Great Mother and the Council of your mission, I know they will do the same."

"Thank you," replied Snake's Tongue.

"There are only two pieces of advice I have to give you," went on Black Sting. "The worker-ant from the riverside mound told me that the red ants do not carry stings as we do. They attack by spraying their poison from the base of the abdomen, which blinds and paralyzes opponents. You must obviously avoid any encounter if you possibly can, but if you are forced to fight your best chance will be to attack from the side and get in close as quickly as possible. The other point is that you will have to leave as light a scent trail as possible for fear of being detected. So be sure to take note of obvious landmarks once you are into strange territory, so that you can find your way back again."

"Yes," answered Snake's Tongue.

"That is all. The Lord of the Stars protect you." And without further formality Black Sting turned back down the passage towards the Council chamber, leaving Dew-Lover to follow.

The huge ant did not do so immediately, however. He first stepped closer to Dreamer and growled, "You'd better not do any dreaming on this trip, soldier. Keep your wits about you—for your own sake.''

"And for yours," interposed Snake's Tongue. "Let him be, Dew-Lover."

The other hesitated a moment, then wheeled abruptly and lumbered after Black Sting.

"Come," said Snake's Tongue. And, with Dreamer hurrying to keep up, he sped with his long, loping stride up the tunnel towards the sunlight.

* 7 *

It was late afternoon in the clearing. The shadows were lengthening across the grass, but the weather had shown no sign of deteriorating, of producing a sudden late-night frost, which can prove so dangerous to both plant and animal life alike at that time of year. The sun continued to bathe the area in its life-enhancing glow, and all of Nature was responding, slowly, cautiously, but positively—filling the world once more with life, with hope . . . with danger.

At the feet of a small birch sapling on the edge of the forest, not far from the base mound, Old Five Legs and several of the other older worker-ants were resting after the day's exertions. They had been engaged in the very delicate task of transferring aphid-bug eggs from their winter storage place deep inside the mound, to a suitable position up on the branches of the birch sapling, where they would soon hatch out and form a new aphid-bug herd. Ants attach so much importance to the honey-dew secreted by aphid-bugs for its magical feeding, healing and narcotic qualities that many colonies maintain their own herds of these tiny, gentle little creatures, keeping the eggs safe and warm during the winter, guarding and nurturing them during the incubation period, and then tending and protecting the herds through the summer, in return for a continuous supply of the elixir. The task of fostering and transferring the eggs is usually reserved for older worker-ants, for it requires care and attention but not too much physical exertion. The lonely job of tending the herds of active, foliage-eating bugs, however, is carried out by younger, more hardy ants and also requires the constant presence of soldiers, for aphid-bugs are considered an appetizing source of food by many other insects and predators.

Five Legs, Never-Rest, Wind-Blow and two or three other workers were relaxing just out of earshot of two soldiers, who were standing guard at the foot of the young tree, whilst nearby a group of half a dozen or so younger worker-ants were also taking their ease, casually nibbling at some gorse seeds after having spent the day clearing a new run to the chosen herd pasture. The older ants were discussing the consequences of the day's events. The story of the red ants' attack on the riverside mound had spread like wildfire, and caused intense apprehension and specula-tion throughout the settlement. In his usual excitable fash-ion Wind-Blow was holding forth on the subject.

"Red ants or no red ants, it's going to make little difference to us what happens, unless we get some influ-ence in the Council. Black Sting is bound to use this as a further argument for having still more soldiers, so whether we end up as slaves of them or slaves of the red ants hardly matters, does it? I mean that's virtually what we are now after all, isn't it? Just slaves. Well, aren't we?" He appealed round the circle.

Five Legs answered mildly, "I think you'd find your existence as a slave of the red ants very different from the one here," and his old eyes twinkled with amusement. He was at an age when he could face whatever fate had in store for him with equanimity.

"Nevertheless," replied Wind-Blow, bobbing his head

up and down with agitation, "it's vital to all of us now, now Thunderer's gone, that we get some say in our affairs. The whole system of organization is going to change. We may never get the chance again. Our well-being depends on it!" He turned to Never-Rest, who, for once in his life, was reclining in quiet repose against a couch-grass stem. "What do you say, Never-Rest?"

"I think," said the latter, with careful consideration, "that it all depends on who takes over the leadership. And," he added before Wind-Blow could jump in with an instantaneous reaction, "I don't believe that's nearly as foregone a conclusion as you might think. Black Sting might seem to be the obvious contender, but I'm not sure that the elders will like the idea of having the chief of the soldiers in charge. And you can be sure that Noble will oppose it too. Of course Black Sting could probably take control by force, if he felt it were necessary, but I don't know if it's in his nature to be so ruthless. He would want to have the support of the vast majority before assuming command."

"If he did become leader," said one of the others, "presumably Dew-Lover would take command of the soldiers. There's a frightening prospect."

"It certainly is!" exclaimed Wind-Blow. "I think I'd rather have the red ants." He waved his feelers excitedly. "But the point is—apart from Black Sting, and possibly Noble—who else is there? Thunderer's gang are all too old. *Someone* has to lead us."

"What do you think, old friend?" asked Never-Rest, looking at Five Legs. "Who do you think would be right?"

Five Legs gazed into the distance and contemplated the question with care, as he stroked a feeler ruminatively with his foreleg. "I don't know," he said eventually, "but perhaps it may come as a surprise. This is a vital moment for our colony. It requires someone of vision to bring us through. In such circumstances one never knows who will emerge." He turned his head and looked over in the direction of the birch sapling. "I wonder what the Story Teller has to say on the subject."

None of the others had been aware that, during the last few moments, a slightly-built ant of indeterminate age had slipped quietly down the stem of the sapling and was reclining a little way off, listening to the conversation. At the last words all with one accord turned their heads in the direction of Five Legs' gaze and a strange hush fell over the group. The newcomer did not respond immediately; merely stayed silent, still. His economy of movement was extraordinary. Not a muscle stirred, not a feeler trembled unnecessarily; only his eyes glimmered with a calm, amused warmth. It gave him an air of totally relaxed alertness that was mesmerizing in its completeness.

Off to one side some members of the group of younger worker-ants noticed the sudden lull in conversation amongst the other party, and the whisper went round: "The Story Teller's going to speak. Still One is going to speak," and the members of the group sidled as unobtrusively as possible to within earshot.

The object of attention remained unaffected by the sudden attention of so large an audience. He might have been dead, so utterly still was his body. The two soldiers at the sapling too had by now noticed what was happening and had approached, but also with discretion. And still the silence continued, no one making any move to encourage the newcomer, as if they accepted that this was a necessary and traditional part of the proceedings.

When finally Still One did speak it was without any preface or introduction, in a low, melodious voice which seemed to carry far further than its volume merited.

"A gigantic oak tree stood in the forest. Old beyond the memory of the Queen of all Queens, huge beyond the vision of the sharpest-eyed soldier, it filled the sky and shadowed the lives of everything that dwelt beneath it, and it seemed that it would stand there forever. But then one day there came a great storm, and the wind tore at the mighty oak tree, and its ancient roots gave way under the onslaught, and it fell to earth with a crash that was heard throughout the whole forest.

"For a while the life that had gone on beneath and within the great tree came to a standstill, for there was no creature and no plant that knew how to exist without its shade. But gradually all the seeds that had lain dormant in the ground beneath its branches began to push up, to grow and to develop into trees themselves. On one side they were dominated by one tree in particular—a cedar—which grew and spread its branches until it too shadowed all that lived beneath it. And it cut off the sun from the other young trees, and its needles fell and smothered their leaves, and eventually they withered and died away until the cedar too had complete domination over the ground on which it stood.

"But on the other side all saplings had equal space and grew at the same speed; they matured and developed together, no one tree having domination over any other, and they stood together, proud, and varied, and independent." The Story Teller paused and looked round at his audience who had listened rapt, from the first word. "Which side would you say profited most from the oak tree's passing?"

There was a doubtful silence, broken only by the soft sighing of the breeze amongst the newly awakened grasses all around. Inevitably it was Wind-Blow who broke it.

"But you must . . . you must have a leader. I mean, every colony needs a leader, doesn't it?" He appealed round the circle. "*Everyone* needs a leader!"

Still One gazed at him in his steady, amused way. "Do you need a leader?" he asked. "Or do you need someone who will say, 'You are your own leader, Wind-blow. You are strong enough to stand without a leader?' "

"But . . . but . . ." Wind-Blow stammered frantically, "we can't *all* stand without a leader. Who will make the rules?"

Still One stayed motionless, contemplating the speaker for several moments, as he invariably did before answering a question. No one thought to break the silence.

"Why do you have need of rules, Wind-Blow?" he asked softly.

Wind-Blow stared at him perplexed, at a loss how to answer. Then Never-Rest spoke.

"Surely we must have rules—laws? Otherwise there'd be anarchy. Everyone would be fighting everyone else over how to do things."

Again the pause. Still One gazed into the distance. Then he said: "There was a bank of stones beside a stream. A still, dead, forgotten bank, covered with the dust of ages. Then one year the stream rose and swept over the bank, bringing life to the stones, rolling them over, flinging them this way and that. And the stones battled amongst themselves, crashing to and fro, struggling for the best position—the large ones seeking to crush the small ones, the sharp ones trying to split the round ones. But gradually the stones changed as they each found the place that suited them best. The large ones sank to the bottom and found they could support the small ones; the jagged ones lost their sharp edges and learned to roll with the round ones. And all the stones were rubbed smooth and polished by the stream, and the colours within them came shining to the surface, and they found delight in rolling together backwards and forwards to the music of the waters. And when the stream receded again it left the bank a beautiful, harmonious, many-coloured place."

The quiet amongst his listeners when he had finished was again complete. They were lulled to a serene, reflective calm by the quality of his voice and the content of his tale, as the brain is lulled by honey-dew. Not many there were sure what the story meant, but somehow it left no further room for argument, no cause for doubt. It was a comforting, reassuring thing.

"What is happening here?" The voice broke across the quiet, and the younger ants jumped respectfully to their feet.

Snake's Tongue stood some little way off, surveying the gathering with curiosity. Behind him was Dreamer and a broad, powerful-looking character well known in the community, called Joker. So engrossed had everyone been in the story that no one had noticed the approach of the small party. Snake's Tongue moved closer, and addressed Five Legs.

"What's going on, old one?"

Five Legs answered calmly. "We'd finished our work quota. We were just relaxing for a moment."

Snake's Tongue studied him speculatively. "Is that all you were doing? Relaxing?"

"We were having a little discussion about the situation now that Thunderer's gone," replied Five Legs. "Just talking, that's all."

"Ah," said Snake's Tongue. His eyes glinted wryly. "I thought you'd had your say about that at the Council meeting."

Five Legs acknowledged the thrust with an amused nod. Snake's Tongue glanced across at the two soldier-ants who had been in attendance on the group. "Everything all right here, soldiers?"

"Yes, sir," answered one of them. "No problems."

Snake's Tongue nodded his head. The gathering began to break up, the worker-ants wandering back towards the mound. Snake's Tongue, however, stopped Five Legs, with a wave of his feeler.

"Just a moment, Five Legs. I need a word with you."

Dreamer stood a few paces off behind Snake's Tongue, watching as the rest of the ants moved off. He had noticed the strange, still quality of the group from afar, so unlike the gossiping, fidgeting little gathering that usually formed during rest-breaks, and he was pondering its significance. Beside bulked the heavy, comforting presence of Joker, who had evidently also noticed something strange, for he muttered to Dreamer, "Looked more like another Long Sleep than a rest-break."

Dreamer nodded, amused. He was happy that Joker was the third ant chosen to join Snake's Tongue and himself on their mission. He was not personally well acquainted with the big soldier, but he knew well the other's reputation as a fighter and a genial companion.

Snake's Tongue was addressing Five Legs again. "We need special rations for an expedition. Aphid-bug eggs, beetle larvae, some honey-dew. Can you arrange that?"

Five Legs nodded. "There is a good supply coming in now. We should be able to find you what you want." He paused. "Could one guess at the purpose of this expedition? Something to do with this story about the red ants perhaps?"

Snake's Tongue nodded. "You would not be far wrong."

"I wish you good fortune then," said the old ant. "It is disturbing news."

"Yes," answered Snake's Tongue. He hesitated and looked quizzically at the other. "That was no ordinary rest-break just now, Five Legs. What was happening here?"

Five Legs twinkled. "Still One was telling us a story," he said. "That was all."

Dreamer lifted his head curiously. He had never met the ant in question but he had heard rumours about the strange, elusive creature known as the Story Teller, who held his fellow workers spellbound with his fables. He had a solitary, reclusive occupation—that of tending aphid bugs—so he rarely came into contact with the hierarchy of the colony. It was rumoured, whispered around the place, that he was an immigrant, a refugee from a previous year's mating brood—that weird hatch of winged ants who emerge from the royal brood chambers only once a year on hot midsummer nights, to fly off into the forest where they perform their mysterious, magical coupling rites, resulting in the formation of new broods, new colonies; a further extension across the earth of the great brotherhood of the species. It was said that Still One was a throwback from one such hatching, that he had shed his wings and crept back to the colony, and made his home there secretly—but no one knew for sure.

"Where is the teller of strange tales?" asked Snake's Tongue.

Five Legs lifted his head and pointed a feeler skywards. The three soldiers looked up. Above their heads a fragile figure was leisurely making its way along a branch of the birch sapling.

"If you needed honey-dew, he's the one to get it for you," said Five Legs. "Shall I call him down?"

Snake's Tongue nodded and Five Legs limped over to the base of the young tree. He called up: "Still One, we need your services. Will you come down again?"

The figure on the tree stopped, looked down, then turned unhurriedly and began to descend. Snake's Tongue turned to the two soldier-ants on guard duty, who were still standing nearby.

"Were you amongst this audience?"

"Yes, sir," replied one of them. Dreamer was still more curious. Soldiers deigning to listen to a humble worker-ant?

"He seems to have a fascination, this Story Teller," said Snake's Tongue, echoing the thought. "What is his secret?"

The soldier hesitated. "I don't really know, sir," he said. "It's just that he . . ." He trailed off.

"What?" commanded Snake's Tongue.

"Makes you think." The soldier looked puzzled as he spoke, as if he were not quite sure what he was trying to say.

"Think?" queried Snake's Tongue. "What about?"

The other seemed even more at a loss. "Things you don't usually think about," he said finally.

"This is getting us a long way," whispered Joker at Dreamer's side.

Old Five Legs was returning from the tree. "Here he is," he said, and stood aside to observe. Dreamer studied the ant who came towards them. There was nothing remarkable about his appearance except that, as he approached, Dreamer was struck by the open look of appraisal with which the other was, in return, examining them. It was as if there were no difference between their respective castes or callings: as if one of the highest ranking soldiers in the colony and the low aphid-bug tender were meeting on quite equal, friendly terms. He stopped in front of Snake's Tongue and waited with a quizzical expression on his face, and Dreamer noticed for the first time the strange, still quality about him, which explained his odd name.

Five Legs was speaking. "Snake's Tongue has need of honey-dew, Still One. A special ration for the members of a rather dangerous expedition. Is there some still in the winter supplies?"

Still One nodded imperceptibly, then Dreamer heard his low, gentle voice for the first time. "Your colleague Dew-Lover has seen to it that there is not much left. But there is a separate store kept for the Royal Quarters. I expect we can find you some."

Snake's Tongue nodded, and was about to speak when Still One added, "You must use it cautiously though."

Snake's Tongue stared in surprise at this enjoinder.

"It is wintered honey-dew and very powerful. Used wrongly or incautiously it can be dangerous."

Snake's Tongue showed an amused toleration at the warning. "I know how to use it, Story Teller. You need not to worry on our account."

The other nodded and then added, "Then it will help you on your mission." It was most strange of an ordinary worker-ant to address so lofty a being as Snake's Tongue with such familiarity, but it was done in such a calm, natural voice that somehow it did not seem an impertinence.

Snake's Tongue looked at Five Legs. "They tell me the Story Teller has a fable to suit every occasion," he said. "Do you suppose he has one for a small force about to venture into the heart of an enemy's domain?"

Five Legs looked enquiringly at Still One, but the latter did not respond immediately. Instead he contemplated each of the three soldier-ants in turn. Dreamer felt disturbed by his intense gaze. Then Five Legs broke the silence with a chuckle, and said, "Tell them how the ants fought the Giant Two-Legs. That might be of interest."

Still One nodded. "Yes, you might find that story has some use for you." And, after a moment's reflection, he began in his quiet, mellifluous tones.

"A party of ants was out exploring for new territory, when, without knowing it, they strayed into the land of the Giant Two-Legs. As they travelled along they were spied by two of the Giant Two-Legs, who were as huge as trees and who could see as far as an ant can march in a day. And the two Giants came tearing after the ants as fast as the wind, making the ground tremble with the thunder of their four feet. And they bent down out of the sky and roared to the ants, 'Your last moment has come, ants. Prepare to die!'

"And the leader of the ants knew that there was no point in trying to fight the Giant Two-Legs, for ants' stings are useless against such monsters. But he was a brave, intelligent ant, and he thought quickly. As one of the Giant Two-Legs bent down to crush him, he called up, 'I am not afraid of you.'

"And the Giant Two-Legs was so amazed at this that he paused, and bellowed, 'Indeed! And why not?'

"And the ant leader said, 'Because I have heard your friend say what a coward you are.'

"And the Giant Two-Legs raised himself up and stared in fury at the other Giant. And then the ant leader ran across and called to the other Giant Two-Legs, 'Come on and fight, Giant Two-Legs! We are not afraid of you.'

"And the other Giant bellowed, 'Indeed! And why not?'

"And the ant leader said, 'Because your friend has told us how feeble you are in battle.'

"And the second Giant Two-Legs raised himself, and stared in fury at the other Giant. And the two Giant Two-Legs forgot about the ants, and flew at each other in their anger, and as the forest thundered with the noise of their battle the ants slipped away.

"But the two Giants soon realized that they had been duped and they abandoned their fight and came roaring after the ants again. And the first Giant Two-Legs shouted to the ant leader, 'So, you thought you could fool us with that story, did you? We are not as stupid as you think.' And with that he lifted his great foot and crushed the ant leader to death.

"Then the two Giants turned to the other ants and roared, 'Prepare to die, ants.'

"But the next most senior ant was also a brave, intelligent ant, and he thought quickly. As one of the Giant Two-Legs bent down to crush him, he called up, 'I am not afraid of you.'

"And the Giant Two-Legs paused and bellowed, 'Indeed! And why not?'

"And the ant replied, 'Because I have heard your friend say what a merciful, kind Giant you are at heart.'

"And the Giant Two-Legs raised himself up and stared in pleasure at the other Giant. And the ant ran across and called to the other Giant Two-Legs, 'We know we have nothing to fear from you.'

"And the other Giant bellowed, 'Indeed! And why not?'

"And the ant replied, 'Because your friend had told us what a friendly, loving Giant you are at heart.'

"And the two Giants glowed with warmth for one another. And they forgot about the ants, and as they embraced each other in friendship, the ants slipped away.

"But again the Giants realized that they had been duped, and once more they came raging after the ants. And the first Giant Two-Legs shouted to the ant leader, 'So, you thought you could fool us with *that* story, did you? We are not as stupid as you think.' And he lifted his great foot and crushed the ant to death.

"Then once more the two Giants turned to the other ants, and roared, 'Now prepare to die, ants, or do you also claim that you are not afraid of us?'

"And the next most senior ant, who was the most brave and intelligent of all, said, 'Certainly we are afraid of you.'

"And the two Giant Two-Legs roared with laughter to

each other, and bent down to crush the ants. But then the third ant leader said, 'Just as afraid as you are of us.'

"And the two Giants paused in amazement and said, 'What do you mean—*we* afraid of *you?*'

"And the ant replied, 'It must be so, for what other reason can you have for wanting to kill us? We are not your enemies; we do you no harm; we are not food for you; we want nothing that is yours. Therefore the only reason you can possibly have to want to kill us is that, in some way, you are afraid of us.'

"And the two Giant Two-Legs stared at each other, puzzled. And then they stared back at the ant and said, 'But why should we be afraid of you?'

"And the ant replied, 'That I do not know. That only you can say.'

"And again the two Giants stared at each other, and again they stared back at the ant and said, 'But we are *not* afraid of you.'

"And the ant replied, 'Then you can have no reason for killing us.'

"And the two Giant Two-Legs thought about it some more, and scratched their heads, and looked still more puzzled and finally said, 'You are right. We do have no reason for killing you.'

"And they went away again, leaving the ants to return to their home."

Still One stopped speaking and waited in his calm, passive way. Dreamer was fascinated. Never before had he heard such a story, told in such a compelling manner. He regarded the strange worker-ant with curiosity. Five Legs was watching the reaction of the listeners with amusement. Then Snake's Tongue spoke.

"Thank you, Story Teller. That was a most interesting tale. We shall remember it."

He turned to Joker and Dreamer. "Well now, we have much to do. Joker, go with Five Legs to the food stores. Dreamer, you and Story Teller will come with me to get the honey-dew. You will need my authority to enter the

Royal Quarters. Let us go." And he turned and headed for the mound.

Dreamer found himself running alongside Still One as they followed Snake's Tongue, surreptitiously observing the other out of the corner of his eye as they went. The worker-ant showed no sign of his thoughts but merely seemed intent on keeping up with the long, loping stride of the big ant in front. But then he spoke quietly, taking Dreamer by surprise.

"Why do they call you Dreamer?"

Dreamer answered simply, "Because I have dreams."

"Powerful dreams?"

"Sometimes."

Still One nodded, "And do you understand your dreams?"

"Not always."

They ran in silence for a moment. Then Still One observed, "Dreams are like stories. There is always a meaning within them if you listen. And always truth to the meaning if you can find it."

No more was said until they reached the store chambers of the Royal Quarters, deep down in the earth in the lowest regions of the colony.

* 8 *

He dreamed that he stood in the centre of a great space. And in a wide circle around him were crowded rank upon rank of ants stretching back to the infinite depths of the darkness, to the farthermost ends of a limitless Council chamber. And he was speaking. He was speaking with such passion, such conviction, such feeling. He was urging bold actions, he was advocating radical ideas, he was declaring a passionate faith. And the multitude around him were listening silently, rapt, nodding to the emphasis of his words. And as he spoke the certainty within him grew and grew, until finally he ended his speech with a great cry of passion, and the massed ranks broke into a clamorous roar that echoed and re-echoed far off into the dark distances and rumbled on to the very edge of the universe.

And he cried out, "That is my purpose! To preach my convictions, to spread my beliefs, to communicate my faith. Surely that is my purpose?"

And the Voice came, as he knew it would, and said: "Yes, that could well be your purpose. But remember that

*your faith may not be the faith of the speaker who follows
you. He will preach different convictions, advocate other
ideas, champion a different cause. And it could be that
they will cheer him too and will turn from you and follow
him until they are persuaded by yet another speaker, and
so on, until there are no more words to be spoken. And
who will be the one to speak to the speakers, can you tell
that?''*

*And he could not. And he was alone again, wondering
where it was that he had heard this Voice before.*

* 9 *

The bright afternoon of the following day saw the diminutive figures of three ants far up the bank of the stream alongside the shadowed vastness of the forest. They had slept long and deeply the previous night, a sleep induced by a heavy intake of fresh food to replenish their starved bodies and by an ambrosial ration of thick, wintered honeydew, which had brought and added intensity to Dreamer's dreams. Strengthened and invigorated, and with the storage cavities behind their jaws crammed to capacity with extra food, they had set out with the sun at its height and the earnest good wishes and exhortations of the elders and councillors speeding them on their way.

Snake's Tongue was leading, his long, easy stride forcing the other two to run almost flat out in order to keep up. Over the period of preparation, Dreamer's admiration for the big ant had increased enormously. His quiet sense of purpose and careful attention to detail had been a source of great confidence and encouragement, and his phenomenal strength and agility were always evident, lurking beneath the taciturn surface, giving Dreamer the impression that he must be almost invincible in battle. It was a false impression he knew, for Black Sting was faster still and Dew-Lover of yet more implacable muscle power; and there were creatures out there in the forest's labyrinthine vastness who could destroy either of them with one blow, but it was a reassuring feeling all the same.

"Pouf! How do we keep up when he's *really* in a hurry?" gasped Joker who was pounding along behind Dreamer. The latter was getting used to his quips and quietly enjoyed the relief of tension that they brought. He was surprised by the sense of affection that the amiable soldier awoke in him and quite uncertain as to how to express it, but he recognized what a wise choice Snake's Tongue had made by adding Joker's morale-boosting presence to the party.

They were now well past the spot where Dreamer had met the little refugee ant from the riverside colony and were travelling on the fairly familiar route which connected the two settlements. Snake's Tongue was setting a fast pace because they had already been held up on several occasions by unexpected obstacles which winter had tossed carelessly across the trail: a torn tree branch here, a new rain gully there; and once they had been forced to make a considerable detour where an entire portion of the stream bank had collapsed into the swollen waters, carrying part of the trail with it. On two occasions also they had taken hasty refuge off the trail, away from the clumsy approach of larger beasts. The first had been the towering shape of a young buck rabbit, who was hopping thunderously about, indulging in an orgy of gluttony on the sweet, young grasses; the second had been the much smaller, but infinitely more dangerous figure of a large rove beetle, which came ambling leisurely along the trail towards them, sending them scurrying off it in the downwind direction.

However, thanks to Snake's Tongue's rapid pace-setting and the vigour in their bodies imparted by their feast of fresh food and honey-dew the night before, they were now well up to schedule, and as the afternoon wore on and they approached their dusk-time objective, the riverside colony, Dreamer's sense of apprehension grew at the thought of coming to that scene of carnage described by the little ant. Perhaps it was this sense of ominous expectancy, or perhaps simply the particular alertness of his senses occasioned by the drama of their mission, that caused him to become aware, long before they reached that first destination, of the faintest hint of an alien scent on the air—a minute whiff of an ant smell, foreign to their own—heavy, sweet, strange. He waited a few moments to be sure that he was not mistaken and then communicated his discovery to Snake's Tongue. The latter stopped and explored the air with his antennae. He looked at Dreamer uncertainly.

"Are you sure? I can smell nothing."

"Fairly certain, sir," answered Dreamer.

"Can you smell anything, Joker?" asked Snake's Tongue.

Joker also scoured the air with his feelers. "Fresh clover and old rabbit droppings," he said cheerfully.

"Hm," grunted Snake's Tongue, "Well, let's go carefully just in case. You go first, Dreamer, and tell us if it gets stronger."

There was no need for Dreamer to do that, however. They had not gone much further before a stronger gust of air brought the scent clearly to the notice of all three.

"You were right, Dreamer," said Snake's Tongue. "Very useful, those senses of yours."

Joker's comment was: "If that's what they smell like, I'd rather they kept it to themselves."

Again Snake's Tongue took the lead, but this time they progressed more warily. The strange scent came and went, but each time in stronger wafts. It was not new—they could tell it was at least a day old—but its powers of endurance were impressive.

The afternoon sun was sinking behind them as they neared their objective and a thin moon was rising through the skeleton tracery of branches over their heads—the Lord of the Stars' own personal beacon, sent at crucial times to illuminate the dark hours. Already its pale, mystical light was beginning to oust the crimson glow of the sunset and weird black tentacles of shadow were stretching across the grass, as if to seize the hurrying figures and bear them off into the trees.

At last the tiny party rounded a curve in the trail and there in front of them, bathed in the last dying glow of the falling sun, was the low shape of the riverside mound. Snake's Tongue stopped, his antennae outstretched to pick up any sign of life.

"Is there anything there?" he asked Dreamer, who stood just behind him, equally alert. But everything was remarkably silent. Unnaturally so, for, apart from the sound of the running water off to one side and the faintest rustle of a breeze amongst the grasses, there were none of the usual busy twilight sounds: the scuttle of insect feet through the undergrowth; the distant chomp of caterpillar jaws on a leaf; not even the sudden swish of feathered wings, as the rulers of the sky sought a last meal before retiring for the night. It was as if the message of fear had pervaded the whole region and banished its inhabitants to other, happier parts.

Snake's Tongue led the way cautiously forward towards the mound. The strange ant smell was all-embracing now, but there was no element of freshness in it and it seemed unlikely that any of the red ants were near at that moment. However the very strangeness of the circumstances inspired wariness. A little way further on Snake's Tongue stopped again, his antennae quivering with distaste at the hint of new scent that had reached them—the scent of death. Sure enough, there to one side of the trail lay the forlorn, empty husk of a dead ant, one of their own species, its corpse stripped quite clean of flesh. Snake's Tongue, with his trained soldier's instinct, immediately passed by, refusing to allow the sight to distract him in his vigilance for danger. Dreamer followed his example, forcing the distressing image out of his mind with a deliberate act of willpower. He knew his dreams would probably recreate it for him with unpleasant vividness later but now was not the time to dwell on that.

He had to repeat the process several times before they reached the mound, for they passed a number of such victims of the massacre. It was obvious that none of the ants caught out in the open when the attack came had stood a chance against their assailants. It soon seemed, however, that perhaps these had endured the more fortunate fate, for as the three living ants climbed the lower slope of the mound and approached one of the entrances, the strength of death grew with every step. On reaching the tunnel mouth Snake's Tongue stopped, unwilling to enter, so powerful was the evidence of the fearful carnage inside. He turned to the other two.

''Wait here,'' he commanded briefly and vanished into the blackness.

Dreamer shuddered and turned to keep watch, thankful that he had been spared the ordeal of entering the terrible place. Joker stood beside him, staring out towards the forest.

''Greedy beggars, aren't they,'' he muttered irreverently. His lack of sentiment was deliberate. It was as if he realized what effect the occasion was having on Dreamer's inexperienced soul, and sought to relieve it. However, nothing could now heal that wound to the younger ant's sensibilities which had been inflicted when he first heard the story from the refugee ant the day before, and which was deepening with every new experience. It was the inescapable scar that Life inflicts on all but the most cosseted of creatures. Dreamer was coming of age.

Snake's Tongue was not gone for long. He re-emerged silently, his face betraying no sign of his feelings. He uttered no word on his findings but merely looked up at the moon, which was now riding high, complete master of the darkened sky, and said, ''Come, now the real journey begins.''

The party skirted the side of the mound and descended the slope on the opposite face. They quickly crossed the remaining grassy space, for on that side the stream curved in to meet the line of trees and the grass gave way to thick forest undergrowth. On reaching the gigantic, looming shadow of the forest edge they paused. This was where the adventure truly began for now they were in quite unfamiliar regions, and woodland regions at that, which no ant from their colony would penetrate far from choice. The darkness and the continuing absence of any sound of life created an eerie, forbidding atmosphere amongst the trees, but the red ant scent clearly indicated the way they must travel, so, with a quick glance at his companions, Snake's Tongue shook his antennae as if to dispel the traces of all previous sensations and slipped into the shadows.

The going was far harder now. There were no clear trails and the ground beneath the trees was constantly changing: here a thick path of moss overlaid with dead bracken, speared through by the new, rising spring fern shoots; here a carpet of wild hyacinth leaves amongst a tangled mass of briar; here a damp, sodden wasteland of last autumn's dead leaves, which had to be skirted, for ants hate moist going, and mistrust the cover such terrain provides for larger predatory insects. There did at least seem little to fear from the latter, however, for the uncanny absence of life around them continued. Once or twice Dreamer was aware of the swish of nocturnal wings far above his head and a couple of times they paused as a distant tremor in the ground told them that a number of the vast mammal order was moving about somewhere; but this gave them little cause for alarm for such giants rarely showed interest in their humble insect species. The absence of other insect life, however, was ominous, for it indicated that red ants had systematically stripped the land of all its new-blossoming springtime population and that scarcely a creature was safe from their aggression. Even the smaller bird and reptile species appeared to have departed to other regions for want of sufficient insects on which to feed. Dreamer felt a grim respect for the extraordinary efficiency of the rapacious creatures they were stalking.

They travelled in total silence for a long while with no change in the conditions around them. Then just as Dreamer was beginning to wonder how much longer he could keep going at such a pace, Snake's Tongue called a halt. Indicating a deep fissure on the exposed root of a nearby fir tree, he said, "Dreamer, scout out that crevice. If it's safe, we'll rest there and feed."

With relief Dreamer obeyed and, having ensured that the crevice was uninhabited, he signalled to the others to enter. They relaxed, swallowing some of the food in their crops. It was mixed with a liberal ration of honey-dew and almost immediately Dreamer could feel the substance's magical effect as it soothed his tired limbs and lifted his drooping spirits.

After some moments, when all three had revived somewhat, Joker broke the silence. "How far do you think their base might be, leader?" he asked.

Snake's Tongue thought for a moment and then said, "Judging from the way they've scoured the countryside, it can't be too far." He gazed at the shadowy forest. "What I can't understand is how they operate—what their system is. We've been travelling in a straight line by the moon and we've joined several of their scent trails, all going in more or less the same direction. Yet we've come across no sign of the ants themselves. They've left no guards behind, established no outposts or satellite colony, even in the mound they overran. They're masters of this entire area and yet we haven't encountered a single one of them."

It was the longest speech Dreamer had ever heard him make. Snake's Tongue rarely revealed his thoughts but this was spoken as a natural communication of ideas to two equally ranked companions. It was a measure of the bond that had been established between them through their mutual isolation in this alien land.

"Perhaps they don't hunt at night," suggested Joker.

"But when do they travel?" said Snake's Tongue.

"They've covered such a wide area and scavenged it so thoroughly that they must either camp out or travel through the night. Either way we must surely come across some of them sooner or later."

"I think it's sooner," whispered Dreamer, his antennae against the ground.

The others froze, their feelers also to the ground. Now they could sense it too: a distant tremor approaching over the forest floor. The vibration grew nearer, accompanied now by sound. The indications were of a large body of insects, but there were other signs too: a slithering, sliding movement, as of heavy objects being dragged along the earth. Then came the scent—the fresh, sickly red ant scent—and mingled with it another scent which all three of the waiting ants recognized: the odour of live crane-fly larvae. The party had evidently raided a crane-fly's hatching place and were taking the larvae back to their base, presumably for food.

The three ants crouched in the crevice, waiting to see if they would be detected. They seemed safe for the moment because the other group was upwind of them, approaching at an angle, and a party on the move, dragging captives, creates so much scent itself that its own senses are diminished. However, the wind might change at any moment or the red ants might have flanking scouts out, and there was no way of knowing how skilled at detection they were. The fact that they still could not be seen, that they existed merely as an ominous conglomeration of scent and sound moving through the half-darkness, made the anticipation all the more nerve-racking.

Then suddenly they came into view, a line of dim silhouettes briefly glimpsed as they crossed a patch of moonlight some thirty ant-lengths off between two tree-trunks. Dreamer counted them as they appeared and vanished again into the shadow. There were between thirty and forty, transporting the bulky shapes of perhaps a dozen larvae between them. The night distorted the distance and it was hard to calculate how big the other ants were but he could see that they were considerably larger than themselves and, from the length of their legs in proportion to the rest of their bodies, probably very fast over the ground. He thought morosely that the three of them would stand little chance in an even-numbered fight with such adversaries.

The enemy continued on their way, oblivious of the presence of the intruders, and now moving away from them further into the forest. Snake's Tongue waited several minutes to let the party get well ahead, then whispered to the other two, "Let's go. We'll follow their trail and hope that it leads directly to their base. I'll go last. Dreamer, you lead the way. There may be others around, so remember, our only hope is to be aware of them before they are aware of us."

"Like a midge-fly is before it's trodden on by a Giant Two-Legs," muttered Joker to Dreamer as they slipped down from the tree root and set off in line.

With a fresh scent trail to follow the going was easier now. The red ants, despite the fact that they were carrying heavy burdens, were making fast progress, which said even more about their size and strength. In silence the threesome kept up a steady, regular pace along the well-trampled path that the party in front was following. They travelled this way for a long time until fatigue and the even monotony of their progress lulled Dreamer's senses to the point where he almost led them into catastrophe.

The ground had altered somehow and was now rising gradually, which increased the strain on the travellers. Dreamer was so intent on keeping an even pace to conserve his breath and energy that he only gradually became aware of a subtle change in the fresh scent trail they were following. The vague difference gently permeated his consciousness, until suddenly he became fully cognizant of it and stopped in his tracks, antennae quivering. There were now *two* sources of the scent, the familiar one on the trail he was following and a steady breath coming from the windward side. They were so similar that he had not taken immediate note of the second source. But now his antennae could also detect a distinct vibration coming from that direction, which was rapidly converging with their own route. He veered sharply off the trail, Snake's Tongue and Joker following without question, and all three plunged into a patch of coarse rye-grass and froze there, only the panting of their bodies and the slight tremor of their antennae indicating their presence.

The approaching vibration pattern was very close now and Dreamer realized that it was in fact another group of the enemy, marching on a separate route which was about to converge with their own, only a few ant-lengths from the point they had reached. Had he not noticed them in time, the two parties would have virtually collided! Dreamer was appalled at his lapse of alertness and he waited in an agony of suspense to see whether they had been detected.

However, the red ants' own state of awareness was evidently worse than their own, for the party—a rather smaller one than the group in front—continued past them and on up the main trail without hesitation. It seemed that their faculties were not as sensitive as those of his own species, or else that those faculties were dulled by their owners' arrogant confidence in their sovereignty over these regions. Either alternative provided at least some advantage to the intruders.

The three ants waited until the enemy group was well out of range. Then Dreamer turned to Snake's Tongue, and said, "I'm sorry, leader. They nearly caught me out."

"You sensed them before they sensed us, that's the main thing," said Snake's Tongue.

"Glad we didn't have to introduce ourselves," muttered Joker.

Dreamer quietly resolved that never again would he allow his concentration to lapse in such a way.

Snake's Tongue explored the night air with his feelers. "I think we'd better rest here, and get some energy back before we run into any more trouble," he said.

So once more they rested gratefully, drank some moisture from the drops trapped between the rye-grass stems and ate sparingly of the food in their crops. All three had by now almost exhausted their store of food and Dreamer wondered how they were going to find more in these starved regions, particularly as it would presumably become more and more scarce the nearer they approached the enemy base. If necessary they could probably find some seeds or edible plant life, but such nourishment was hardly suitable for ants on the march—and possibly on the run—who required a large supply of energy.

The shadows around them were softening and the thin moon seen through the branches high over their heads was paling, as the Lord of the Stars once more withdrew his protective cloak of darkness from the world and allowed the dawn to creep hesitantly in. The air was very cold now and its damp chill crept into their limbs as they rested. Snake's Tongue shivered and stretched his lengthy frame.

"We must go," he said. "Keep alert for any sign of life. We must find some food before long, if only to hide for the return journey. Dreamer, see if the way is clear."

As it happened, it was a form of life which discovered them, and a very unpleasant form. Just as they had vacated the shelter of their grass clump and Dreamer was hesitating at the edge of the trail with the other two behind him, a heavy thud and a groan from Joker make him whirl round.

The sight that met his eyes was terrifying. Joker was lying prone on the ground and over him towered the huge figure of a large tree-spider, its immense jaws poised to strike. The only reason it had not done so immediately was because it was partially distracted by Snake's Tongue, who was just out of reach of its long, hair-covered limbs and whose remarkable reflexes had spun him round, sting at the ready, at the first moment of impact.

The monster was fully three times the size of any of the ants and had evidently dropped out of the foliage above their heads from a considerable height, which was why they had not been aware of its presence. Tree-spiders do not normally prey on ants, finding more appetizing food high amongst the branches of their normal habitat, but such was the dearth of suitable victims in these parts, even apparently at that height, that this one was evidently no longer choosy about what it ate. It must have witnessed their entry into the protective clump of grass and lain in wait above until they came out again.

Never in his life had Dreamer confronted such a formidable opponent. He had heard all the stories of course, of momentous encounters with similar adversaries—such tales were the very stuff of ant lore—and he was aware that his world was also the domain of infinitely more powerful and voracious species than his own; but he had always seen them at a distance, high over his head or speeding aggressively across the horizon, never directly encountered them at such proximity. He remained frozen to the spot in a state of shocked paralysis, until a fierce command from Snake's Tongue shook him into action.

"Distract it, Dreamer!" shouted the big soldier, who then whirled away to one side.

Dreamer had no notion of what his leader planned to do, but instinctively he obeyed and, more as a reflex movement than with any calculated plan of action, he lunged forward towards the gigantic shape, his sting automatically curled forward beneath his body. The spider's great head had swung round following Snake's Tongue but now, as it sensed Dreamer's approach, it swung back again, a strange rumbling hiss coming from somewhere within the cavernous depth of its body. The enormous mandibles, which were easily capable of crushing an ant's body at a single embrace, gaped towards him. Dreamer realized that everything depended on keeping out of their range. He danced forwards, presenting his puny sting, and then leapt back again, shouting insults in a wild display of aggression. He was dimly aware of Joker, half stunned, attempting to crawl out between the beast's legs, and then suddenly of the long, tensile figure of Snake's Tongue materializing again on one side with incredible speed, leaping for one of the hindmost legs and clinging to the hairy surface with feet and jaws together.

As Dreamer continued his crazed dance of distraction in front of the monster's head, Snake's Tongue drove his sting upwards and forwards towards the bottom joint of its leg, just above the claw-like foot. The sting struck the hard carapace of the leg just above the joint and was deflected off to one side, almost causing him to lose his balance. He hung on grimly and struck again, once more failing to find the vulnerable spot. The spider kicked its leg ponderously, trying to shake him off, but his weight was sufficient to inhibit this movement so it next swung its huge head round towards him. He was on its hindmost leg, however, and the creature could not reach that far without bringing its leg forward and dangerously unbalancing itself. As it aimed its jaws futilely in Snake's Tongue's direction, Dreamer once again rushed in, threatening its front, and it was forced to swing back again.

Snake's Tongue lunged again and again with the base of his abdomen at the vulnerable leg-joint until at last he felt the satisfying thrust as his sting penetrated the narrow gap and entered soft flesh. With all his power he injected a long jet of poison and then leapt clear.

The spider gave a great hiss as it felt the searing pain in its leg and it whirled towards Snake's Tongue, those gigantic pincer jaws, containing their own lethal brand of poison, parted ready to strike. Snake's Tongue reared on his hind legs just out of range, taunting the creature. He knew his poison required a short time before its paralysing powers took effect, so the spider was still mobile and even more dangerous now it was enraged.

On the far side Dreamer was now relieved of the beast's immediate attention. He could see Joker still dazedly attempting to struggle out between the spider's trampling feet. That first instinctively inspired counter-attack had taught him an enlightening lesson: that no dilemma seems quite so hopeless if faced with a positive reaction. Now he put that lesson into effect in a more calculated and cool-headed way, and, following Snake's Tongue's example, he attacked the nearest leg, aiming for the lowest joint. He jumped and clung to the thick hairs on the great limb, aware of the sheer solidity of the member and of the powerful odour excreted from its surface. Again and again he thrust, seeking that vital cleft between the sections. After several abortive attempts his sting at last penetrated and he injected his poison with as much force as he could muster. Then he leapt clear. He was not, however, quite so fast as Snake's Tongue in doing this, and in his inexperience he had chosen to attack only the second leg of the four on his side, which left him within closer range of those great jaws. The sharp pain in the spider's leg brought it lunging in his direction once more and as he turned to flee its mandibles clamped around his body.

What saved him was the haste with which the spider had struck. Had it had time to aim properly, it would undoubtedly have gone for the vulnerable joint between head and thorax or between thorax and abdomen. As it happened, its wild strike made contact with the retreating rear of Dreamer's abdomen, some way above the sting where the carapace was at its thickest. The jaws gripped firmly around his body but failed to pierce the hard protective covering immediately, so that it could not inject its deadly poison.

It was now Joker's turn to enter the action. Initially stunned by the first impact of the spider's heavy body as it dropped from above, his head was now clearing in the few vital seconds' reprieve that his companions' attack had won for him. He was still half under the beast, scrabbling instinctively to get away between its legs, but now, as his senses returned, he dimly realized that with the creature's jaws diverted to Dreamer and with Snake's Tongue again rushing in to attack its leg on the other side, he was in an advantageous position to do some damage himself. He was actually lying beneath the spider's most vulnerable part, the undersurface of the soft, slender section which joined the thorax to the abdomen and allowed its body flexibility. In the sideways swing of its head as it attacked Dreamer the spider had exposed this part and the crouching movement of its body during the same lunge had brought its

underbelly lower, within range of Joker's sting. He now
rolled over on to his back and, with all the strength left in
his bruised body, struck upwards at the vital spot. His
sting pierced the skin and he injected as much poison as
was possible from such an unnatural position. The spider
gave an instant lurch, knowing it had been wounded in a
critical place. Releasing its hold on Dreamer, it swung
round to deal with this new assault. The poison from the
first two attacks was now having its effect and the beast's
legs were not behaving quite as they should have done. It
staggered, trying to maintain its balance, and Snake's
Tongue and Dreamer, sensing victory, both renewed their
attacks simultaneously. Dreamer, his lesson learnt, this
time followed Snake's Tongue's example and went for the
rear leg out of reach of the jaws. Neither had a strong dose
of poison left after their initial attacks and Dreamer was in
considerable pain from the monster's bite around his abdomen, but both were able to inflict further minor wounds on
its leg-joints before it kicked them off and staggered,
hissing, out of range.

The three ants crouched exhausted, watching the huge
beast as it lumbered dazedly around the undergrowth.
Joker's lunge had caught it in a vital place and as the
poison slowly infiltrated its system, bringing with it a
numbing paralysis, the spider sensed that it would soon be
at the mercy of its opponents, and its eyes took on a
forlorn, almost appealing expression.

The ants waited, content merely to observe and regain
their strength, as their attacker blundered this way and
that, crashing against grass stems and twigs, until it subsided into a heaving, defeated mass amongst the undergrowth. They felt no malice now that the contest was over
and the victors determined. This was Nature's way; the
stark, but essential processes were merely being fulfilled.

When the sounds of the spider's movement in the undergrowth had ceased Snake's Tongue did not immediately
approach it: his first thought was that the noise of their
struggle might have attracted the attention of some of the

red ants. His antennae erect, he listened for a long moment to the sounds of the forest, but all seemed as it should be. Then he looked towards the other two. They were both bruised and exhausted, but otherwise seemed unharmed. He turned his attention back towards the spider. Moving slowly, with the greatest caution, he approached it. The beast was by no means dead. It was breathing steadily and its eyes, though glazed and not focusing properly, could still dimly follow his movements. It knew, however, that its end was near. Such was its size, that it was quite possible it would have survived its injuries had it been granted time to recuperate. But Snake's Tongue had no intention of allowing this, firstly because he did not wish to leave so fearful a menace at liberty near the route by which they would have to return, and secondly because it now offered the supply of food which they so desperately needed. He signalled with his antennae to the other two to come forward and then approached the spider's head to make sure the creature was indeed incapacitated. When he saw that it was only able to make the slightest of movements in reaction to his advance, he moved round to its flank. The others knew without being told what to do and all three climbed between the long, outstretched legs, and, without a word, attacked the slender, vulnerable joint between thorax and abdomen with their mandibles.

The grisly deed was soon accomplished. So numbed was the spider by now that it probably felt little before it succumbed. There were a few spasmodic, involuntary twitches as the ants bit through its vital arteries, but then stillness, and within a few moments its huge form lay in two sections, completely severed.

Snake's Tongue studied his two companions. Joker lay sprawled on the ground, too dazed and exhausted even to make the expected quip about their deliverance. Dreamer too rested, nursing his aching sides where the spider's jaws had scarred the carapace. Snake's Tongue himself was relatively unmarked but even he, seasoned soldier that he was, had been shaken by the episode. He went across to Joker and touched him exploratively with his feelers.

"All right, Joker?" he asked quietly.

The other nodded weakly, then summoned his energies and lified his head. "Nothing to it. When are we going to do some *real* fighting?"

Snake's Tongue nodded, relieved, and turned to Dreamer. "Well done, Dreamer," he said. "You fought well."

Dreamer felt no elation at his leader's praise. He was too worn out for that and he realized what a lucky escape they had had. But he also realized, vaguely and without any particular sense of satisfaction, that they had in fact acquitted themselves respectably; that each had responded without hesitation in the crisis and played his part with honour. It boded well for the future of their mission and further strengthened the bond of loyalty between them.

"We will rest and then feed," decided Snake's Tongue. "Then we must move on. The sun will soon be up."

They fed hungrily as soon as their strength had revived. Spider flesh is not to ant's best liking but they were in no position to be fastidious and they knew they were unlikely to have such an opportunity again. They needed the nourishment, not only to replenish their energies but also the supply of poison for their stings, which had been virtually exhausted in the fight. When they had eaten their fill and tucked away selected morsels in their crops for future consumption. Snake's Tongue left the corpse and scouted around the immediate vicinity. He soon found what he was looking for: a shallow, cavelike depression beneath a large stone lying nearby. He signalled to the other two and together they dragged the remains of the spider into the aperture and then covered them over with dead leaves and twigs, finally scattering the whole with humus scratched up from the ground to disguise, for a while at least, the scent of death.

That done, the three ants returned once more to the path of the red ants, Snake's Tongue leading this time. As he hesitated on the edge of the trail, scanning the air for signs of danger, Joker turned to Dreamer at his side.

"Thanks, young one," he said in a low voice. "You're a better fighter than you look. I didn't relish being a spider's dinner just yet."

Dreamer's stride was a little more jaunty, despite the ache in his sides, as the three set off again through the trees and the brightening glow of the rising dawn.

* 10 *

Bug-Rump was drunk. It was hardly his fault. He had been left to clean out the store chamber where the royal store of winter honey-dew was kept. After Snake's Tongue's expedition party had been given their supply, the small remainder of the precious stuff had been carried in thick congealed lumps down to the Royal Quarters themselves. The two soldiers of the Royal Guard who were constantly on sentry duty over the chamber now departed and Bug-Rump was left with the last dirty job—as Bug-Rump usually was.

His task was to clean the final traces of the sweet sticky substance from the walls and floor of the little chamber, leaving the place ready for the new deposits of spring honey-dew. The job involved scraping the earthy surface with mandibles and claws and carrying the resultant unsavoury mixture of earth and coagulated honey-dew by mouth to the outside of the mound, where it was deposited amongst the grass stems on one of the slopes. Inevitably a certain amount of honey-dew would melt away from the soil whilst in contact with the warm juices of an ant's mouth, and it was a strong-willed worker-ant indeed who could refrain from swallowing a little of the delectable stuff, forbidden though it was. Bug-Rump was strong neither in will nor in body. He was one of the first-born of last year's larvae brood—always the most stunted in growth—and he had survived through to this year more by luck than by judgement, having by chance discovered a tiny crevice in one of the warm inner hibernation chambers into which he could just squeeze and which was too small for any larger worker to covet. Here he had spent the winter in relative comfort, only to emerge after the Long Sleep to find himself once more one of the drudges of the community by reason of his diminutive stature.

Bug-Rump's resistance to honey-dew was negligible, as his humble status rarely allowed him to come into contact with it. In this instance he had succumbed to temptation rather more often than was wise on his several trips backwards and forwards between the chamber and the outside, and by the time his task was almost completed he found himself in a distinctly intoxicated stage, staggering about the little chamber with a happy smile on his face, a dazed look in his eyes and a sequence of bizarre hallucinations in his brain.

Then suddenly one of these dreamlike images materialized into a frightening reality. A huge black shape loomed out of the darkness, a heavy foot descended on his back and a low voice rumbled close to his head: "What do you think you're up to, my friend?"

Bug-Rump desperately tried to stand still and focus his wayward senses on the speaker. He dimly recognized the voice and scent as belonging to Dew-Lover and something in the hazy recess of his brain told him that he was in trouble, but he wasn't quite sure why, nor did it seem to matter very much. He mumbled semi-incoherently, "Gorra clean out honey-dew," while staggering under the weight of Dew-Lover's foot.

The latter's voice sank to a vicious, menacing growl: "Clean out the honey-dew, eh!"

"Yeshir—clean iddup."

The pressure on his back increased so that poor Bug-Rump's legs were sagging precariously under him.

"Where are the Royal Guards who should be on duty here?" demanded the voice.

"Gone shir. Told me, clean up honey-dew, an then gone."

"Did they give you authority to eat it up as well?"

"Not eat it, shir. Jus' clean iddup. Nothing lef'—jusha shticky mess." Bug-Rump waved a feeler around the chamber, promptly overbalanced and sat down with a bump.

"Well, there's certainly nothing left now you've been here," growled Dew-Lover, running his antennae around the walls. "Where is it all? Don't tell me the supply was finished."

"All finish. All gone—down to Royal Quarters. Lasht bit gone to exp . . . expedish . . . expedishion—an now clean plashe up."

"Expedition?"

"Snake's Tongue's expedishion—find red ants."

Dew-Lover paused thoughtfully. "How did Snake's Tongue know there was some left here?"

"Dunno, shir. Still One brought 'em."

"Still One?"

"Yesh. Story Teller."

Dew-Lover's eyes glinted dangerously in the darkness. "The Story Teller, eh? And did he tell you to stuff yourself silly with it?"

"No, shir. Royal Guard jus' said give 'em honey-dew an' clean plashe up."

Dew-Lover was silent for a moment. He was deeply angry. He had managed to keep himself well supplied with his favourite form of nourishment for much of the winter, by the simple expedient of helping himself from the colony's main store whenever he felt the need. The guards there never dared to question his right to exceed the nor-

mal ration. Consequently he had been able to spend most
of the Long Sleep in a very pleasant state of semi-
intoxication. However, the supply there had run out some
while ago, and his arousal had therefore been a cold,
cheerless one in more ways than one. And now to discover this wretched little creature, so obviously under the
influence of the bewitching substance that had been denied
to himself for so long, put him in an evil fury, and
Dew-Lover in that state was a very dangerous ant indeed.

"You know the penalty for stealing from the Royal
Stores?" he growled.

"No stealing, shir. Jus' clean iddup," whined Bug-
Rump helplessly.

Dew-Lover dropped his voice to an even more menacing
level. "Don't argue with me, you miserable specimen. I
know when someone's been thieving honey-dew, and royal
honey-dew at that. And the punishment is death."

Bug-Rump's voice took on an edge of real fear now as
the extent of his predicament began to penetrate his befud-
dled senses. "Not stealing, shir. No stealing. Please . . ."

"Silence!" roared Dew-Lover. He turned to the two
soldiers with him, who had been waiting brought at the
threshold of the chamber. "We'll see what story the Story
Teller has to tell about *this*. Bring this drunken little runt
along." And he marched up the passage, leaving the
soldiers to half carry, half drag poor Bug-Rump after him.

Outside amongst the grassy stretches of the clearing the
springtime activity was gathering pace, busy groups of
ants moving here and there in all directions; heaving,
dragging, carrying, digging. To the eye of the casual
observer there might have appeared little rhyme or reason
to all the hectic motion, but in fact it was precisely ordered
and organized, every ant knowing exactly what his task
was and how he had to go about it.

Up on the birch sapling Still One was absorbed in the
tending of his little clusters of aphid-bug eggs, moving
them around to the driest, warmest spots on the bark

surface, cosseting the healthiest ones and picking out those that were undersized to be taken back and added to the food supplies. The adult bugs themselves wandered placidly about him, sturdy, easygoing little creatures, whose sole purpose in life seemed to be to eat and sleep, lay their eggs and recreate their honey-dew for the benefit of other species.

If Still One was aware of the approach of Dew-Lover and his soldiers, the latter supporting the semi-inert body of Bug-Rump, he showed no sign of it.

Dew-Lover stopped at the base of the tree and growled up at him, "Come here, Story Teller."

Still One looked down without expression and then obeyed, descending unhurriedly. The huge soldier-ant confronted him at the base of the tree trunk, towering over the slim figure.

"Are you responsible for this?" He indicated the lolling body between the two soldiers.

Still One studied the sight for a moment, then turned his eyes with their mild, seemingly unconcerned expression back to Dew-Lover. "Responsible?" he asked.

"For allowing this miserable creature to get himself into such a drunken state."

Again Still One looked at Bug-Rump. "Oh, poor Bug-Rump," he said quietly. "Have you been weak-willed?"

"Stealing from the royal stores is not weak-willed, my friend. It's treason." Dew-Lover's voice had sunk once again to its dangerous low rasp.

Still One regarded him impassively. After a moment he said, "He can't have been stealing. I saw the last of the honey-dew being taken down to the Royal Quarters."

"Then how do you suggest he got himself into this condition?" demanded Dew-Lover.

"He must have absorbed some of the residue in the soil while cleaning out the chamber. It's almost impossible not to on that job."

"Absorbed?" sneered Dew-Lover. "Absorbed? He's stuffed himself with it! He's half unconscious on the stuff!

Look at him." And, grasping the unfortunate little ant under the head with his great mandibles, Dew-Lover held him, half dangling, in front of Still One. Then he let go and Bug-Rump collapsed in a quivering, pathetic heap at Still One's feet.

The latter stroked him gently with his feelers and murmured. "Poor Bug-Rump."

"Poor Bug-Rump!" repeated Dew-Lover scathingly. "Do I take that to mean you sympathize with him?"

Still One replied, "He is unused to the effects of honeydew. He won't feel very well when they have worn off."

"They won't get the chance to wear off," growled Dew-Lover. "The penalty for what he's done is immediate death."

There was silence. Still One regarded the enormous soldier in his imperturbable way. The other stared back with menace, daring him to offer a challenge.

Then Dew-Lover said, "Were you responsible for removing the last of the honey-dew?"

"I am not in charge of the supplies," replied Still One. "I only help to produce them. I was acting on orders from Snake's Tongue."

"I know where the orders came from." Dew-Lover thrust his massive head down to Still One's. "But you told me a while ago that the honey-dew was all finished."

"That's true. The ordinary supplies were finished," answered Still One. "There was only just enough in the royal store to last the winter."

"Then how was it there was enough left for Snake's Tongue? And how was it there was enough left for this creature to cram himself with?" He kicked the semi-inert body at his feet. Still One said nothing. "Well?" roared Dew-Lover.

"I'm sorry there was none left for you," said Still One in his quiet voice.

Dew-Lover drew back his head angrily. "Me! I'm not talking about me. I'm talking about him." Again he kicked the body. A thin whimper broke from Bug-Rump. "He's had enough for six!'' He lowered his head once more. ''And you . . . you told me it was all finished.'' His voice was a vicious whisper.

Not a muscle stirred in Still One's body, not a flicker of his thoughts showed on his features as he stared back at the huge head looming barely a feeler's length from his own.

''Well?'' grunted Dew-Lover, ''What have you to say?''

''Nothing,'' answered Still One. ''There is nothing to say.''

''What? You mean you haven't even a story for the occasion? I thought you always had a story.'' Dew-Lover straightened up. ''Well then, let's see if we can give you something more to build a story on.'' He turned to the two soldier-ants. ''Pick him up.'' He nodded down at Bug-Rump. The soldiers obeyed, supporting the frail figure once more between them. ''Hold him in front of me.'' They did so. Dew-Lover straightened his forelegs, towering over the semi-inert body, and curled his thick, heavy sting forward towards the worker's underbelly. He looked at Still One and said, ''It is the law of the colony that he should die for what he has done. I shall now carry out that sentence. Unless . . .'' he added with malicious amusement, ''you can find a story to dissuade me. Well? Have you such a magical tale, friend Story Teller?''

''I will tell you a story,'' answered Still One softly.

Dew-Lover hesitated, taken aback. He stared at the other suspiciously for a moment, then relaxed his rigid stance. ''Are you playing games with me?'' he growled.

''You asked me for a story,'' said Still One. ''If you will listen then I will tell you one.''

''It had better be a good one,'' replied Dew-Lover threateningly, ''or I might just transfer the sentence to you.''

''That is for you to decide,'' said Still One. He paused a moment, then began.

''There was a tiny seedling in the ground on the side of a mountain. And in the spring it began to grow. But close beside it on the mountain stood a rye-grass stem. And it saw the seedling growing and it said, 'Who are you to grow in my space? That I will not allow.' And it spread its blades and cut off the sun from the seedling, and the seedling withered and died. But beside the grass stem stood a fern. And the fern saw the grass stem spread its blades and it said, 'Who are you to spread your leaves in my space? That I will not allow.' And it spread its fronds, and cut off the sun from the grass stem, and the grass stem withered and died. But beside the fern stood a hawthorn bush, and beside the hawthorn bush stood an ash tree, and beside the ash stood a huge elm. And each one spread its branches to cut off the sun from the one beneath so that all below the elm withered and died. But then the mountain on whose side all these had grown saw the elm spread its branches and said, 'Who are you to kill all the plants which grow on my slopes? That I will not allow.' And the mountain cast its shade and cut off the sun from the elm, and it sent down its waters to tear at the roots of the elm, and it hurled down its rocks to beat at the trunk of the elm, and the elm tumbled and perished. And then the sun looked down and saw that there was nothing left growing on the mountain on which to cast its warmth. And so it departed the heavens, and there was darkness everywhere.''

He stopped speaking and in the silence that followed it seemed indeed as if the warmth had gone from the sun although in fact it was still shining. Dew-Lover stood staring at Still One as if the power had gone from his limbs, a strange expression of bewilderment on his face. Then that expression was replaced by a look of absolute fury—whether because he could not understand the implications of the story or whether because he understood all too well, it was impossible to say—but with a roar of rage he stepped up to Still One and struck him a blow with his huge clawed forefoot, which sent the other tumbling head over heels in the dust. He lay there, half stunned, an evil gash on the side of his head, as Dew-Lover came up and stood over him.

"Try and make a fool of me with your stories, would you?" he bellowed. "We'll see about that. There are no mountains hereabouts to do your fighting for you!" And he kicked the prostrate body forcing a gasp of pain from Still One.

"What is the trouble here?" The voice momentarily diverted Dew-Lover and he turned in its direction. Old Five Legs had approached, unnoticed in the commotion, with Never-Rest at his side.

"I'll tell you what the trouble is, old one," growled Dew-Lover viciously. "Rebellion, that's what it is. Your workers thieving at the royal supplies. And this one trying to make fools of his leaders with stupid stories. It's rebellion, my friend, and I wonder where it started from." He lowered his head characteristically in Five Legs' direction. "Could it be that they get their example from their spokesman, who makes seditious speeches on the floor of the Council chamber?"

Five Legs stared at the half conscious bodies of the two worker-ants. "If it's these two you mean," he said calmly, "I think you've probably chosen the two ants least capable of rebellion in the entire colony."

The fury kindled once more in Dew-Lover's eyes. "Indeed?" he replied dangerously. "And how do you know what is in the hearts of each worker? You have direct access to their innermost thoughts perhaps."

"Only the Lord of the Stars has that," replied Five Legs. "But I think I know many of them fairly well."

"Then you and the Lord of the Stars had better do some very fast explaining," said Dew-Lover, "because all I see is rebellion. And you know what my answer to that is." And he turned once more to Still One, lifted the inert body by the head with his great mandibles and held it aloft. "Well?" he demanded and curled his sting forward ready to strike.

At that moment, when Still One's life apparently hung

in the balance, it seemed as if the Lord of the Stars did indeed take a hand in the proceedings, but with an event that eclipsed in drama anything that was happening in that little group. A sudden series of panic-stricken shouts and scuttlings from the edge of the forest nearby made everyone turn their heads. Ants were fleeing in all directions out of the low line of undergrowth bordering the clearing and their cries could be clearly heard: "The Tawny Killer-Bird! The Tawny Killer-Bird!" Then, before anyone in the group could move from their frozen postures, there came a great rustling and shaking amongst the trees, and bursting into the clearing, with its yellow eyes glinting and its red-gold plumage flaming in the sunshine, hurtled the forest dweller that ants fear perhaps more than any other.

The Tawny Killer-Bird is one of the few bird species who have an appetite for ants and are not afraid to attack their nests in order to find the juicy larvae buried deep inside. This was a cock bird, lean and vicious after the winter and quite undiscriminating in its hunger. Its gigantic golden shape, with its dark, shining green neck and head and its splendid arch of streaked tail feathers, sped this way and that around the clearing with enormous strides of its long taloned legs, the curved beak snapping with the speed and ferocity of lighting at the ants fleeing from its path. Then, following the general direction taken by the frantic insects, it suddenly saw the base mound itself. It checked its pace for a moment, cocked a fearsome eye at the teeming hordes upon the hillock, and launched itself in a gleeful assault, sprinting a full pace to the summit, scratching at the grassy surface and pecking dementedly at the scrabbling, struggling mass of insect life exposed upon it.

Deep inside the mound, where he was holding a conference with some of his officers, Black Sting felt the sudden tremors shaking the earth around him and fell silent, his antennae quivering to pick up a clue as to what was happening. Then he whipped into action.

"Racer, collect every soldier available and get them to the surface! One Eye, warn Noble and the Royal Guard to protect the Royal Quarters if they're not already on their way. The rest of you, follow me!" And he was away, speeding up the tunnel towards the surface.

As Black Sting and his band of officers climbed above the outside ground level and into the mound itself, they could feel the reverberating earth tremors even more clearly and now the passages were filled with a terrified mass of fleeing ants through which they had to fight their way. From the shouts around him Black Sting soon learned the nature of the catastrophe and he felt a cold chill of despair that was utterly unfamiliar to him. He knew that there was scarcely any way in which he and his soldiers, however brave or numerous, could challenge such an assailant.

However, the thought did not cause him to hesitate, merely to redouble his efforts to fight his way upwards, roaring, "Out of the way! Clear the way!" over the frightened yelling of the crowd.

The vibrations and clawing sounds from above grew even more violent and showers of earth and small stones were now falling from the passage roof and walls upon the ants beneath, adding to the general pandemonium. It seemed for a moment as if Black Sting's way would be barred completely by a solid wall of ants and earth, but then suddenly this barrier appeared to explode and disappear from his astonished gaze, to be replaced by a dazzling flood of daylight as a huge, taloned claw simply ripped away that whole section of the mound's surface. As the rumble of earth and the screams of terrified ants faded down the hillslope Black Sting shouted to the officers behind him to follow and raced for the great gaping hole now open in front of him. Again the talon struck a little lower this time, and another large section of the tunnel's floor crumbled down the slope. Black Sting found himself rolling and tumbling down in its wake, other bodies falling alongside. Scrabbling and clawing at the loose earth, he fought his way to one side until his feet miraculously came into contact with firm, rooted grass stems and he was able to hang on and pull himself onto a relatively stable surface. He took a firm foothold and looked about him.

It was a stupefying sight. The gigantic bird was perched on the very summit of the hillock, above and to one side of Black Sting's position. Its looming shape, taller than the height of the mound itself, blotted out the sun, and its nearest talon—the one which had done the damage to Black Sting's tunnel—was now tearing with fearful results at an area of hillside some twenty ant-lengths up from where he was standing. Showers of earth mingled with the crushed bodies of unfortunate ants caught under the beast's claw were flying down the slope and already a massive part of the hillock's upper section had been destroyed. The bird evidently knew what it was seeking, because now it was ignoring the fleeing mass of ants and every so often its long neck would stretch down and it would bury its great hooked beak into the exposed earth, rooting around for more succulent prey. Black Sting knew that the brood chambers, with their packed ranks of soft, vulnerable larvae, were set deep in the earth far below the ground level but even so, if the bird was determined enough, it was quite capable of destroying the entire mound and digging right down to the brood chambers and the Royal Quarters themselves in its ravenous search.

It was now that Black Sting proved what a superb fighting ant he was. It was not a conscious act of bravery that prompted him nor the automatic call to duty of a being who knew no fear. It was rather the instinctive reaction of one who understood no other way to respond to danger than to meet it head on with all the faculties at his command and to entrust the outcome to fate. With only a vague idea of what he was going to do he began to climb the slope directly above him. Fighting his way up through the grass, loose soil and stones and the still fleeing, scattered waves of ants, he reached the summit, perhaps a quarter of the way round its circumference from where the Tawny Killer-Bird was causing so much damage. He could

see now that many of his own soldiers were milling around
the feet of the monster, clinging to its talons, scrabbling up
its legs, spearing ineffectively again and again the hard
yellow, scaly skin with their stings. He was aware too, out
of the corner of his eye, of the big form of Dew-Lover
lumbering towards the bird from further round the mound;
but he did not wait for his lieutenant to catch up. He knew
that the other's strength would be of little help in this
instance.

With a cold anger glinting in his eyes Black Sting sped
across the top of the mound to join the battle. He could see
that his soldier's puny stings were quite useless against the
thick hide and plumage of their attacker, but somewhere in
the back of his mind he had an idea that the creature was
not totally invulnerable and that, if any ant had a chance of
finding its weakness, he had.

As he approached the huge, earth-stained talon upon
which the bird was standing, Black Sting roared to the
frantic soldier-ants around it to make way for him. With
relief in their eyes they fell back to allow their leader to
pass. He ran at the bird's leg and leapt at its ridged surface
just above the smooth, hard curve of the outer claw.
Withholding the use of his sting, he threaded his way up
the limb between the lunging bodies of the soldiers upon it
and reached the lower fringes of plumage encasing the
thick upper leg. Once on the overlapping, ribbed surfaces
of the feathers themselves he could make easier progress
and he climbed higher and higher, closing his mind to the
suffocating odour of the beast which now assailed his
senses. He could feel the movements of its body like earth
tremors beneath his feet and he was dimly wary of the
shouting and the turmoil falling away below him, but he
did not pause to look, sticking grimly to the task of
climbing ever higher towards his goal.

Halfway up the flank he sensed danger as a large shadow
flitted repeatedly across his vision and he realized the bird
was flapping its wings as it fought to maintain its balance
on the mound's crest. He changed course slightly away

from this threat to climb the steep, overhanging curve of the creature's breast, and soon he was past the wings and the colour of the plumage under his feet changed from a rich, golden brown to the shimmering green and black of the neck. Now came the most hazardous part of his journey, for he was suddenly taken by surprise as the sky spun dizzily over his head, his weight shifted, threatening to topple him from his grasp, and the air rushed past his body. He realized that the bird was making another of its lunging beak-stabs at the ground beneath. Black Sting hung on grimly for an interminable moment, as the shouts and the spatter of flying earth sounded once more around him, then he was soaring upwards again to the same dizzy height. He did not wait for the ride to be repeated a second time, but, with the last remains of his strength he heaved himself up the final stretch of the giant's neck and on to the crest of its head.

It must have been here that the Tawny Killer-Bird at last became aware of his presence, for suddenly all motion beneath him ceased and he could sense the creature pausing in its work as it tired to determine what the small irritation on its brow might be. It shook its head to try and dislodge it and once more Black Sting had to cling on for dear life to avoid being flung to the winds. But nothing was going to deter him now for he could see his goal in front of him—that one single organ that he instinctively knew was the beast's only vulnerable spot—the glistening, translucent curve of its eyeball, longer than his own body and partially hidden from him by the fleshy stretch of its protective lid.

The Tawny Killer-Bird stood motionless again, seeking to discover if the irritation was still there, and Black Sting seized the opportunity. He ran forward over the edge of the brow to the very corner of the gleaming orb where the two lids met. There he spun round, clinging to the fine strands of down at the edge, so that the base of his abdomen hung poised over the glassy surface of the eye itself. The bird, sensing the movement, instinctively closed

the protective shield of its lids but Black Sting held on,
awaiting his moment. As the lids inquisitively parted again
he struck downwards. The point of his dark, curving sting
pierced the transparent surface of the eye's cornea and
sank, half its length deep, into the soft, moist texture. The
lids immediately closed again, trapping Black Sting's body
between them, but if anything this gave an added impetus
to the jet of poison he sent squirting deep into the tissue of
the eye. Then he struggled frantically to free himself from
the crushing grasp around his abdomen before the reaction
came.

Perhaps it was as well that he could not do so immediately, for he may well not have survived the ensuing
eruption of sound and movement that followed his attack.
With a screech that split the heavens the huge bird reared
upwards, its wings beating the air into a miniature whirl-
wind, its talons pounding the earth in a frenzied dance of
rage and shock. It half slithered, half flew down the side
of the mound, its claws tearing still more earth from the
ravaged surface, and then flailed around distractedly amidst
the grass as it sought to ease the burning pain in its eye.
Black Sting clung on with all his force as earth and sky
spun around his head in a demented blur. He was aware
only of a holocaust of sand, wind and motion which
seemed to have no end, until suddenly the pressure around
his body was released and he was falling dizzily through
space, turning over and over, until he finally hit the ground
with a thud that shook every particle in his body and
immersed him in a welcome, oblivious darkness.

They carried his inert form with tender care back to the
shattered mound. Past lines of silent, watching ants they
brought him, past the black earth-falls and the tumbled
piles of stones, up the corpse-strewn flank of the hillock
and into the sanctuary of the darkness inside. Down into
the depths of the earth they took him, until finally they laid
him in an innermost chamber, bathed and tended his battered body and performed their secret ant's rituals. All

through that day and the following night they mouthed their ancient orisons to assist his own formidable recuperative powers to do their work.

At one point late in that long night there came a message to the chamber and a hush fell over all the ants there. They lowered their heads and drew back their feelers in humble reverence as a huge, regal form loomed quietly in the dark, paused for a moment beside the still figure, whispered with some of the dignitaries present and then melted away again back to the Royal Chamber.

Then at last, some time in the morning of the following day, Black Sting stirred, sighed, twisted an antenna and finally moved his head to look around him. It took some time for him to realize, in the numbed confusion of his mind, that the darkness was not in his head but about him. He knew that something catastrophic had happened but he could not remember what it was. He sensed the quiet movement around him and felt the dull pain in his body but knew not the source of either. Then, as he tentatively stretched his bruised limbs, testing them, he was aware of a presence approaching him and of Dew-Lover's voice growling at his side.

"Are you awake, leader?"

"Where am I? What happened?" murmured Black Sting.

"You're safe," came the answer. "We brought you back. You're all right."

Then he sensed others approaching and he heard Great Head's voice coming out of the unreal depth of the darkness: "How are you, brave soldier? You've had a terrible fall. How are you feeling?"

Then he remembered. He remembered the Tawny Killer-Bird and all that had happened. He tried to raise himself up saying, "What happened? The bird—what happened?" but the effort caused a searing pain through his head and he fell back swooning again.

"Stay," said Great Head. "You must rest. There is nothing to fear now. The Killer-Bird will not trouble us again for a long time."

Black Sting thought of the many dead and wounded of his kind, caught in the bird's onslaught. He thought of the fearful damage done to the mound above his head. He remembered the threat of the red ants, now so much more dangerous with the colony in its maimed, vulnerable state. "There is so much to do," he murmured.

"Yes, yes," replied Great Head calmly. "But not now. There is plenty of time. First you must get better. Here, the Queen of Queens has sent some of the last of the honey-dew to help you in your recovery. Eat now, and rest, and later we shall start afresh."

And he slept again, dreaming weird, hallucinatory dreams that spoke of worlds and powers and happenings far beyond those about him.

* 11 *

He was battling alone with a gigantic spider. It towered above him, slashing clumsily at him with its huge mandibles. But he evaded them nimbly. He felt strong, alert, unafraid. The darkened undergrowth around was his terrain and he used it to advantage, darting from stem to stem, lunging unexpectedly down behind a leaf, undaunted even by the further looming shapes of more spiders approaching behind the first. He picked his moment and leapt forward, clinging to the beast's hairy leg and swinging his abdomen up, up, until the sting pierced the soft underside of his opponent's throat. With a hiss and a shudder the creature wheeled away and staggered off into the shadows and he turned to meet the next one. Again the confrontation, giant and midget, the sparring, the thrusting, the advance, the evasion. And again the final nimble sally, the unexpected thrust, and the victory of skill over brute force. And so on, monster after monster, confronted, challenged and vanquished, until the dawn came and there were none left to fight and he stood there, master of the ground.

And he cried out: "That is my purpose! To challenge evil. To confront our foes. To battle with all the strength and skill and courage that is in me and to defeat the enemy one by one, until there are no more left to defeat. Or perhaps even until I myself am defeated and must perish. Surely that is my purpose?"

And the Voice replied: "Yes, it is possible that is your purpose. But remember that your enemies too have their purpose. And to them, you are the enemy, you are the evil. And they too will be ready to fight until they perish. And it may be that the fighting will go on until there is no one left to fight. Who is there who can fight for the end of the fighting—can you tell that?"

And he could not. And he was alone again, struggling into wakefulness, trying to remember whence the Voice had come.

* 12 *

The three ants had not rested until high-sun that day, when sheer exhaustion had forced them to halt for a while. They had chased a woodlouse out of a crevice in a dead tree branch lying off to one side of the trail and there, in relative security, they had dozed uneasily by turns while one or another of them had kept watch. The wind had risen early that morning and the sun had retreated behind a racing barrier of wild spring clouds. The trees of the forest had come to life, whispering, groaning, gesticulating at one another. It seemed to the ants, unused to being in the centre of such a vociferous uproar so far from the shelter of their mound, as if the woods were protesting at their own intrusion, that every crash and whistle was directed specifically at them, and the thought had given an added urgency to their scurrying feet all through the morning. When they finally rested no one slept easily through all the continuing noise and movement, as Dreamer's own disturbed murmurings and stirrings testified, and Joker chaffed him about his dreams as they set off again on the trail.

Snake's Tongue was even more silent than usual as he led the way along the well-defined route. Amongst all the commotion of the wind around him, he was concentrating on using greater than ever caution for the signs were more and more obvious that the red ants commonly frequented these parts: there was still less evidence of other forms of life around, and the converging side trails were becoming more frequent, each one adding its own trace of the distinctive red ant spoor to the general scent on the main track. Strangely though there was no further sign of any red ant parties themselves and paradoxically Snake's Tongue found this rather disturbing, though he did not communicate his worry to the other two.

Despite their aches and their nervousness at the display of Nature's force around them, the three were working well as a team now. The various trials and dangers they had encountered had fostered a trust and a mutual dependence between them. Each one knew the other's worth, each had proved his courage and justified the faith placed in him, and now there was an unquestioning acceptance of one another's role in this lonely mission.

They had been on their journey now for an entire revolution of the sun and although their encounter with the spider had temporarily replenished their food supply, they were beginning to wonder how much further they would have to march. The terrain had been changing gradually throughout the morning. The ground had been rising imperceptibly but steadily, the trees becoming less lofty and less dense, allowing the undergrowth beneath more scope for growth and variety. The scents of unfamiliar plants and bushes wafted past the ants' antennae, foreign bird calls sounded from time to time in that other world above their heads and even the soil had a texture and a smell that was strange to senses so conditioned by the riverside habitat. They travelled for a further period, the ground rising more and more steeply, until they could see ahead of them a broad expanse of light and sky where the trees appeared to come to an end. The wind dropped as they approached this boundary, as if heralding a significant arrival, and with a mounting sense of anticipation and excitement the three cautiously climbed the final slope, until they broke out of the trees and the undergrowth, mounted a further rising, grassy space dotted with budding gorse and heather clumps, and finally came to a halt on the crest of a ridge which for all they knew might have been the edge of the world.

It was not, of course, but it provided a vantage point on a part of the world that was altogether unfamiliar and astonishing. They were standing on the summit of a bank that was perhaps twice the height of their own base mound. Below the bank the land was level and stretched away to an infinity far beyond the range of their limited vision. From this ground a series of scents and sounds new to their experience reached their quivering senses: the smell of peat and dry moorland turf; the lonely cry of the curlew punctuating the ceaseless, ecstatic trill of the skylark; and the secret, distant message of the wind stalking the wide heath.

But more startling than all this was what lay in the foreground. Only perhaps two large tree-lengths from where they were standing, rising out of the flat, rippling grassland like a great rock anchored in the sea, stood a vast ant mound. Higher and wider than anything within the capabilities of their own species to construct, it was a monstrous edifice of mingled earth and sand, pine needles and dead grass stems, broken here and there by uneven patches of living grass and the occasional sprouting flora which had taken root upon its surface. And upon this surface, teeming in their hundreds, mounting and descending in purposeful, ordered lines, spreading out across the surrounding countryside in lordly phalanx and with arrogant step, were the enemy they had come to find.

Dreamer stared in wonder at the astonishing sight. It was a revelation to him that there were members of the same order of life as himself upon the earth who could exist so differently and in such a different landscape.

At his side Joker too was staring. "Not afraid of much, are they?" was his eventual whispered comment.

And certainly the red ants exhibited a confidence and a lack of caution which indicated that they did not have much to fear within their domain. Apart from a few lone, stationary figures placed at strategic points about the mound, who were obviously sentinels, there was very little attempt at either concealment or precaution on the part of those out in the open. Then on closer observation, the watchers noticed that these groups did not consist solely of the big russet-bodied insects. Most of the large parties progressing backwards and forwards from the mound consisted of a central core of smaller, brown-hued members of their own or a similar species, surrounded by a cordon of the red ants. And it was these poor, oppressed creatures who were evidently burdened with most of the colony's tasks of heavy labour, while their escorts merely acted as guards and supervisors. It was the smaller ants who transported building materials, waste matter, food and supplies back and forth; it was they who cleared trails and excavated drainage channels, who dug the tunnels and repaired the surface of the great mound, who in fact performed all the menial and domestic tasks under the haughty eye of their warrior masters.

"They're using them as slaves!" whispered Dreamer appalled.

"That's why they took the larvae from the riverside colony," muttered Joker. "To breed them as workers. Idle lot, aren't they?"

"Not so very different from our own system," said Snake's Tongue. The other looked at him curiously. "We just have a worker caste instead of using other species." But he did not elaborate on the statement.

Dreamer considered the idea with interest. It threw a new light on its exponent. Little by little he was learning more about the strange, reticent personality who was leading them and each new facet came as a surprise, as if somehow it was a quality inappropriate to a purely military being.

Snake's Tongue meanwhile had returned his mind to another subject of more immediate import. It was puzzling to him that, even accounting for the apparent lack of caution on the part of the alien ants, the three had been able to approach so closely without encountering any of them. The sense of unease which had been troubling him during the last stage of their journey now redoubled. He stared ahead towards the huge mound, trying to discover why none of the otherwise ubiquitous activity was happening in their direction. Then, with that sinking feeling in the stomach which always accompanied the realization of an awful truth, he suddenly understood. He turned, slowly and calmly, almost knowing what he would see.

Sure enough, behind them, evidently having emerged from the trees at the forest edge and effectively cutting off all chance of escape, stood a motionless rank of perhaps twenty of the enemy. Utterly still and silent, they watched like strange deified apparitions who had appeared from nowhere to stand in judgement on these rash intruders into their kingdom.

At his side Dreamer and Joker became aware that something was amiss and they too turned. They stared without speaking at the forbidding sight. Inevitably it was Joker who broke the tension.

"Do you suppose it's a welcoming party?" he muttered.

"Stay where you are," said Snake's Tongue. He took a few paces forward towards the line of ants and stood alone, waiting.

From the centre of the line a lone red ant stepped forward. Two others joined him, one on either side, and with an easy, authoritative gait the three approached up the slope. As they came nearer Dreamer was able to study these strange creatures more carefully. Fully half again as big as themselves, they had immensely long legs, which carried their elongated bodies high off the ground, and they bore their wide, powerful mandibles and short, thick antennae at a lofty angle, which increased their air of aggressive arrogance. The ant in the centre, who was evidently in command, was slightly larger than the other two and he moved with an easy, athletic grace which, were it not that it boded so ill for an enemy, would have been quite beautiful to watch. The trio came to within a grass stem's length of Snake's Tongue and stopped. Snake's Tongue held his ground and the six ants regarded each other for a long moment. Then the leader of the red ants spoke. His voice had a strange, rasping quality to it, containing none of the undulating muscle tones used by their own species, but it was nevertheless not an unpleasant sound.

"You are very small for such fighters."

Snake's Tongue hesitated, puzzled, "Fighters? I don't understand," he said.

"You slew Wide-Jaws the tree-spider without injury to yourselves. This is impressive."

"Ah," said Snake's Tongue. "Is that how you found us?"

"We heard the noise of your battle and sent scouts to see. We have watched your progress here."

Snake's Tongue nodded. "That is impressive too. We had no knowledge you were watching us."

The red ant's antennae hovered questioningly in Snake's Tongue's direction. "You are either very brave or very foolish," he said. "Why have you come to certain death?"

"We only came out of curiosity," answered Snake's Tongue. "We mean you no harm."

The other gave a short, sharp bark of amusement. "You mean *us* no harm! And what harm could three such creatures threaten us with?" Snake's Tongue did not reply. The red ant went on: "Curiosity is a strange motive for such a foolhardy journey. Where have you come from?"

Snake's Tongue hesitated again. Should he discuss the reason for their coming? There seemed little point in not doing so, especially as the red ants already knew from which direction they had travelled. "We have come from beyond the riverside colony which you destroyed four sun-ups ago," he said. "We wished to discover who such fierce killers might be."

The other stared at him impassively. "Well, now you know," he said. "What do you hope to gain by the information?"

"We have orders to return and inform our Council," replied Snake's Tongue.

"Your Council?" asked the other curiously.

"Yes. The body that is chosen to rule us."

"Ah." A flicker of amusement crossed the red ant's features. "Chosen. How quaint. Do you have none amongst you powerful enough to rule by strength?"

"Certainly," answered Snake's Tongue, "but we do not consider strength to be the only quality necessary for a leader."

The red ant looked vaguely puzzled. Then he asked, "And what will your Council do when you do not return?"

"I don't know," said Snake's Tongue truthfully.

"How far and how big is your colony?"

"That you must find out for yourselves," he replied.

The red ant studied him contemplatively. "We shall," he said. "Come. It is time for you to meet our own leader. The Spider awaits your presence."

He nodded to one of his companions, who turned and signalled with his antennae to the waiting line of ants at the forest edge. The line began to move forward towards them. "Follow me," said their commander, and without looking to see if his order was obeyed, he skirted round the three smaller ants and began to descend the ridge. The other two with him indicated to Snake's Tongue to follow. Realizing that there was no chance of escaping and no point in disobeying, he did so, with Dreamer and Joker following and the line of red ants at some distance behind.

The commander of the little force was striding out with his long, graceful gait towards the huge mound, and even Snake's Tongue had to run almost flat out to keep up with him.

"Why is your leader called The Spider?" he asked as they went.

"You will see," the other tossed back. "Strength is the only quality *he* requires to hold his position. You had better pray you don't experience it." And he quickened his pace as if to discourage further conversation.

Snake's Tongue allowed the others to catch up with him, the two red ants following a few paces behind. He muttered in a low voice, "Keep a look out. Remember our route. Take note of anything you see."

"Wish I knew what use it could be," muttered Joker back.

"You never know," replied Snake's Tongue. "Don't lose hope."

"No talking!" barked one of the red ants behind and the three of them concentrated in keeping up with the leader and observing their surroundings.

Had the circumstances not been so desperate these would have been fascinating. They were travelling a well-worn path through a jungle of high, coarse grasses and heathland plants that were quite unfamiliar to them and it soon become obvious that the amount of activity they had been able to see from their viewpoint on the ridge was only a fraction of what was actually going on within and under this labyrinth. It was dissected by a maze of trails and pathways leading this way and that in all directions, and upon these routes a vast complexity of organized activity was taking place. Working parties of all types and sizes were moving hither and thither; ordered contingents of soldiers marching with measured step; shuffling groups of enslaved worker-ants bearing loads of building materials; lone messengers hurrying on urgent missions. Only on the particular trail by which they had approached had all movement been prevented by the simple expedient of placing guards at strategic points to turn back any who sought to come that way. Their own progress appeared to attract little attention for there were many such parties of smaller ants under the guard of the ruling species around and it was only their relative self-possession and independence of bearing which might seem unusual.

Dreamer found himself wondering how on earth this vast population was able to feed itself, but that question too was soon answered as they drew nearer to the great mound and trails began to converge upon their own at a wider angle, evidently leading from regions far distant to those from whence they had come. Upon these routes they encountered more and more frequent parties bearing food supplies: larvae and pupae from the raided homes of insects of a myriad of different species; the inert corpses of small beetles, mayflies, aphid bugs; the dissected segments of an enormous caterpillar; even bodies of the red ant kind themselves who had perished on some distant battle. It was evident that they foraged far and wide for food, systematically stripping the countryside region by region, leaving each totally denuded of insect life before moving on to the next. The ruthless efficiency of the system made him shudder and he wondered whether there was any limit to the population growth of this great colony. For the first time on the mission Dreamer began to experience a real sense of fear. Even the encounter with the spider had been preferable in its urgency and excitement to this cold, silent uncertainty which faced them now.

The party was approaching the mound. They caught glimpses of its towering flank through the grasses in front of them and soon they were climbing its lower slopes where the vegetation was thinning out. The path grew steeper and steeper, making it harder to negotiate the busy traffic upon it. The cliff face of the great ant-made mountain towered almost vertically above them and the flat heathland fell away beneath as they climbed. The black, gaping mouths of tunnel entrances appeared and dropped away beneath them, at the same time swallowing up many of the other insects moving about the slope so that the general activity thinned as they climbed higher. Then at last they reached a level shelf or small plateau situated perhaps two-thirds of the way up the mound's flank, and here the leader stopped. The three smaller ants and their two escorts climbed up behind him and also halted. The line of soldier-ants behind had already come to a halt some way down the cliff face, leaving the smaller party to continue on its own. Now the six ants stood on the edge of the level space, staring towards a dark, cavernlike orifice in the cliff side. Half a dozen other senior-looking ants stood grouped around the cave entrance and there was considerable coming and going of various individuals intent on urgent-seeming business.

"Spooky-looking place," whispered Joker beside Dreamer. "The Spider's lair, do you suppose?"

One of the ants at the cave mouth came towards them and held a brief murmured conversation with their captor's leader. Then he looked curiously at the prisoners for a moment, turned and went back to the cavern, disappearing inside. The other turned to them.

"You are about to meet The Spider," he said. "He will probably wish to ask you some questions. I advise you to answer them and to do nothing to provoke his anger. It is a frightening thing." And he turned back to the cave mouth again.

There was an expectant silence around the little plateau. Dreamer felt a scent of finality, as if this was the last moment left to him of the life he had known, as if the sunlight was about to vanish forever. He stared down at the distant panorama of landscape presented from this dizzying vantage point. He noted the wild grass rippling into the hazy distance and the clouds galloping majestically across the sky and was reminded of his recurring dream during the Long Sleep, the dream of climbing the high mountain. He almost expected to hear his Voice in reality for the first time, booming from the heights of the peak above him.

But it was a different voice he was to hear. There was a sudden stiffening in the demeanour of the ants around the cave mouth and they began to fall back respectfully to the sides. The blackness of the opening seemed to grow darker still as an enormous bulk filled it. A strange bronchial hiss could be heard echoing within the confines of the cavern as if, for its originator, the very act of breathing was something to be aggressively attacked rather than naturally performed. Then out from the cave emerged the biggest ant Dreamer had ever seen. It was not simply the monumental physical presence which made such an impact, though this in itself was inspiring enough. There was also something about the creature's personality—a massive implacability, a total assumption of omnipotent right and authority—which was mesmerizing in its complacency, frightening in its inflexibility. One could see instantly why he was called The Spider. There was that same squat solidity, that same impenetrable doggedness. Even the stance was similar, with the enormous body slung low between wide-splayed legs rather than poised alertly at the apex in the usual manner, as if actual movement were the last consideration; as if it were the world that always came to him, rarely the reverse.

This monster stood for a moment before his cave, peering at the daylight as if it were an intrusion on his sovereignty. Then he looked across to where the little party of trespassers stood with the captors. He moved with leisurely impassiveness towards them, his size seeming to increase with every step. The ant who had led them there stepped forward to meet him and, standing dwarfed in his shadow, muttered to him in a low voice. He then stood aside and The Spider approached until he loomed above them within almost a feeler's touch of Snake's Tongue. The strange rasp of his breathing was curiously hypnotic as he studied the threesome for a long, unnerving moment.

His voice, when it came, was a cavernous rumble. "They tell me you were sent to find out about us."

"Yes," answered Snake's Tongue.

The Spider stared at him from his great height.

"They tell me you defeated Wide-Jaws."

"Yes."

Again the stare, again the ominous pause. Then: "Perhaps you would like to make an occupation of slaying spiders?'' The question was followed by a sudden, startling bellow of amusement. ''Well?'' he asked.

''Only if they threaten our own lives,'' answered Snake's Tongue in a calm voice.

The Spider nodded contemplatively. ''Only if they threaten your lives,'' he repeated slowly. Then he lowered his gigantic head until it was almost touching Snake's Tongue, the thick, heavy antennae arched over the other's back. ''Well, do you think you could kill this spider so easily?'' he growled in a voice like distant thunder.

Snake's Tongue hesitated. ''I can't imagine there are many ants on the face of the earth who could do that,'' he replied.

''You are right.'' The Spider withdrew his head from its threatening position and his voice returned to its formal tone. ''Where have you come from?''

''Our own colony,'' answered Snake's Tongue.

''Where is that?''

''Beyond the riverside mound you conquered four sun-ups ago.''

''How far beyond?''

''That I cannot say.''

There was a pause. The Spider looked down at him without expression.

''How large is your colony?''

''Larger than the riverside one.''

''How much larger?''

''That also I cannot say.''

Again the pause. The rasp of The Spider's breathing seemed to be the only sound in the living world. Then, with astonishing rapidity for one built on such a cumbersome scale, his great forefoot lifted and came down on the back of Snake's Tongue's thorax, flattening him to the ground beneath its weight.

Rapid though the movement was, Dreamer had seen Snake's Tongue's reflexes in action and he knew that his leader could have avoided it. But he chose not to, allowing himself be pinned to the ground, quite helpless. Both Dreamer and Joker instinctively followed his passive example and did not react to the move.

"Then let *me* tell *you*," said the Spider venomously. "Your colony is just a few sun-ups' journey for my soldiers from here. It is large enough for me to require more than half my fighting force to destroy it. And it has enough larvae in its brood chambers to provide me with many slaves and keep my army supplied with food for many days. That much information we have already discovered from the unfortunate inhabitants of the riverside colony." The great weight lifted from Snake's Tongue's back. "So you see there is nothing I need from you. And no reason to keep you alive."

Snake's Tongue got carefully back to his feet. "And no reason to kill us either," he said, looking up at the huge ant.

The other cocked a quizzical feeler at him. "Why should I not kill you?" he demanded. "You are less nuisance to me dead, than alive as captives."

"Then let us go," replied Snake's Tongue.

"Let you go?" came the amazed reply.

"Why not?" asked Snake's Tongue. "Unless of course you are afraid to."

There was an uneasy stiffening amongst the ants within earshot. Something stirred in Dreamer's memory, puzzling him; and then he suddenly remembered Still One's story of the ants and the Giant Two-Legs. Had Snake's Tongue too remembered it, he wondered. Was he consciously putting it to use? He waited, breathless, for The Spider's reaction and was conscious of Joker, frozen, equally expectant, at his side.

The Spider stared at Snake's Tongue for a long, tense moment. Then he roared once more with amusement. "Afraid?" he bellowed. "Afraid of you! Why should I be afraid of *you?*"

"No reason at all," answered Snake's Tongue. "We wish you no harm, even if we could do you any. Therefore you have no reason to be afraid. And, as I say, no reason not to let us go.''

The Spider looked round at his subordinates on the plateau. "Did you hear that, soldiers? This is a clever ant we have here. He says we have no reason to kill him, because we have no reason to fear him. That is a clever argument." He looked back at Snake's Tongue, his eyes glinting. "It seems to me that you are so clever we might indeed have reason to fear you. What do you say to that?"

"I say, what is there to fear in another's cleverness? Unless of course you make an enemy of him."

Again The Spider paused thoughtfully. Then he asked, "What do they call you, ant?"

"Snake's Tongue."

He nodded. "Very apt. Well, Tongue-of-the-Snake, let me tell you this." He lowered his head menacingly once again to Snake's Tongue's level. "*Every* creature who is not of our kind is enemy to our kind."

There was a silence as still as death itself, as the two ants, one as solid as rock, the other as nimble as water, stared at each other, eye to eye.

"That is very sad," said Snake's Tongue quietly.

The Spider raised his head once more, an expression of irritation on his features for the first time. He was tiring of this game of words which he could not seem to win.

"I will not let you go," he growled, "for the simple reason that I do not intend you to return and warn your colony about us. I have plans for your colony." He glowered malevolently round the three of them. "For the moment my sides are mainly engaged elsewhere, but when I am ready, and when the moment is ripe, then your colony shall learn all about me. I shall look forward to meeting your elders in person." He looked at Snake's Tongue for a moment, as if daring him to make a reply. Then he said, "However, Tongue-of-the Snake, I shall not kill you immediately. I have further use for you and your rash friends."

His great head swung round to where the ant who had led them there was standing. "Fleet, you are in charge of these three. Take them deep down and guard them well. We shall desire more information from them in time.''

"Yes, Spider," replied the ant, stepping forward.

The Spider's head came back towards Snake's Tongue. His voice suddenly dropped to a dangerously low, calm tone. "But before you go," he said, "I want you to understand, my clever friend, that I am not one to be trifled with."

Before anyone quite understood what was happening, the huge ant had lifted his forefoot again and taken the end of one of Snake's Tongue's antennae between the twin claws. Then his great mandibles also clamped around the slender organ, and, with a sudden vicious wrench of those tremendous neck and thorax muscles, he snapped the feeler like a dry reed and ripped away the entire end section.

The shock and the speed with which it happened were so great that for a moment no one moved. For Dreamer, ever afterwards, the incident had in retrospect a strange, unreal quality about it, as if it had occurred in one of his dreams. An ant's antennae are his most vital and sacred accoutrements. They are the instruments of his awareness, his chief means of self-expression, the insignia of his personality. That act of mutilation was the most cold-blooded desecration of Snake's Tongue's identity that the imagination could conceive.

Snake's Tongue himself was so taken aback at the suddenness of the assault that he remained frozen to the spot for several seconds. Then he staggered and the motion seemed to free everyone else from the bonds of their inactivity. Dreamer and Joker simultaneously ran forward to his side to support him; the rest of the red ants around the plateau moved and shifted uneasily, turning away and continuing with their business.

The Spider himself wheeled away unconcernedly, growling. "The tongue of the snake is perhaps not quite so effective when it has lost one of its forks," and he stalked with a ponderous lack of haste back to his lair.

Snake's Tongue stared at Dreamer and Joker, a dazed

expression in his eyes. Then the pain seemed to strike him, to clear his head, to shock him back to consciousness and he firmly regained his balance, tossing his head as if to shake his numbed senses back into place. The injured feeler, with perhaps a third of its length torn away, drooped pitifully, the exposed end moist and raw. Joker examined it.

"Not too bad," he said. "It's a clean break. It'll heal fairly quickly." He turned towards the ant called Fleet. "That is you if you'll find us some balm for it," he said in blunt tones. "Wild thyme or dock will do. Or don't you believe in treating the prisoners you've injured either?"

"We will find you something," answered the red ant, a hint of diffidence tempering his normal haughty tone. He signalled with his feelers to the two other soldiers behind them and then turned back. "Follow me," he said, "and don't attempt to escape. The next wound will be a more serious one."

He led the way to one side of the plateau. Joker and Dreamer looked to Snake's Tongue but he waved them on with his uninjured feeler. "Go on," he said. "I'm all right."

With one on either side of him he made his slow and painful way after Fleet. The other two red ants brought up the rear. The small party descended over the side of the plateau to the flank of the mound once more, dropped some way down and then entered one of the tunnel mouths. The darkness closed in and they found themselves within the great edifice that was the heart and centre of the red ants' existence.

* 13 *

In the secret recesses of the gorse clump, which stood alone between the mound and the stream, a scurry of surreptitious activity was taking place. Never-Rest, Wind-Blow and other older worker-ants were slipping in from the various corners of the clearing, mingling and muttering in the dry, secluded space at the centre of the clump and peering nervously through the spiky forest of gorse fronds towards the misshapen bulk of the damaged mound beyond. Word had been whispered around the trails and along the tunnels of the mound, secret messages had blown backwards and forwards through the community, and finally, in that mysterious, almost telepathic way that ants have, the consensus of all the discussion had brought the leaders of the worker's caste here to this agreed meeting place.

The sense of nervous expectation did not dissipate until the word went round: "Here he comes! Five Legs is coming." And into the group, with unhurried calm, came the old ant followed discreetly by Still One. The dozen or so ants there gathered round Five Legs and silence fell as they waited for him to speak.

He looked around the little gathering, studying the mood, noting the tense, apprehensive expressions. Then he said, "I've brought the Story Teller with me. I hope no one objects. I thought he might have something of use to say."

There was a general nodding of heads and murmuring of assent. Then Five Legs went on. "I think you all know why we've met. There has been a real feeling of worry amongst all the worker-ants about the Council's views on the rebuilding of the mound. I have never encountered such a genuine spread of unhappiness throughout our kind in all my summers."

More nods and murmurs of agreement. Five Legs continued: "This is a terrible time for us all. We have had a hard winter. Many of us have not awakened from the Long Sleep and those that have are in a weak and undernourished condition. With Thunderer gone, our colony is in a leaderless and uncertain state and the threat of the red ants hangs over us like a storm cloud. And now, to add to our troubles, there has been the terrible tragedy of the Tawny Killer-Bird's attack, which has damaged our home and killed many more of our kind. Such a disaster has not happened since the time, many summers ago, when it is said that the waters of the stream rose and flooded the mound, killing half its inhabitants. The fact that this time we have survived at all, that the mound was not completely destroyed and Our Great Mother and all her brood slaughtered, we owe to the sheer bravery and brilliant thinking of one single ant—Black Sting. On that we are all agreed and are eternally grateful." Again there was a murmur of agreement.

"And of course," he went on, "It is now our responsibility to repair the mound and bring the colony's life back to normal as quickly as possible. It will be a big task, that we recognize. However the Council has decreed that it be undertaken under conditions which give us grave cause for concern. They have set a time schedule which means that, even were our numbers at full strength and in peak condition, we would have virtually to double each worker's labour quota; and yet at the same time they have agreed, in the light of the red ants' threat, to request Our Great Mother to select the major part of the new brood of larvae for development as soldier-ants rather than workers, and to delay their hatching for that reason.''

Five Legs paused and looked round the gathering. The faces were solemn and attentive. No one seemed to want to interrupt him, so he continued. ''Now, as you know, the feeling has been slowly growing throughout the last two summers that perhaps we worker-ants should have a little more say in the ordering of our affairs; more influence in the life of the community. We don't wish to challenge the existing order or to pose a threat to the Council's authority, but the general opinion seems to be that there should be more recognition of our worth, more acceptance of the fact that the part we play in the colony's life is as important as anyone else's.'' Further mutterings of accord. ''And now, in this time of crisis when we have such a vital role to play, the rumblings of dissatisfaction appear to be coming to a head. I wonder whether anyone else would like to say something on the subject.''

The ants broke into a general murmur of discussion. Inevitably it was Wind-Blow who first spoke aloud, addressing the group in his compulsive, excitable fashion: ''We simply *can't* repair the mound in the time the Council has demanded. Not in our present state and with our present numbers. It's just not possible! We'd lose half our force through sheer strain and exhaustion.''

''I agree,'' spoke up another. ''It's a very dangerous job. It's going to need proper planning and preparation. If we rush at it there are going to be more catastrophes.''

''That's right,'' said someone else. ''What we need is consultation between all parties. Not just orders.''

''Absolutely.'' ''Quite so.'' ''Just what I think.'' The sound of agreement was unanimous. Then Never-Rest spoke up in his thoughtful, reasoned tone.

"I don't quite understand the need for the urgency in any case. Of course we want to put the mound back to order, but as far as the red ants are concerned, I don't see that it makes any difference what state it's in. It won't make it any easier to defend when it's repaired."

"That's true." "Quite right," went the murmur.

"In fact," went on Never-Rest, "we might wear ourselves out putting it back together again, just in time for the red ants to march in and take it over without so much as a thank you."

"It seems to me," said another, "that everyone is in this together. If the red ants attack then we're going to have to fight alongside the soldiers and die alongside them too. And in that case, if they want the mound repaired, then they ought to be prepared to work alongside us."

There was a tremendous outburst of approval at this—so much so that Five Legs had hastily to urge restraint—with an apprehensive look towards the mound.

Wind-Blow followed up the clamour, gabbling in his urgency. That's right. This isn't the time for orders and injunctions. This is a time for consultation and teamwork. We all face the crisis together. We should have a say in the decisions. We've said it before, we should have a voice in the Council!"

"That's it! That's right!" "A voice in the Council!" The agreement was emphatic, the mood suddenly determined and positive. The uncertainty had crystallized into a decision. Five Legs nodded and looked around to where Still One was standing quietly in the background.

"Do you have anything to say, Still One?" he asked. The noise of the meeting subsided. Everyone looked, waiting expectantly for Still One's response. As always it did not come immediately. When it did, it was in his usual still, soft voice, from his position on the outside of the group.

"I think a voice in the Council would be a very reasonable thing to ask for."

Nods and murmurings of accord. Then he added, "But what do you do when the request is refused?"

The ants looked at one another. They muttered and whispered to each other. Never-Rest spoke up: "It's true, they most certainly will refuse. Five Legs has already made the suggestion at the first general meeting and none of them liked it at all."

Five Legs looked to Still One again. "What do you say, Still One?" he asked.

Still One stared up through the spiky mass of the gorse bush to the distant light of the sky beyond. "It is their right to refuse," he said.

There was a ripple of puzzlement and consternation.

"Right? Why is it their right?" demanded Wind-Blow. "We have a right to insist!"

"Absolutely." "Quite so." "We must insist," ran the mutter.

"There is no such thing as the right to insist," said Still One.

They stared at him, perplexed.

"No such thing?" queried Never-Rest.

"They have their right to their opinion. We have the right to ours. No one has the right to insist that their opinion prevails, only to state it and let persuasion decide the issue."

"Persuasion?" queried Never-Rest. "How can we use persuasion? We have no influence, no voice, no representation. It is the right of persuasion that we are seeking."

"Exactly." "That's it." "That's the point!"

Still One stood motionless, in his eyes a distant, secret intimation. Then he said, "A great rock stood on a hillside. Hard, grey and solid, it had stood there since the dawn of time, firmly embedded in the earth, covered with moss and lichen, so that it looked part of the hillside itself. And the moss and the lichen that clung to its surface protected it from the frost and wind in winter and the sun's heat in summer, so that the longer the rock rested there the more secure it felt in its permanence. And under and around the rock, lay a myriad of much smaller stones and pebbles. They were also a part of the hillside but they had not the solidity and permanence of the rock, nor were they protected by moss and lichen from the elements. So they said to the rock, 'Please, mighty rock, could you spread your moss, and send down your lichen to us so that we too may be protected and last like you till the end of time?' And the rock replied, 'No, indeed I shall not—for you are mere pebbles, lowly stones—whereas I am a splendid rock. What right have you to permanence?'

"So the smaller stones discussed the matter amongst themselves and decided that they would move to other parts, for they could not be worse off elsewhere. And they allowed the wind to blow them and the rain to wash them, until they rolled down the hillside to more respected regions. And suddenly the rock found that the hillside was crumbling beneath it, that its foundations were no longer as firm as it had believed and that its weight was now too great for the weakened soil to bear. And with a roar like thunder it toppled from its ancient resting place and went rolling down the hill, faster and faster, until it smashed into countless pieces at the bottom. And the pieces were scattered across the ground, as small, and as humble, and as exposed as any pebble."

He stopped talking and as always his words were followed by a silence of contemplation.

Then Five Legs said, "But we are not stones. We don't wish to leave the mound. We love our colony."

There was a ripple of nodding heads. Still One answered.

"Of course. The story is only to show that the great are as dependent on the humble as are the humble on the great."

Further thoughtful pause.

"But how does one make the great see that?" asked Never-Rest.

"The ways are there," replied Still One. "But it is not for me to advocate them. I may only speak for myself."

"But who will advocate them?" demanded Wind-Blow. "How will we know the ways?"

"When the feelings are strong enough," answered Still One, "when enough minds are thinking the same, then the way will become clear," and he turned away and went out of the shadowed place into the daylight, a lone, fragile figure.

The rest of the worker-ants' leaders looked at one another uncertainly. "What do we do meanwhile?" asked one.

"I think we should send a deputation to the elders," said Wind-Blow. "We can at least put our case as forcibly as possible."

"Yes, yes, a deputation, a deputation," ran the murmur.

Five Legs nodded. "Very well," he said. "Who wishes to come with me to talk to the elders?"

And so it was that a party of half a dozen or so of the senior worker-ants, headed by Old Five Legs, met half a dozen or so of the senior Council members, headed by Great Head, in one of the smaller Council chambers deep inside the mound. And the elders of the Council listened politely and attentively to what the workers' leaders had to say, and because they were versed in the ways of diplomacy and skilled in methods of negotiation, they did not show the rage they felt at this challenge to the time-honoured traditions; they displayed no sign of their sense of outrage that the accepted order should be questioned at such a moment of desperate crisis. They merely set their jaws, nodded their heads and stared at the floor, promising to give the matter their consideration. And the worker's leader went away uncertain, but feeling that perhaps something might come of their approach.

It was not until they saw the look of anger and disapproval on Black Sting's face as he went about the clearing, still limping stiffly from the effects of his fall—deploying his soldiers, doubling the guard on the various work parties, issuing directives for the work to begin on the mound—that they knew their petition had been to no avail.

*   *   *

As it happened, it came about as Still One had predicted sooner than anyone could have foreseen. The way did become clear, not through argument or any specific decision, but through a natural unanimous response to an event which occurred early on in the rebuilding of the mound. At first the worker-ants went to work obediently—with sullen, unwilling grace, it is true—but they went. For the first few days they worked, steadily and exhaustively—heaving vast masses of earth back up the hillside, digging, shaping, under the watchful, suspicious eyes of the soldiers. Then— whether it happened through faulty design or through general carelessness under the strain of the circumstances, no one ever discovered—suddenly, on the afternoon of the third day, the major part of the section that was being rebuilt broke away from the main structure. With a deafening roar, it went tumbling back down the hillside once more, carrying perhaps two dozen worker-ants with it.

When the terrible sound had ceased, the dust had cleared and the shock abated, the work of rescue began immediately; and after the unfortunate victims had been dug out of the great landslide, it was discovered that half of them had perished and the rest were all injured or scarred in some way or another. These latter were carried off to be cared for, while Black Sting and the elders surveyed this new extent of damage, muttering and shaking their heads between them. Then the command went out for work to begin once again.

And it was now that the revolt occurred, quietly, spontaneously, without any pre-consideration. The worker-ants simply looked at each other, the unspoken message flashed around the work parties, all minds reached the same simultaneous decision and, ignoring the shouts and commands of the soldiers, they began to gather in a great silent crowd, out in the open at the foot of the mound.

Black Sting, Dew-Lover, Great Head and the other leaders surveyed the gathering mass from a vantage point outside one of the tunnel mouths about a third of the way up the mound. The worker-ants stared back at them, grim, sullen, defiantly determined. They made no move to communicate, no gesture of intention, merely stood their ground, challenging their leaders to do their worst.

Great Head shook his huge old skull helplessly. "What has happened to us? What has happened to us?" he muttered in despair. "Never in all my summers have I known such a thing. Open revolt! And at such a time of crisis. Where is loyalty? Where is honour? Our Great Mother will die of sadness when she hears."

Dew-Lover looked at Black Sting. "Let me go down there with some soldiers," he growled. "I'll soon get them back to work."

Black Sting shook his head. "We have to handle this cautiously. It could get out of control if we aren't careful." He turned to Great Head. "If I may make a suggestion, leader," he said. "I think the best thing to do is to play the waiting game. I think we should return into the mound, leave a guard at all the entrances and just see what effect time and hunger and cold will have. I don't imagine they'll resist for long."

The old ant looked at him, worried. "Perhaps you're right. I hope you are. We may not *have* very long. The red ants could be here at any time." He stared out towards the forest. "I wish Snake's Tongue would return."

"They'll be back soon, I'm sure of it." Black Sting reassured him. "I can trust Snake's Tongue. Meanwhile let's see what effect discomfort and the night will have on these foolish ants."

So the leaders went inside the mound and left the worker-ants masters of the clearing, but exposed to the elements and the predators of the forest and the Lord of the Stars' darkness.

* 14 *

He was relaxing out amongst the dry summer grasses, on the bank above the stream. These were the good days, the rich days at the height of the summer, and he was out there with his friends taking life easy, luxuriating in the warmth, the sweet smells of the earth, the soothing ripple of the water and the glories of the golden world around them. Joker was there, and Snake's Tongue and Still One also—and Old Five Legs, and even a lazy, relaxed Black Sting reclining nearby. Several others too, amongst them, strangely, Fleet and one or two of the red ants. And the talk meandered languidly back and forth, the laughter followed frequently and there was no sense of caste, rank or authority of any kind—merely an easy, warm, equal friendship that brought with it an immense sense of pleasurable well-being. And each ant had something to say, adding to the contribution of the ant before, so that the discussion progressed to ever more fascinating depths and the ideas blossomed with ever more thrilling implications, all taking delight in the midst of one another.

After a while he rose casually from his place and wandered at ease to the stream's edge, gazing down into the shimmering depths of the water, and at the same time far into the blue mysteries of the sky reflected there. And he whispered to the water: "That is my purpose. To live at ease with all of my kind; to abandon struggle and argument, questing and ambition; to be at peace with the world. Surely that is my purpose."

And the strangely familiar Voice rippled from the water: "Yes, that is a splendid purpose. But how do you persuade the world to be at peace with you?"

And it was gone, and he awoke to darkness, and to cold, and to the voices of the enemy.

* 15 *

They could tell by the subtle changes in the temperature that they had been held captive for three days and nights so far, and the fourth day was now commencing. They were being kept in a small chamber deep inside the vast mound where they had been brought that first terrible day of their capture, when Snake's Tongue had lost part of his antennae in such a hideous way. He was much recovered now. The injury had given him great pain the first two days, causing fever and strange hallucinations, but their captor, Fleet, had seen to it that various herbs and remedies had been supplied with which to treat the wound and it was healing well. Snake's Tongue did admit to having lost a part of his sensory faculty, but otherwise he made no complaint, merely maintained a stoical silence. Dreamer knew, however, what a terrible deprivation the assault must have been, particularly to such a splendid fighter as Snake's Tongue, and both he and Joker were tactfully solicitous of their leader's well-being.

They were being treated reasonably well, albeit with

scant respect. There was a regular guard outside their chamber of two red ants, who paid them little attention, but at least left them to their own devices. The fact that prisoners outnumbered guards did not seem to concern their captors in the slightest. They were obviously confident of their own vastly superior fighting abilities, and secure in the knowledge that the passages outside were always swarming with others who could be immediately called on to help and trusted to frustrate any attempt at escape. Indeed the general attitude of the big ants to their many captives seemed extremely casual. The three prisoners could tell from the various sounds in the darkness that work parties made up of smaller brown ants were constantly moving back and forth along the tunnels outside, all only very loosely guarded by a small, relatively relaxed number of red soldiers, and yet they never detected any signs of rebellion or flight. It seemed that the likelihood of success was so remote and the threat of retribution so strong, that none considered the attempt worthwhile.

The one member of the enemy with whom they had regular contact was Fleet, who was always in attendance when their guard was changed or when food or medications were brought. He at least evidently took his responsibility for their security seriously. But there also seemed to be another motive for his diligence. Behind his lofty, distant manner there appeared to lurk a secret curiosity about his prisoners, a reluctant instinct to communicate which he could not quite repudiate. Dreamer sensed somehow a loneliness in the powerful ant, a subconscious dissatisfaction, which in a strange way paralleled his own questing nature and made him feel a paradoxical affinity with the other. Fleet would enter their chamber with the guards who brought food: a lowly diet of seeds and dried vegetable matter—not for them the rich plunder of meat brought in by the raiding parties—and, when the guards had left, would hesitate for a moment on the threshold as if unwilling to leave. If one of them asked him a question he would answer with a vague, reluctant air, but he would never reject it. Once or twice they were able to draw him into a brief discussion about the comparative lifestyles of their two different ant-kinds, and in this way they learnt quite a lot about the alien insects.

One significant conversation explained a great deal about the system of the red colony, although it made uncomfortable hearing for the three captives. Snake's Tongue began it by asking, "Why have we not seen any worker-ants of your own species?"

Fleet replied, "Because we do not breed worker-ants."

"None at all?" asked Joker, puzzled.

"We need all our brood to increase our fighting force."

"But why do you need to keep increasing that?" asked Snake's Tongue. "Why can't you keep it at a stable strength, and supply it with your own workforce?"

"How should we feed ourselves then?" asked the red ant. "We need to increase our forces so that we can conquer new territories and thus find new food supplies. How else can one maintain a colony?"

Snake's Tongue hesitated, perplexed. "Do as we do," he replied. "Simply maintain the colony at the strength that your surrounding territory can easily support."

It was Fleet's turn to be puzzled. "You mean you never expand your colony?"

"Why should we? The nearby habitat provides enough food in the form of seeds, fruit, carrion and insect larvae for us to feed our present population without ever having to travel more than a night's journey from the base mound. Why should we wish to go further?"

Dreamer could sense the red ant contemplating this bizarre philosophy in the darkness. Then he said, with a hint of scorn, "How very unambitious you must be."

Snake's Tongue said quietly, "If ambition means constantly having to destroy other colonies, constantly having to enslave other species, then yes, we are unambitious."

"Very chivalrous, no doubt," replied Fleet loftily, "but how then do you ensure that you are not yourselves destroyed?"

"Until we encountered you, we never considered there was such danger; at any rate, not from our own kind."

"Well, now you have learnt differently. Perhaps it means that we are not of your kind."

"Do you believe that?" asked Snake's Tongue.

The other hesitated. When he spoke, Dreamer thought he could detect a less confident note in his voice. "Certainly our leader does. To him, all who are not of this colony are the enemy—no matter what size, species or order. You must realize that. No amount of discussion will change *him*."

"And you?" asked Snake's Tongue.

"I follow my leader," was the instant reply.

"Then there is little hope for our own colony?"

"Not unless it can find some miraculous new method of defence."

Snake's Tongue pondered this. "How long will it be before you reach there?" he asked in a low voice.

"A little while yet. We are busy at the moment conquering new territories in the sun-up direction. When we have finished there, we shall assemble the major part of the army and turn to you." Fleet's voice became more abrupt. "Now, I have talked enough. I must go."

He turned to leave the chamber, but Snake's Tongue stopped him with a last question. "There is one thing I would like to know."

"What is that?"

"When does the conquering end? When you tire of it or when you reach the end of the world?"

There was silence. Then Fleet answered, "That you must ask The Spider." And he was gone.

There was quiet in the little chamber, broken only by the casual mutter of conversation of the guards outside and the distant rumble of activity throughout the great mound. All three ants were lost in their own individual reflections on the exchange which had just taken place. Dreamer felt once again that frightening sense of finality, of the end of hope, that he had felt as he waited on the plateau of The

Spider's first appearance. Remembering further back, he recalled too that same sense of awe at the realization that pure, self-interested evil existed as a force to be reckoned with which he had experienced on first hearing of the red ant's assault on the riverside colony.

As usual it was Joker who broke the silence and put their thoughts into perspective. "Good to know one has such friendly neighbours."

Dreamer, as always, warmed to the mild quip. He had come to know the other well during their long hours of confinement. The bond had grown between them as they talked away the idle hours and he had revealed to Joker more of his innermost thoughts and instincts than he had done to anyone before. He had discovered a sense of relaxation and trusting confidence in the hefty soldier's utterly dependable presence and he was coming to realize that he valued this relationship perhaps more than any other formed in his brief life.

Meanwhile Snake's Tongue had retreated quietly to the end of the chamber further from the entrance. He now murmured to the other two to come close. Then, in a low voice that the guards could not overhear he said, "We have to make an attempt at escape somehow. The colony must be warned, otherwise there is no chance for it."

The others considered this. "How can we possibly escape?" whispered Joker. "The place is swarming with red ants. Outside too. We can't outfight them; we can't outrun them. What hope is there?"

"There is always hope if one can find it," replied Snake's Tongue. "I've been giving it some thought since we've been here, and I've also been doing some observing. I'm not so sure the red ants are such invulnerable fighters, at any rate in a confined space. Remember what Black Sting told us about their methods? They spray their poison rather than inject it, which is why they don't carry stings. And that's why they're more effective at long range. 'Attack from the side, and get in close,' Black Sting said. Well, suppose the three of us tackled the two

guards within the confinement of this chamber? They are
built for speed over the ground, rather than manoeuvrability
in a small space, like the tree-spider. We defeated that. I
think we could defeat them.''

"But then what?" asked Joker. "How do we get out of
the mound and back home again?"

"I've been listening to the sound of the work parties,"
answered Snake's Tongue. "The main activity is at the
beginning and end of the day. That's when the big groups,
either of captive day workers or night workers, leave the
mound or return to it. Our chamber is obviously off a
minor tunnel that isn't used much, but from the sounds it
seems to me that here is a junction with a much bigger
tunnel just a little way along from here. Even with my
damaged feeler I can sense the work parties moving past
there.''

"Yes," said Dreamer. "It's about ten ant-lengths from
here. The largest work parties consist of about twenty
captive worker-ants and half that number of soldiers.''

He could sense the antennae of the other two hovering
curiously in his direction.

"That's very good, Dreamer," said Snake's Tongue.
"Those feelers of yours are useful. How far off can you
detect one of the parties approaching?"

"If it's a large one, perhaps thirty ant-lengths down the
main passage. The vibration pattern is quite strong.''

"And can you tell whether they're moving up or down
the tunnel?"

"Yes. The upwards direction is this way." Dreamer
patted the back wall of the chamber with his feeler.

"Clever young thing, isn't he?" commented Joker.

"Can you tell us what their names are too?"

But Dreamer was too interested in Snake's Tongue's
train of thought to feel more than a momentary glow at the
praise. The big ant continued.

"That should be enough. The suggestion I have is this:
that we wait until the main activity is commencing. Then,
when Dreamer senses one of the large parties approaching

up the main tunnel towards the outside, we deal with the guards. We slip along to the junction and hope to join the work party without anyone noticing. Then, once we're out in the open, we'll just have to see where the party goes and take our chance."

The other two contemplated the scheme. "It's going to be risky trying to join the work party without any of its guards sensing us," said Joker uncertainly.

"I think we could do it," said Dreamer cautiously. "From the vibration patterns, it seems that the red ants concentrate themselves at the front and the rear of the groups with the worker-ants strung out in the middle. It should be possible to join in at the centre without them noticing, providing of course none of the workers gives us away. Also there's something else which should help us."

"What's that?" asked Snake's Tongue.

"I don't think their senses are as sharp as ours. I've noticed that Fleet and the guards are never quite as sure as we are of precise movements in the dark. If one of us moves quietly it always seems to take them a moment to work out exactly where our new position is."

"Yes," said Snake's Tongue. "I've noticed that too. What about their sense of smell? Do you think that's as strong as ours?"

"No," replied Dreamer. "Fleet still hasn't learnt to recognize each of us by our scent. He has to wait until we speak to know who is where. Whereas, we know instantly when it is he who has entered."

"Good. We must use every advantage we have," said Snake's Tongue.

"They can't be totally unaware," said Joker. "They knew about our fight with the spider."

"That's hardly surprising," answered Snake's Tongue. "We made enough noise to alert the entire forest. What is interesting, though, is the way they were able to keep us observed from then onwards without us knowing. They can evidently move very skillfully when they have to. Our problem is not only going to be escaping from the mound, but getting home again without them catching up with us. I suggest that we should make our attempt to escape with one of the night work parties. Then we shall have the night to travel through for the first part of the journey, when our sharper senses will be to our advantage.''

"Which night, leader?" asked Joker.

"How about tonight?" said Snake's Tongue.

There was a pause. The theoretical discussion about escape prospects had been exciting, a relief from the tedious hours of waiting. Now the immediate prospect of actually putting the plan into practice brought home the reality with sobering clarity. To Dreamer their chances seemed frighteningly slim.

Joker was obviously thinking the same thing. "Doesn't give us much chance to get ready," he said.

"We're as ready now as we'll ever be," answered Snake's Tongue. "All we have to do is plan how to tackle the guards. The rest we'll have to take as it comes; we can't know exactly what will happen. But the longer we wait, the less warning we shall be able to give to our colony and the more danger there is that The Spider will decide he has no more use for us.''

And so it was decided. They held a whispered discussion about their tactics for the attack on the guards, then there was nothing to do but wait until the evening burst of activity, their suspense and nervousness growing perceptibly with every hour.

Dreamer spent much of the time speculating about this strange species who so threatened the survival of his own kind. There was something unexplained about them, some mystery that he could not quite define. It was puzzling that they appeared so omnipotent within their domain and so utterly ruthless about extending its boundaries, yet that his own colony had only recently become aware of their existence. Was it that they had not long been established in this region? Was it that this gigantic mound was the product of only one or two brief summers' activity? There was certainly an oddly haphazard and temporary quality about its appearance. It did not have the solid, well-beaten and naturally overgrown look of their own ancient hillock, however huge it was. He fell to pondering about the red ants' lifestyle and breeding habits and he suddenly realized that he had heard nothing about their Queens; there had been no mention of the Royal Quarters, the brood chambers or even of the Queen of Queens herself. Surely she had some influence over the colony's lifestyle? Surely even The Spider was answerable to her authority? Yet it seemed to be a taboo subject; one that was simply not mentioned or taken account of during the normal day-to-day activity.

It then occurred to him that he had seen or heard no sign either of any elders. At their first meeting, Fleet had shown amusement at the idea of a ruling Council, which seemed to indicate that that was not how they did things here, but even so it was odd that they had not encountered any elderly ants. The Spider himself was certainly large but he did not seem particularly long-lived. Dreamer sensed that here somewhere was an important missing element in their knowledge of the strange insects, but for the moment it was a mystery he could not solve.

Some time towards evening Fleet returned with two soldiers, bringing the second feed of the day. As usual he hovered for a moment after the soldiers had left and Snake's Tongue was ready with an immediate comment. He prodded the small pile of seeds and greenery with his good antenna. "We're getting tired of this vegetarian diet," he said. "You might at least have brought us some of that spider's meat, after we took so much trouble to kill it for you."

Fleet sounded amused when he replied, "You're welcome to it. We're not fond of spider meat. But I'm afraid you'll have to wait. We left it where you hid it. If any parties go out in that direction in the near future, I'll request that they bring some back for you. But only as your entitlement for killing the spider, you understand. We don't make a practice of feeding meat to prisoners."

He was about to leave, when Dreamer impulsively threw out a question on the subject which had been troubling him. "How many Queens are there in your colony?"

The red ant hesitated. "How many?" he repeated cautiously.

"Yes," said Dreamer.

"I don't understand."

Dreamer was at a loss; the question seemed simple enough. "Well . . ." he said, "how many are there for breeding and where are the Royal Quarters? We never hear them mentioned."

Again there was that strange, searching silence. Dreamer could sense Snake's Tongue and Joker showing an alert interest in the exchange.

Fleet answered with a question of his own. "Do you have more than one Queen?"

Again Dreamer found the question puzzling. "Of course," he replied. "We have only one Queen of Queens naturally, but there are several younger Queens. How else would the colony survive?"

"Where do these other Queens come from?" asked Fleet.

Dreamer hesitated. It seemed an extraordinary query. Snake's Tongue took it up. "They are the offspring of the Queen of Queens, the next generation."

"Ah," said Fleet. He pondered this for a moment. "You mean they return to the nest after the mating flight?"

"Some of them," answered Snake's Tongue. "The rest go off to found colonies of their own."

"And your . . . Queen of Queens, as you call her, she allows them to return? She is not afraid of their usurping her position?"

"Of course not. She is the supreme being, the Great Mother. All worship her; why should she be afraid?"

There was a long moment of silence. This was evidently a quite new concept to the red ant. Snake's Tongue then asked cautiously, "Do you then have only one Queen?"

"Yes," came the answer. "She is the founder, the

creator of the colony. She would not tolerate others intruding on her position."

"Then does she rule alone?" asked Snake's Tongue.

"Rule?" repeated Fleet curiously. "The Spider rules. Her only role is to breed. To breed soldiers as fast as possible. To give us our strength."

"Does she have no contact with the Spider then, or any of your elders?"

"Elders?"

"Your old ants, your wise ones."

"We have no old ants. Our Queen only founded the colony three summers ago. And why should wisdom only come with old age?"

Further silence. To the prisoner these things were a revelation; and to Dreamer especially, many things were becoming clearer.

Fleet was continuing: "When you mention contact, do I take it that your leaders consult with your Queen?"

"Certainly," answered Snake's Tongue. "She is the ultimate ruler, the last of her generation. She is directly descended from the first Queen of All Queens, who founded our colony countless summers ago. She knows and understands more of life than any elder can possibly do."

"So they go to her for advice?"

"Yes. Does The Spider not go to your Queen for advice?"

"No one goes to her. She would kill them instantly. Her task is to protect her brood."

There was a horrified pause. "Even from her own kind?" asked Snake's Tongue.

"Who knows? Even her own kind have a taste for young larvae in times of hunger."

The three smaller ants considered the implications of this apparently barbaric regime. Dreamer then asked, "Where then are her quarters?"

Fleet replied, "Far down under the mound. Deep in the earth where she first dug her nest."

"She never leaves there?"

"No. She lives there almost cut off from the mound

itself. There are only a few narrow passages used by the captured slaves who are trained to look after her. They bring her food and help tend the larvae. She will dwell there for her whole life, hatching and caring for her brood.''

"And when her life is finished?'' Dreamer asked the question spontaneously, only realizing after he had done so what a crucial one it was.

Fleet's answer came in a flat, unemotional voice. "Then the colony is finished.''

Again there was silence. Dreamer felt a sense of horror and at the same time of deep tragedy as he contemplated the image of the gigantic creature doomed to spin out her solitary, suspicious existence in the dark confines of her self-made prison far beneath their feet, where her only objective was to produce ever more of these fierce fighting insects to rampage their conquering way across the land, until she was too old and exhausted to replenish their forces and brought the whole massive created structure to an end with her own demise.

Snake's Tongue was evidently thinking similar thoughts, for he commented quietly, "A sad system.''

"Perhaps,'' replied Fleet, matter-of-factly. "It is evidently not as long-lasting as yours, but neither would it seem to be as vulnerable. And, though it maybe a brief existence, it is a glorious one.''

"Is glory what matters most?'' asked Snake's Tongue.

Dreamer could sense the red ant stiffening proudly. Yet he did not react aggressively. "To us, yes,'' he said. "There may be other ways, but that is how we are. It is Nature's way. It is as the Lord of the Stars intended.'' And he turned and left abruptly, as if he wished to have no further discussion on the subject.

The three pondered the matter for a long moment after he had gone. Then Joker summed up the situation with a dry comment: "Seems an awful lot of bother for nothing.''

"Yes, indeed,'' answered Snake's Tongue. "However, it's not much consolation to us. If the colony was only founded three summer's ago, then it has a good few more to last. Which means they'll have a lot more territory to conquer.'' He paused. There was a tiny, almost undetectable hint of emotion in his stern soldier's voice, as he said, ''Well, we *do* have a Queen to report to.'' He quickly controlled the lapse and added brusquely, ''It's imperative we try to escape. We must eat as much of this food as we can and then make ready.''

Not another word was said as they ate and filled their crops with extra food. They then rested and waited for the night outside to approach.

* 16 *

That first night out in the clearing had been a cold one. The worker-ants had huddled together in groups for warmth but they had a long, uncomfortable time of it. The early hours of dawn had been the worst, before the temperature began to rise and when the brightening light left them feeling exposed and helpless to the eyes of passing predators.

Old Five Legs stretched his stiff painful joints in the reluctant knowledge that they could not survive many more such nights in the open. However, he reflected, at least they had not had to endure the fatal consequences of a night frost. He peered towards the darkened shape of the mound. Everything seemed quiet there. He could just make out the shadowy figures of the guards posted at every tunnel mouth. They were going to make very sure that none of the workers got back to the comfort of their quarters, he thought.

He looked around him at the gently stirring, muttering groups of ants nearby. It was hard to tell what the prevailing mood might be after this first testing period. Had the defiance worn thin through the cold and the discomfort? Or had the sense of determination survived? What we need, he thought, is a good feed: that would bolster morale. He called to the other senior worker-ants nearby. They held a brief, low-voiced discussion and then the others dispersed around the clearing to organize food-scavenging parties.

Just as Never-Rest was leaving Five Legs asked him, "Where is Still One? Have you seen him this morning?"

Never-Rest waved a feeler towards the birch sapling some way across the clearing, near the edge of the forest. "He's with his beloved aphid-bugs. *They're* not going to suffer because of the revolt." And he went off on his mission.

Five Legs set off at his own pace for the birch sapling. On the way he stopped here and there to converse with some of the groups of worker-ants, enquiring after their well-being, sounding out their resolution. He was pleased to find that the rigours of the night had, if anything, strengthened the general determination. There was a grim resentment against their treatment, a deep-rooted anger that their feelings should be rejected in so autocratic a manner; and nowhere was fear in evidence, nor was it ever suggested that their cause was hopeless, though Five Legs knew that deep down many must secretly be feeling both.

He reached the sapling and gazed up into the delicate green mist of budding spring foliage. Sure enough the slim figure was there, pottering about on one of the lower branches. Five Legs called up and the other peered down over the edge of his branch.

"Greetings, Five Legs," he called back. "How are you after that long night?"

"Stiff, cold and bad-tempered," replied the old ant. "Can I have a word with you?"

"If you can manage to climb, why don't you come up here?" replied Still One. "I can give you something which may make you feel better."

Five Legs did not hesitate long. It was a while since he

had bothered to climb a tree, and even longer since he had mingled with an aphid-bug herd, but he remembered the joys of both from his youth and suddenly the invitation seemed very appealing. He flexed his ancient leg muscles and began to climb.

As he went, puffing and heaving, the ground with its attendant smells and noises fell away beneath him, and the clean, bright air of that altogether different upper world surrounded him. He reached the junction where Still One's branch met the main trunk and paused to recover his breath. He stared down through the young, bursting web of leaves at the diminished, scurrying world of the clearing below, and he thought: yes, I know why you like it up here so much. You have a perspective on it all from here. And an escape as well. That's something we could all do with from time to time.

He headed along the branch towards the distant figure and soon he was weaving his way between groups of aphid-bugs. They paid him little attention as he passed; merely stared at him with their large, contented eyes, munched away at the young greenery, and nuzzled their clusters of tiny, rounded eggs, which clung stickily to the leaves and the fissures and crevices of the bark. Eventually Five Legs came to where Still One was busy arranging one such cluster in a more secure formation in the joint between two leaf stems. The old ant gave a sigh of relief and made himself comfortable against a twig stump. He gazed around him, nodding appreciatively.

"It's a pleasant spot you've got yourself here. And a pleasant job too."

"Yes," said Still One simply, without stopping his work.

Five Legs watched him for a moment. "You don't think you should be refusing to work also?" he asked.

Still One nodded towards his herd. "There is no reason for them to suffer because of our problems. And we may have need of their honey-dew."

Five Legs nodded. Still One pushed and prodded until

he had the eggs arranged to his satisfaction, then he went to a nearby fissure in the bark surface, scraped at something with his mandibles, returned and laid a small lump of coagulated honey-dew at Five Legs' feet. "Eat that, he said. "Freshly gathered yesterday. That will make you feel better."

Five Legs hesitated. "Have we the right, do you think? I know we're in revolt, but old habits die hard. I'm remembering what nearly happened to poor Bug-Rump."

"They have our sleeping quarters—we have their honey-dew. It's a fair exchange," replied Still One with a twinkle of amusement. "And we'll only take the ration we're entitled to. We'll see that theirs is preserved. Dew-Lover can come for it whenever he likes."

"That's what worries me," said Five Legs. "He probably will. And in a vile temper too."

"Yes," answered the other. "He has a difficult disposition. Poor Dew-Lover, it must be hard to live with."

"Hard for others to live with. I wish I could feel your sympathy for him." Five Legs took the honey-dew and tasted it, relishing the clean, sweet tang of it as it melted and trickled down his throat. "The first of the year," he murmured. "That's a marvellous taste."

Still One watched him as he sat savouring the sensation, feeling the soothing warmth flooding through his tired limbs, the calming glow washing the worries from his brain. "That's better," he sighed contentedly.

"What did you want me for?" asked the younger ant after a few peaceful moments had passed.

"Ah, yes," answered Five Legs, dragging his mind back to the realities of the situation. "I don't know how long we're going to have to wait out here, but it's been a long night and it's going to be an even longer day. I want your help to keep up morale. We can keep everyone busy to some extent, with foraging parties and so forth, but there's bound to be lot of sitting around with little to do, and that's when imagination starts to work, fear creeps in and resolve begins to crumble. I thought some of your stories could be of great use then to keep up the weaker ones' spirits, help the simpler ones to understand what this is all about.''

''Certainly,'' replied Still One. He paused. That strange immobile quality had fallen upon him. ''Do *you* understand what it's all about?'' he asked.

Five Legs pondered. ''Sometimes I think I do. Sometimes I'm not so sure any more. The trouble is, there's no precedent for what's happened. In all my summers I've never known such a thing. I could never have conceived of a spontaneous rebellion taking place like this.'' He paused for a moment, lost in serious contemplation. ''But what I do know,'' he added, ''is that it's important, whatever it is.'' He looked across at Still One. ''Do *you* know what it's about?''

As always, the moment's silence. ''It is about the right to choose,'' said Still One eventually.

''The right to choose?'' queried Five Legs, puzzled.

''I've noticed that a creature will seek to preserve his life under almost any circumstances. The only time he will readily risk it—cast it away even—is when you take away his right to choose. Perhaps because that *is* his life.''

Five Legs nodded. ''Yes, I think you're right.'' He thought a moment longer. ''But it's very hard for all to have the right to choose, because all choose differently.''

''Ah,'' murmured Still One, ''but therein lies the secret. The whole secret of a peaceful world.'' A small, rotund aphid-bug wandered up and nuzzled him gently. He stroked it absent-mindedly with a forefoot. ''If everyone were to choose his own way—for himself alone—and none were to seek to impose his way on another, then the strife would cease. For what is certain is that there are as many different ways as there are creatures on the earth.''

Five Legs thought about this for a moment. ''But are there not times when a way *has* to be imposed, for the benefit of everyone as a whole? For instance, are we not trying to impose our way on the Council now?''

''No,'' replied Still One. ''The workers have made a

spontaneous decision that they do not wish to obey the Council's will unless certain conditions are met. The Council is free to meet those conditions, or not, as it chooses. The conditions are not being *forced* upon it. Of course it means both sides having to make compromises ultimately, but the point is that they will have *chosen* those compromises themselves, in the light of the other side's wishes, not had compromises imposed upon them, against their own wishes.'' The aphid-bug wandered on its way, and Still One gazed into the distance. ''There is a very small story about it. Shall I tell you?''

''Yes,'' answered Five Legs, his honey-dewed brain telling him that nothing could be better than one of Still One's stories at this moment.

''Three ants were out on a journey over strange territory,'' said the Story Teller in his gentle tones. ''They followed a trail over a long distance until they came to a spot where the path divided into three and each of the three new paths went off in a different direction. And the three ants each wanted to take a different path. And they discussed the problem, and the discussion turned into an argument, and the argument turned into a fight, for each of the three wanted the other two to go on his path. But, just when it seemed that they were about to kill each other over the issue, one of the ants called a stop to the fighting and said, 'Look, if we feel so strongly about it, let us each take a different path. Surely it is not worth dying for?'

''So they took their leave of one another, and each set off on his chosen path, and each travelled a long and difficult route, until at last they came to the end of their paths. And there—lo and behold—they had all come to the same place.''

Silence. Five Legs nodded dreamily. ''I like that story,'' he said. ''That is a good story.'' He sighed. ''It sometimes makes life very difficult though, when there are so many different paths and so many different opinions over which to take.''

The Story Teller twinkled. "Yes, indeed," he replied. "But, as I said, that *is* life."

A voice cut across the peaceful scene from below: "Five Legs, are you there?" There was an authoritative command in its tone. Both ants peered down ovr the edge of the branch. Black Sting stood at the foot of the tree with Great Head at his side and Dew-Lover and two soldiers at his rear. "We wish to speak to you."

Five Legs looked at Still One. "Oh dear," he said, "I knew this interlude was too pleasant to last. I'll have to go down and face them." He hesitated, contemplating the other. "You're a strange ant, Story Teller, but a wise one. I trust you more than any of the others. May I ask you to come with me?" He added wryly, "That isn't just an order of course—you have the right to choose—it's just that I'd like some moral support."

Still One acknowledged the joke with an amused nod and said, "Since you choose to ask me, then I choose to come."

"Thank you," said Five Legs and turned to descend the tree.

When they reached the base Black Sting waited for them to approach, stern, unmoving, magnificent. At his side Great Head took a step forward. The two most venerable members of their respective castes faced each other with the composure that age and experience brings.

"We thought it was time we had a talk, Five Legs," said Great Head. "Just a private talk between you and us to see if we couldn't resolve this situation between us. The elders of the Council have asked Black Sting, in the light of the danger in which our colony finds itself, to take Thunderer's place for the moment as leader and he has agreed. We thought that perhaps you and he ought to discuss the matter before things became any more, er . . . unpleasant."

Five Legs glanced at Black Sting. The big soldier stared back, grimly inexpressive. "Certainly," replied Five Legs. "Would, er . . ."—he found himself uncertain as to whether to address Great Head or Black Sting directly. "Would you object if the Story Teller stayed with me?"

It was Black Sting who answered. "You may have who you wish. We want to talk with those who represent the workers' opinions."

Five Legs nodded. "As long as you realize that we have little influence over those opinions," he said. "This was a spontaneous, unanimous action. No one ordered it."

Black Sting acknowledged this with a brief nod. "All the same, you are their spokesman. You have their respect."

"What do you wish to discuss?" asked Five Legs.

Black Sting went on: "Snake's Tongue's party has still not returned. It is now several sun-ups since they left. I can only assume that they've been captured or killed, or at any rate prevented from returning in some way. Any one of those possibilities means that they have probably encountered the red ants. Now, I've got soldiers posted out in the forest as lookouts, but all they can do is give us some warning of the red ants' approach, which may come at any moment. It's surely madness for us to be in such a state of disarray, to be squabbling over internal matters, at such a time as this. What is the point of winning concessions over points of the colony's organization if the colony is destroyed in the process?"

Five Legs considered the statement carefully. "Perhaps," he said slowly, "the members of my caste consider those concessions to be even more important than the safety of the colony."

Black Sting's eyes burned with angry incomprehension. "More important?" he demanded. "More important than the achievement of generations of ants? More important than the survival of Our Great Mother and her young Queens and all their brood? More important than the existence of their own entire community?"

"Perhaps they feel that they have no real place in that existence. Perhaps they feel that their community has no respect for their own existence."

"But what of that existence?" Black Sting was totally bewildered. "What of their own lives? Are they prepared to lose those to win a mere moral argument?"

Five Legs looked round at Still One, who stood just behind him. "As Still One says," he replied, "freedom of choice is perhaps the one issue over which a creature *will* perhaps give up his life." He stared over at the mound with its great, gaping rift, where a dozen ants had died the day before. "I don't know," he said. "Which is preferable, death in the execution of the Council's ambitious designs, or death at the whim of the red ants? You must ask the worker-ants themselves."

Black Sting looked towards the fragile figure behind Five Legs. Strangely, the two ants had never communicated before. "You are the one they call the Story Teller?" he asked.

Still One nodded—the tiniest movement.

"Is it your stories that have begun these wild ideas?"

The usual pause. Then Still One answered, "A story cannot decide the destination. It can only illuminate the way a little."

Black Sting studied the smaller ant for a moment. Then he turned back to Five Legs. "I have respected you, old one," he said. "I had thought you cared for the well-being of our colony."

"Indeed I do," answered Five Legs gruffly: there was a sudden impediment in his throat. "But the well-being of a colony means the well-being of its individual members. Perhaps we feel that no one cares enough for that." He cocked a feeler in Black Sting's direction. "It's not much that we're asking, you know."

Black Sting lifted his proud head. "It is a great deal. It is the overturn of our whole traditional system of organization. It is the undermining of the chain of command by which we survive."

Five Legs shook his head sadly. "We don't wish to overturn, or to undermine anything. We only want our voice to be heard." He looked towards Great Head as if to appeal to the one with whom he had most in common. But the latter could only shrug and look unhappily away.

Black Sting raised his antennae in an imperious gesture of finality. "Well, let us see what another night out in the cold will do to your followers' resolution," he said.

He was about to turn away when Dew-Lover, who up till then had been glowering from the background, lumbered forward saying, "One moment, leader." He stopped in front of Five Legs waving his feelers towards him suspiciously. "I smell honey-dew. Have you been taking it?"

"A little," replied Five Legs. "Still One gave me some to ease my stiffness; I had an uncomfortable night. But no more than my ration." He added pointedly, "You needn't worry, Dew-Lover. The supply is being collected and preserved as usual."

The huge ant glared at him and then at Still One, a resentful anger burning in his eyes. "It seems to me that you ants are all too free and easy with the colony's honey-dew," he growled viciously. "Is that what you mean by the well-being of the workers, eh? Unlimited access to the honey-dew supplies."

Five Legs said nothing. Black Sting wheeled away. "Come, Dew-Lover," he said impatiently.

Dew-Lover gave a final, lingering look at the two worker-ants, which seemed to say that they had not heard the last of the matter, and turned to follow Black Sting and Great Head back towards the mound.

Five Legs watched them go, sighed, and said, "Ah, it is a hard thing to try and change the traditions of time, is it not, Still One?"

The latter nodded. "It is. But they will change whether one seeks it or not. That is what time is for." And he turned and began to climb his birch tree once again, leaving Five Legs to report what had been happening to the other worker-ant leaders who were hurrying across the clearing towards them.

*   *   *

It was later that day, when the sun had risen to its highest point and the worker-ants exposed out in the open were keeping a nervous lookout aloft for the swooping shadows of feathered hunters, that the retribution came. And not from any high-flying creature, but from the most earth-bound of their own kind: Dew-Lover himself.

Five Legs was limping about near the gorse clump, organizing the digging of shallow trenches to provide some protection against the cold during the night, when he was interrupted by that easily recognizable voice growling behind him.

"All right you cunning old schemer, let's see how clever you really are."

Five Legs turned to see Dew-Lover glowering at him from a few paces away, where he had just emerged from the grass stems. With him was his habitual escort of two hulking soldiers.

"Come with us," ordered the huge ant.

"Where to?" asked Five Legs.

"You'll find out," replied the other and gestured with his feelers to the soldiers, who moved forward and aggressively prodded Five Legs after him as he moved off towards the mound.

The worker-ants left behind muttered and bobbed anxiously amongst themselves until Wind-Blow, who had witnessed the incident from some way off, came hurrying up to demand what had happened. Then he rushed off again amid a flurry of distraught imprecations to tell the others.

Meanwhile Five Legs was led up the lower slopes of the mound into one of the tunnel mouths and down through the darkness of the passages to an obscure chamber within. By the time he reached it he was panting with the effort of having to keep up the pace that the soldiers had imposed. As he was thrust inside the chamber he was immediately aware of Still One's scent in the blackness.

"You here too, Story Teller?" he asked. "Are you all right?"

"I'm all right," replied the other's voice quietly.

"Don't be so sure about that," hissed Dew-Lover's voice from near by. Five Legs was aware of the soldier's heavy scent hanging oppressively around him as the other came close and thrust his head towards him in that intimidating way that he had.

"Right now, old one, you and I are going to have a little talk. This treasonable nonsense has gone on long enough. If it had been left to me, I'd have had you and the rest of the workers' leaders killed right out there in front of them all at the very first sign of rebellion. That would have put an end to it quickly enough. However, luckily for you, more cautious counsels prevailed." He thrust his head still closer and his voice sank to a vicious rasp. "But that doesn't stop me from dealing out a little punishment on my own account. Perhaps then you'll think twice about challenging the authority of those above you." A savage kick knocked Five Legs' two forefeet suddenly from under him and he fell heavily to the ground.

He lay there for a moment, the breath knocked out of him. Strangely, although he felt pain, he felt no real fear. If this is the way I am to go, he thought, then so be it. I am old now and tired. I have had my time; it doesn't matter now. But then he remembered Still One, and thought: it is not the same for him though. He still has youth and strength. He can still be of use to the colony.

He raised himself up and said, "You can do what you wish with me—it doesn't matter—but why have you brought the Story Teller here? He has done nothing."

"Oh, has he not indeed?" Dew-Lover growled. He swung about to where Still One was standing. "It seems to me he has done a great deal. It seems to me that he has been generously bestowing his honey-dew—*our* honey-dew—on all and sundry who fancied it. It seems to me that, with his stories and his honey-dew, he has been one of the chief sustainers of this upstart revolt." His heavy feelers hovered questingly about Still One. "I wonder how much fresh honey-dew he has been helping himself to in the process—eh?"

Still One answered quietly. "I do not take honey-dew."

Dew-Lover hesitated. "What? Why not?"

"I feel no need for it."

The soldier retorted scornfully. "Nonsense! Everyone takes honey-dew if they can get it."

"Not everyone."

"Don't lie to me, you cunning little maggot! You have the smell of the stuff about you whenever I meet you."

"Naturally. I work with it."

"And you make very free with it too. Well, we'll soon see how much you have inside you at this moment." Dew-Lover turned to one of the two soldiers. "Where are those crushed yew berries?"

Five Legs felt a pang of anxiety. Ants take the juice of yew berries as an emetic, but only in minute quantities as an overdose can prove fatal. "Be careful!" he exclaimed. "That is poisonous if you take too much."

"Everything is poisonous if you take too much," said Dew-Lover. "Even honey-dew. Isn't that so, Story Teller?"

"It is so," replied Still One.

"Then we'd better make sure you haven't taken too much of that. For your own sake." Dew-Lover took some of the pulpy, bitter-smelling mess which the soldier had brought forward between his mandibles and, pinning Still One against the wall of the chamber with one heavy forefoot, rammed the substance hard into the other's mouth. Still One choked and spluttered, fighting to clear his throat, but the more he fought the deeper the huge soldier thrust the noxious stuff down his gullet. Gasping and retching, Still One ceased struggling and slid down the wall. Dew-Lover turned to the soldier. "More," he commanded.

Five Legs clambered to his feet and lumbered forward. "No!" he exclaimed. "You'll kill him!"

Ignoring him, Dew-Lover turned back to Still One with a fresh dose between his jaws. Again he thrust the stuff hard between the other's own mandibles. With all his feeble strength Five Legs hurled himself against the soldier's great body and his weight temporarily threw the other off balance, causing some of the pulp to drop. Dew-Lover turned on his assailant with a roar, grasped the old ant under the head with his mandibles, and slammed him viciously against the wall. Then he reared up in front of him and drove his thick, heavy sting deep into Five Legs' belly.

Five Legs felt the agony of the thrust even through his stunned, fading consciousness. He gave himself up, almost with relief, to death. He heard the new voice which rang across the scene as some distant intrusion from another world.

"Dew-Lover!"

Dew-Lover hesitated on the point of injecting his poison. Slowly, reluctantly, he withdrew his sting and turned towards Black Sting whose voice had stopped him. The latter stood in the chamber entrance, his eyes glinting in the darkness, his antennae tensed to pick up the details of the situation. Five Legs lay, stunned and wounded, where Dew-Lover had left him. Still One was vomiting in a corner with terrible agonized heaves, as if he would retch out his very entrails.

For a long moment Black Sting did not move. The sound of heaving breath, of Still One's retching, and the scents of the various ants present, mingled with the odour of blood and yew berries, told their own tale. In those few moments Black Sting experienced a revelation that was to change him for evermore. He who was so used to violence, to pain, and to death—he who was trained in the uncompromising ways of discipline and of battle—when faced now with this spectacle of two ordinary worker-ants so assaulted in this wretched place, felt a sense of pity and of responsibility that all the horrifying examples of war in the open could never evoke. He stepped forward and with a burst of rage slashed across the side of Dew-Lover's head with his mandibles. Dew-Lover staggered back, the blood pouring from the wound.

"Get out!" Black Sting hissed. "Get away from here

and if you come near me again before it has been decided what to do with you, I shall kill you.''

The huge ant skulked past him and staggered off into the darkness. Black Sting turned to the other two soldiers, who were cowering against the walls. ''Fetch medicine and treatment for these two at once. And I warn you, if either of them dies your own lives will be forfeit.''

The soldiers scurried off to obey. Black Sting went to Five Legs, and touched him with his feelers. ''How are you, old one?'' he asked. But Five Legs only mumbled incoherently in reply. Black Sting turned to Still One, whose retchings had subsided to a weak gasping. The soldier realized that he could do nothing here for the moment and with a grim face he turned and left the chamber.

Still One came as near to death as it was possible to come. Paradoxically, it was the very excessiveness of the poisonous dose Dew-Lover had administered which saved him. It had caused him to vomit so immediately and so violently that relatively little of the stuff had actually entered his system. All the same, it was a close thing. For two days and nights he lay, scarcely breathing, in the chamber to which they had brought him, while they administered antidote and kept his body warm. Five Legs too lay nearby in the same chamber, where they attended to his bruises and to the wound in his abdomen. His condition was not so critical, for Dew-Lover had not injected any actual poison after his thrust, and the old ant's tough constitution aided a surprisingly quick recovery, but all the same he had to endure considerable pain for a while. His main concern, though, was for the wan figure that lay nearby, and he was forever fussing and chivvying the ants in attendance, who soon got heartily sick of his presence.

However, eventually Still One's breathing became firmer, and his heartbeat stronger, and soon he was able to take a little liquid sustenance without immediately rejecting it—

and even despite his protests, a little of his own honey-dew—
which speeded his recovery greatly.

From time to time Black Sting, Great Head and other
elders would slip in briefly to see what progress the inval-
ids were making, and the senior worker-ants—Never-Rest,
Wind-Blow and the others—were frequently in attendance.
It was they who, at the instant of Five Legs' apprehension
by Dew-Lover, had sent a hurried deputation to Black
Sting, thus bringing about his timely intervention. They
were now able to inform Five Legs that the workers had all
been allowed back into the mound and that everyone was
only awaiting his recovery to begin discussions about their
conditions for a return to normal living and working.

For it seemed that the painful incident had had the effect
that all their protests and demonstrations could not achieve.
Black Sting's stern defence of the old autocratic traditions
had crumbled at the revelation of his lieutenant's vicious
action, and indeed the wave of revulsion that had spread
through the whole community—amongst worker-ants and
Council members alike—had brought it home to everyone
how interdependent they all were for their safety and
well-being: one caste with another, one rank with another,
each individual with every other. It was the unanimous
verdict of the Council, after consulting with the Queen of
Queens, that Dew-Lover should be banished from the
colony—sent forth from the mound to survive as best he
could alone in the forest—and that the worker-ants should
immediately have their request granted for representation
within the Council's ranks.

To this end, as soon as Five Legs was well enough to
participate, Black Sting called a meeting of the leaders of
all sides to decide what form this membership should take.
It was agreed that Five Legs, as the chosen leader of the
worker-ants, should be admitted to all meetings of the
Inner Council, and that he should bring a deputation of his
own choosing to the larger gatherings of the General Council. It was furthermore agreed that as many soldiers should
be involved with the reconstruction of the mound as was

necessary to complete it in the fastest possible time, without meanwhile endangering the general security.

And so once more work began on the damaged hillock. And this time with an even greater urgency—for further evidence had come in of the red ants' far-ranging activities. . . .

* 17 *

It is extraordinary how news gets round the countryside. Via tiny whisperings in the grass, messages on the breeze, scents and sounds in the undergrowth, the tidings of particularly momentous happenings can be transmitted across enormous distances in an almost miraculous way. The variety of insect life in particular—as well as of the other larger species—is so great, their ways of communication so various, their means of travel so diverse and so wide-ranging, that information can be spread abroad via countless intermediaries in ways that the originators could never foresee.

Vague rumours and rumblings of the red ants' scourge of the land had been filtering through to the colony ever since the first dramatic report of the attack on the riverside mound. Now that the general springtime activity was in full flood everywhere, more specific accounts were coming in. Refugees from other ravaged settlements spread their distraught messages far and wide; news of sightings from the air of red ant parties on the march became more and more frequent; stories of dreadful encounters deep in the forest were spread and magnified to spinechilling proportions. There were even odd messages relating specifically to the progress of Snake's Tongue's little force. Their course through the forest had been witnessed, even though the terrain had seemed to them so devoid of life; reports of their stupendous battle with the tree-spider had filtered through; and it was even rumoured that the red ants themselves had been alerted by the fight and had sent scouts to observe the party's progress.

Snake's Tongue, Dreamer and Joker were of course unaware that all this was going on. Deep in the fastness of the enemy's mound, cut off from all forms of communication with the outside world, it seemed to them that none could know of their plight, nor of the fearful impending danger presented by their captors as they steadily built up their forces, and extended their boundaries. It appeared vital that they escape and spread the warning, not only to their own kind but to the world in general.

As they waited for the evening to fall and the change of work parties to commence, the tension increased moment by moment, until Dreamer found himself longing for the time to come, simply to alleviate the suspense. He went over their plan for dealing with the guards a thousand times in his mind, and at the same time his antennae were constantly alert for the slightest increase in activity outside in the passages.

Then eventually came the change he was expecting. The general tramping of feet became more frequent, the size of the groupings larger. He whispered to Snake's Tongue that the moment was approaching.

The three ants quietly took up their agreed positions: Snake's Tongue against the wall to one side of the chamber entrance, Dreamer and Joker against the opposite wall, the former nearest to the opening itself so that he could sense when the moment was right. For an interminable while they waited, as the working parties marched back and forth along the main tunnel past the end of their own passage, growing gradually in size and frequency. The two guards outside seemed quite unaware of anything happening, as they lounged and muttered between themselves. At last Dreamer, his antennae against the ground, received the signals he was waiting for. A distant tremor from some way down the main passage indicated that a large, widely spread party, comprising mainly captive worker-ants, with a small advance escort of red guards, was approaching.

Dreamer immediately gave a groan as if in pain and, calling out to the guards, moved back towards the centre of the chamber. The guards stopped their chatter and one of them entered to find out what was the matter while the other hovered in the entrance. As the first one passed him, Joker leapt at him from the side, flinging his body against the higher, longer form of the red soldier, lunging with his sting at the other's underbelly. The moment Dreamer heard Joker make his move, he too ran round and attacked from the other side. The enemy ant hissed and reared up, attempting to bring his assailants within range of his spray of poison, but with one on either side of him clinging with claws and mandibles, he could not bring the base of his abdomen to bear and he roared for his companion to assist.

The latter was already on his way to join the fray and it was now that Snake's Tongue took his, most dangerous, part in the action, for he had to tackle the second guard unaided. With that extraordinary speed of his, he hit the guard in the side of the body, sending him staggering across the chamber, and then was on him like a veritable army of ants, biting, clawing, stabbing.

The battle was short, sharp and ferocious. The red guards, though big and immensely strong, had little chance against the surprise and speed of their opponents. Both Joker and Snake's Tongue had got in that first vital jab with their stings, and the creeping effect of the poison increased the ungainliness of their opponents' blundering manoeuvres within the narrow chamber. The acrid smell of the red ants' own poison filled the air as they aimed it indiscriminately into the darkness, but the smaller ants had

taken care to keep themselves well out of the direct line of
fire. Again and again, Joker and Dreamer struck at the first
guard and injected their poison, until he lay helpless on the
floor of the chamber, violent convulsions jerking his body.
Joker relinquished his grip, whispered to Dreamer to hold
on to the big ant, and turned to where the scuffle of
Snake's Tongue's fight was taking place.

Snake's Tongue was having a harder time of it, for his
opponent was an extremely powerful beast, and having
rallied after that first onslaught, was fighting back at his
single opponent with a ferocity which required all the
latter's speed and agility to evade. However, when Joker
joined battle on the other flank, the enemy soldier found
himself outmanoeuvred and it was only a matter of moments before the effect of his attackers' repeated sting-
thrusts reduced him also to a passive, heaving form on the
floor.

Gasping with their exertions the three smaller ants hesitated for a brief moment, listening for any signs that the
struggle had attracted further attention, but all was quiet,
except for the tramp of the work party's footsteps, which
by now was vibrating past the immediate end of their own
small passage.

"Quickly!" whispered Snake's Tongue and he slipped
into the tunnel, leaving the other two to follow. The
narrow thoroughfare was empty as the three hurried the
few paces along it to where it joined the main passage.
Here Snake's Tongue hesitated a moment to ascertain the
situation. They were fortunate: not only was the work
party with which they were immediately concerned strung
out in a long line on either side of the junction, but several
other smaller parties and individuals were travelling in the
opposite direction, so there was a considerable concourse
within the passage.

The three stepped out into the jostling crowd, joining
the general upward direction of the work party. No one
commented. Those red ants who were around were either
travelling in the opposite direction or were some way

ahead or to the rear and did not notice the addition of three extra slaves to the general throng. The other captive brown ants seemed too preoccupied and generally dispirited to care about or even notice any change in their numbers and the three were able to merge in unobtrusively with heads down and feelers lowered in the prevailing submissive fashion.

As they went higher and higher the passage was joined by others, and the crowd thickened until they were part of a huge flood of activity intent upon either reaching the daylight or escaping from it. When they finally emerged into the open air they found that the dusk was well advanced, but even so the fading light dazzled their eyes after their long confinement in darkness.

They were perhaps halfway up the slope of the immense mound, but facing in another direction to the one from which they had originally approached it, looking now across the rolling limitless expanse of heathland, where not a tree broke the skyline. The air was strangely heavy and oppressive, in contrast to the fresh, windswept atmosphere which had heralded their arrival, and towering mountains of darkened cloud dominated the immense expanse of open sky in a way which the three ants from the lowland, forest-shadowed regions had never seen before. It was a spectacular and intimidating display which, to Dreamer in particular, seemed almost supernatural in its grandeur. He cast a worried look at Joker who was just behind him and the latter muttered, "Storm coming up; could be useful," which reassured him somewhat.

Now they were able to observe the column of ants of which they were a part. It consisted of perhaps two dozen workers, strung out at irregular intervals, with a group of half a dozen or so red soldiers at both the front and the rear of the line. The whole party was headed down a well-established run which descended over the irregular, loose-packed earth and scree of the mound's slope. Dreamer glanced back at the ants following and thought he detected the odd curious look from those nearest in the line, but they were generally too apathetic to pay much attention to the intruders in their ranks. He looked about him, taking in the rest of the activity on the hillock's flank. Work parties of various sizes were progressing backwards and forwards in similar manner, while large hunting parties consisting solely of red soldiers moved past at a faster, more confident pace. Smaller red ant groups and individuals trotted here and there on particular missions, and there was a general atmosphere of highly organized industry.

However, there was something very different about it all to the activity which took place around his own home base. It was hard to specify but Dreamer, having now been amongst the alien insects for several days, could detect a subtle undertone of tension and deep-rooted unease, which all their arrogant display of invincibility could not disguise. It stemmed, he supposed, from the strange ephemerality of the species' system of procreation, with its inbuilt mechanism of self-destruction. He shuddered to think what would happen if they ever learned to surmount this deficiency in the way that his own kind had.

As he was pioneering this an astonishing event transpired. A sudden warning hiss from Snake's Tongue, just ahead, made him look up. Coming towards them up the run, already past the advance party of guards was a group of three red soldiers. Their leader, easily recognizable by his superb, graceful stride, was Fleet.

There was no way that the three fugitives could take evasive action. The run was only wide enough for two ants to pass at a close distance and the small party were almost upon them. All they could do was lower their heads and keep going and wait for the apocalypse to happen. Dreamer's heart sank at the sheer misfortune of such a chance encounter. But then came the miracle.

He was aware of Fleet casually scanning the party of workers as he came. He was aware of the sudden lift of the other's antennae, and the flash of recognition in his eye as it fell upon Snake's Tongue. He was aware of it passing on towards himself and Joker, and of the tiny, involuntary hesitation in the red soldier's gait. And then he was past, and his two companions with him, and no further sign did he make.

Dreamer was to remember that moment often in the days to come. Had Fleet reacted in the expected way, the pattern of future events would have been a very different one. Dreamer was never quite able to explain or understand why the red ant had behaved as he did. He only knew that the incident belonged to the great subliminal stratum of life and experience of which he was recently becoming more and more aware.

Whatever the reason, they were still unapprehended, no hue and cry sounded at their backs and with every step they took further down the hillside their sense of relief and astonishment increased, until at last they were travelling through the jungle of grasses over the level ground itself and were able to turn their minds to the next immediate problem.

A hold-up occurred at a junction of paths ahead of them and for a moment the party came to a brief halt to let another group pass by in front. Snake's Tongue seized the opportunity to have a quick, whispered consultation with the other two.

"We're going in the wrong direction," he muttered. "And I don't see how to break away without being spotted. Our best hope is to wait until we're well away from the mound and then take our chances individually, when each of us sees a moment. It will mean breaking up, but it gives a better chance of at least one of us getting away."

"Can't we meet up again somewhere?" whispered Joker, voicing Dreamer's unspoken plea.

"Aim for the spot where we killed the spider," replied Snake's Tongue. "Fleet said it was still there, so there will be food. Also it didn't sound, from what he said, as if they have regular parties out in that direction at the moment. So, provided we keep ahead of any search parties, we should have a chance."

"Depending on how long he keeps quiet about our escape," said Joker. "He saw us, you know."

"I know," replied Snake's Tongue. "That I don't understand." He glanced over his shoulder. The group was moving off again. "There's a storm coming," he whispered hurriedly. "Take advantage of it. And we'll try to meet at the spider place around dawn. But don't wait longer than sun-up: one of us *must* get home to warn them!"

"Stop talking! Move on there!" The harsh command rang out behind them. Snake's Tongue turned instantly and moved off again and Dreamer followed, knowing they could probably not communicate again and feeling suddenly very alone and vulnerable.

The light was fading fast which gave him confidence. The galloping storm clouds were hastening the retreat of daylight and an ominous wind was beginning to moan and rustle among the grasses around them. Dreamer wondered vaguely what action the work parties took when the weather broke. Most insects take refuge when it rains, either scurrying for their homes or, if they are too far away, hiding under leaves or in crannies amongst the vegetation. A direct hit from a raindrop can be an uncomfortable experience for a creature the size of an ant. However this time, Dreamer thought, it was a risk the three of them would probably have to run if they were going to take advantage of the elements to make their escape.

He was scarcely aware of Snake's Tongue's going. The party had travelled well beyond the much-trampled regions in the immediate vicinity of the mound and was progressing along a single narrow trail that appeared to be running almost parallel with the distant shadow of the forest's edge. Then, just as the first few warning drops of rain were beginning to spatter around them, the path took a sudden turn inwards towards the trees and it was here, on the bend where they were momentarily out of sight of the guards at both ends of the columns, that Snake's Tongue vanished. One moment he was there, running just ahead of

Dreamer, the next, he was gone, only the faintest rustle in the vegetation at the side to indicate his passing.

Dreamer felt a momentary twinge of panic at the disappearance of his leader. He glanced back quickly to see if Joker was still there and was relieved to find the reassuring bulk of the cheerful soldier still behind him.

"That was neat," whispered the other. "Our turn next. Good luck, young Dreamer."

Dreamer nodded and whispered back, "See you for a feast of spider meat." Then he concentrated on looking ahead for a suitable place to break away.

The chance did not come for some time. The path was running dead straight now and the grasses on either side had thinned out providing little immediate cover. However, they now seemed to be heading straight towards the trees, and the pace had speeded up, motivated by the general desire to reach cover before the rain increased. Dreamer could not tell whereabouts in the forest they were going to arrive, for the mound was well out of sight behind them now, but his general sense of direction told him that the original trail by which they had approached the enemy's base was a considerable distance away to one side.

The storm broke while they were still some way off from the tree-line. A sudden flash of lightning momentarily illuminated the darkening gloom around them, throwing the giant shapes of the trees ahead into stark relief against the blackened sky. A moment later came the threatening rumble of the thunder as the heavens growled their anger at the world.

It is a general superstition among ants that thunderstorms are a sign of the Lord of the Stars' fury at some particularly abominable deed somewhere in his domain and that at such a time his wrath can fall on all who have incurred his displeasure. Being the essentially just power that he is, however, such occasions are also held to provide opportunities for the deserving. As the work party ran at full speed for the cover of the trees, with the rain splashing at an ever-increasing rate about them, Dreamer prayed that he was of the latter category and looked about urgently for his chance to escape.

Joker, however, apparently beat him to it. As the party reached the darkness under the first of the trees and hurried to find shelter amongst the roots Dreamer glanced back and, with a mixture of fear and elation, realized that he was alone. The other had seen his chance during the dash and vanished.

It was now that another of those surprising revelations of psychology that were constantly educating Dreamer in the unpredictable ways of the world occurred. He found himself cowering with three or four other captive ants in a small unprotected space in the lee of an exposed tree root. The rain was now falling heavily, as they could hear by the distant heavy swish of its impact upon the leaves and branches above their heads, but immediately around them was a temporary quiet as the canopy held off the deluge for a few moments. The rest of the party were also taking shelter in nearby places and Dreamer, his antennae alert as they now took over the main responsibility for informing him in the near-darkness, could tell that one of the two groups of red ants was close by to one side. As he searched for clues as to the whereabouts of the other, he felt a gentle feeler-tap on his back. He turned to find there the ant who had been next in line, immediately behind himself and Joker. He had not taken much notice of any of the other captives before, but now, as the lightning flashed across the heavens once again, he saw a gentle, inquisitive little face peering at him from the shadows.

"That's the way you should go," whispered the stranger, pointing back over his shoulder with a feeler. "The advance guard are over there, in the other direction."

Dreamer hesitated, taken aback, half suspicious. Then the other whispered again: "That's the way your friend went. There's a trail in that direction, if you can find it. I should wait till the rain breaks through overhead and then run for it."

Dreamer felt a warming flood of gratitude at this unexpected help-offering and he mumbled his thanks. The other waved them aside and said, "Go when there's another thunder crash. That will cover any sound you make. Good luck. I wish I had your courage."

The chance came almost immediately. The peal of thunder which followed that same streak of lightning coincided with a renewed gust of wind and a torrent of waterdrops breaking through from the branches above them, and for a few moments the sound and fury about them was numbing in its magnitude. Dreamer felt the push of the other ant's feelers behind him and then he was out in the midst of the frenzy, running for his life.

The next few moments again had the quality of one of his dreams. As he ran, blindly, frantically, expecting at any moment to hear the sound of shouts and pursuing feet behind him, Nature indulged in one of her most spectacular displays—solely it seemed for his benefit—as the storm passed directly overhead. The thunder roared its exhortation at his fleeing figure, the lightning lit up the huge gesticulating shapes of the trees around him, the wind hissed and howled from the branches over his head and the rain hurled its great parcels of water in his wake as if veritably to wash him on his way. Twice he was hit directly by one of the drops, which flattened him to the ground, left him soaked and gasping with shock; but then he was up and running again, the icy mantle of water streaming off his body, the sodden ground clinging to his scurrying feet. Only vaguely was he conscious of his direction, and he fleetingly wondered whether Joker was anywhere near and how he was faring in this holocaust, but he had no time to worry about it: his own survival was his sole, frantic preoccupation.

Eventually, however, he was forced to seek refuge and take his bearings. Sheer exhaustion was making his running clumsy and incautious and when he blundered headlong into a rushing torrent of water that almost swept him bodily away down a precipitous bank, he realized—after having dragged himself back to firm land again—that no use was being served by crashing blindly on any further. He veered off to where the grey mass of a stone reared its glistening head above the ground, ran around to its lee side and squeezed himself into a narrow crevice beneath it.

His heart thumping and his breath coming in great gasps, he listened for signs of pursuit. But the noise of the elements effectively drowned out all but the closest of individual sounds, and it seemed that there was little chance of anything being able to keep track of a quarry in that bedlam. He peered about him, seeking for clues as to his whereabouts. The only indication he had in the brief lightning flashes was a vague emptiness beyond the trees to one side, which indicated that he was still close to the forest edge. This gave him encouragement for it meant that he had been running more or less parallel to this boundary and was at least headed back towards the only forest trail he knew; that by which they had come.

Dreamer swallowed a little of the food in his crop, retained from their last meal in captivity, and contemplated his situation. Only now was he able to observe the full majesty of the storm about him. Never before had he been out in the open during such a display by the elements; he had always taken refuge in the home-mound at such times, along with all the others of the colony. Now he was witnessing it at close quarters—indeed was almost a part of it—and he began to realize for the first time how truly gigantic the forces of Nature could be and why all creatures held the unseen Lord of the Stars in such awe. He felt utterly, appallingly alone. He remembered, however, the teachings of his earliest days, which were that he who truly dared, he who held his own life as little, had nothing to fear, and he knew that, as soon as he had gained his strength again, he would have to venture out once more into that dreadful tumult.

And so he did. He rested a few moments, chose a line of direction which would take him away at an angle from the forest's edge, picked out a landmark in the next lightning flash—a briar clump some twenty ant-lengths away—

and then waited for the next lull in the storm. When it came—when the wind fell a little and the rain was not driving quite so hard—he left the shelter of his crevice and sprinted for the briars. Slithering and stumbling, buffeted and soaked, he reached his objective, crouched beneath a leaf and peered out for his next patch of shelter.

And so it went on. Stage by stage, blindly trusting to his instincts and his natural sense of direction, he made his exhausting way through the forest. The downward slope of the ground helped him; and the thickening of the vegetation, although it did not aid his progress, told him that at least he was travelling further from the red ants' base. He lost all track of time and had no idea how far he had come. His enforced vegetarian diet during the days in captivity had left him in no condition for strenuous exercise such as this, and tiredness and hunger began to take their effect so that he was stumbling instinctively along in a half conscious state.

Then at last he had a stroke of luck which gave him encouragement and renewed energy. In the middle of one of his wild dashes from one spot of shelter to another he suddenly realized that he was running on firm, even ground for a few steps. He stopped, peering into the darkness for a clue. His antennae told him that, even amongst the general rain-sodden smell of the earth around him, there lingered faint traces of old insect scent. Then a flash of lightning— this time from further off—showed him that his suspicions were correct: he had stumbled across a trail. Whether it was the one by which they had come he could not tell, as all individual traces of their own scent would have been washed away, but it seemed to be leading in the right direction and it offered much easier going. Thankfully he decided to follow it. It did not offer so much cover of course, but the storm seemed at last to be abating a little and he chose to brave the hazard of the falling rain in return for the smoother ground. Several times he was struck by hurtling raindrops but he was so soaked already that, apart from the momentary shock and discomfort, it made little difference. He hurried on with new hope.

Then came an even greater boost to his morale. He had been on the path for some time, making good progress, aided by a steady decrease in the storm's ferocity, when he suddenly heard a hoarse shout behind him which brought him to an abrupt halt.

"Hey, slow down, can't you? Give me a chance to catch up!"

With a warmth flooding his heart such as he had rarely felt before, Dreamer waited for a bedraggled and panting Joker to come stumbling up to him. The two ants joyfully embraced antennae in the middle of the track.

"You were going at such a pace! I thought I'd never catch you!" gasped Joker.

"I didn't hear your steps with all this rain," said Dreamer, the pleasure choking his throat. "How long have you been behind me?"

"Quite a way. I picked up your scent some time ago. You've made better time than me. I'm lucky to be here at all."

"Why?"

"I took the wrong line to begin with. I almost blundered out of the forest again back near their mound. And then I had to lie low for a bit. There were several parties of red ants about. They've discovered our escape. They were out looking for us."

Dreamer's heart sank again. "That means they must be behind us! They could be following our trail right now!"

"More than likely. But I think we got a start on them. They were dashing backwards and forwards along the forest's edge, trying to pick up our trail. They didn't realize we had entered the forest so far along. But it can only be a matter of time before they're after us; they know where we'll be headed."

"I wonder if it was Fleet who raised the alarm," Dreamer conjectured.

"Not necessarily," said Joker. "It wouldn't have taken

them long to find the guards anyway. Come on, we must move fast. Those red beasts are far too speedy for my liking.''

He set off again down the trail with Dreamer panting behind him, the latter's antennae now much more alert for signs of pursuit behind.

As they went the storm continued to abate until the thunder had dwindled to a mild grumble in the distance and the rain had eased to a gentle drizzle. There was even a faint glow through the clouds from time to time, as the moon struggled to reassert her presence in the heavens. Despite the ominous fear of pursuit behind them, Dreamer felt a sense of security and renewed calm as he loped along behind Joker's comforting bulk. The experience of being so totally alone in those strange parts with the terrifying ferocity of the storm about him was one which he would never forget, and now that he once more had companionship in the midst of danger he realized what a precious thing it was to him, and in the secret core of his soul was deeply grateful.

They had been travelling for some time, stopping only for the briefest of rests, when Joker called over his shoulder, ''I think this is our old trail. I keep thinking I recognize parts of it.''

Dreamer had been suspecting the same thing. It was an instinctive feeling rather than any precise recognition, brought about by subtle indications: a fleeting combination of herbal scents, the shape of a tree-trunk, a particular curve in the path. He began to think hungrily of their hidden store of spider meat and to wonder whether Snake's Tongue had made it there before them. If imagination wasn't playing tricks on them and they were indeed on the right path, then the place couldn't be far off. He only hoped that the red ants hadn't anticipated their first destination and sent a party by another route to cut them off there.

They almost passed the spot. If Snake's Tongue had not been alert, listening to their approaching footfalls, they might well have run right past it. His hiss came as they were passing a patch of rye-grass at the side of the trail and brought them up sharp. They peered towards the dark outline of the grass clump from which the sound had seemed to come, and only then did Dreamer recognize it as the one in which they had hidden from the party of red ants on their approach journey and the place where the spider had attacked them. With an exclamation of delight he plunged towards it, Joker following close behind, and they were reunited with their leader as he stepped forward out of the shelter of the grasses. For once Snake's Tongue allowed his own emotion to show and it was evident that he was as pleased to see them as they were to see him.

"Well done, well done!" he kept repeating as they touched feelers in joyful greeting. "We made it! How are you both?"

"Exhausted," gasped Dreamer.

"And famished," added Joker. "Is the spider's body still there?"

"No," replied Snake's Tongue. "But there's something better. The grubs have got to it and they've laid their eggs there. There's quite a feast. Come."

He led the way to where they had hidden the spider's corpse and revealed where he had scraped away the protective covering of leaves and humus. The empty husk of the spider's carapace lay there, stripped almost clean of flesh, and within the hollow shell lay a pale, succulent mass of eggs with here and there the wandering figures of hatched maggots in attendance. The two hungry ants wasted no time. Ignoring the small, shambling forms of the grubs themselves, they pounced on the delicious orbs and ate ravenously. It was the first animal protein they had eaten in a long time and their bodies absorbed the energy-giving food gratefully. In between mouthfuls they briefly told Snake's Tongue of their escape, and of Joker's discovery of the red ant search parties.

Snake's Tongue's face was grave in the pale light of the approaching dawn. "That's bad," he said. "I had hoped they wouldn't discover our disappearance for some time. But I suppose that was too much to expect. Perhaps Fleet did raise the alarm after all.'' He glanced back towards the trail. ''I'll go and listen on the trail. Fill your crops and then join me.'' And he was gone with that astonishingly rapid, darting motion of his.

''Not much wrong with him,'' observed Joker, his mouth full.

''I'm glad,'' said Dreamer. ''I was frightened that he might not be here.''

''Take a lot to stop that one,'' said Joker. He brushed some of the sticky egg substance from his mandibles with a foreleg, and sighed happily. ''That's more like it! I'd forgotten what a proper feed tasted like.'' He drank from a raindrop on a nearby stem.

Dreamer too was feeling much better for the nourishment and his spirits had risen accordingly. Now, however, he also became more attuned mentally and his thoughts turned to the danger of pursuit. ''We'd better get back to him,'' he muttered, cramming a last few of the tiny eggs down into his crop.

Joker did likewise and the two hurried to where Snake's Tongue stood motionless on the track, his one good feeler to the ground, listening.

''What can you hear, Dreamer?'' he asked, his voice grave.

Dreamer laid his long, slender antennae on the ground and listened intently. The sounds of the forest were all around: the rustle of foliage as the wind stirred the vegetation; the patter of waterdrops falling from the still-sodden trees; the distant, heavy impact of a deer's hooves far off. Then he became aware of another signal, a faint but steady vibration, filtering through the other sounds from far back along the trail. He listened carefully for a few moments, then lifted his head and looked at Snake's Tongue.

''It's them,'' he said simply. ''There's a party following down the track.''

Snake's Tongue nodded. "I thought so," he said. "How many, do you think?"

"I'm not sure," said Dreamer. "They're too far back. But they're coming fast."

"Right," replied Snake's Tongue. He looked at them each in turn. "We've a long way to go. Are you ready to run?"

Dreamer and Joker nodded. Without another word Snake's Tongue turned on the narrow trail and, with the refuge of the darkness vanishing moment by moment around them, set off at a heart-pounding pace towards home.

* 18 *

Fleet's reaction, when he had caught sight of the three fugitives amongst the work party leaving the mound, had surprised himself as much as it had them. He could never afterwards quite explain how a highly trained and committed soldier such as himself could have permitted them to continue unchallenged in the way he had. It was a purely instinctive, spur of the moment response which, as soon as it had happened, he could not retract. There was something about the three smaller ants, with their strange lifestyle, which had touched a chord deep within his conditioned, uncompromising being. Their conversations together while they had been in his custody had aroused unsuspected emotions within him, had touched on aspects of life which he had hitherto never allowed himself to consider, and in that split second when he held their fate so completely within his grasp he could not bring himself to be the instrument of their destruction.

Immediately after the incident, however, he realized that he had placed himself in a very awkward position by not effecting their recapture. He was responsible for their safe-keeping and to have to admit to The Spider that he had failed in that duty would be to incur his leader's awesome wrath. However, he had no choice but to do so, and he knew that his best chance was to make an immediate clean breast of his failure, though not of course of his subsequent spontaneous compounding of that failure.

Upon entering the mound he sent the two soldiers with him off on some mission and headed for the chamber where his captives had been held. He arrived to find that the attack on the guards had only just been discovered. Several soldiers were milling disconcertedly around the two inert bodies. Such an action on the part of captive ants was virtually unknown within the colony and the soldiers looked uncertainly to Fleet for guidance. He ordered them to collect search parties and to wait for instructions while he went to face his leader.

His immediate and contrite admission was probably what saved him from the full repercussions of The Spider's ire, and also the sheer improbability of the captives' bold escape. On hearing the news the gigantic insect stared for a long moment at his subordinate in sheer disbelief that three such paltry creatures could have effected a coup of that nature against his own magnificent forces. Then he roared his condemnation at the unfortunate Fleet, who bowed his head in suitably humble contrition.

When he had worked the fury out of his system The Spider thought for a moment. Then he turned his grim eye once more upon his officer. "Well, we shall have to take a look at this intriguing colony, which breeds such impudent ants," he said. "As soon as I can muster sufficient forces I shall turn my attentions in that direction. Meanwhile, you had better go in pursuit of those three presumptuous escapers, and if you don't wish to pay the penalty for your negligence you had better see that you catch them. Go."

Fleet went. He knew that now was not the time for further aberrations of his duty and that, if he was to reinstate himself in his leader's—and indeed his own—

estimation, then he must do everything in his power to rectify the situation. He immediately sent out various advance search parties to try to pick up the trail of the fugitive ants in the midst of the gathering storm, while he himself assembled a small party of chosen soldiers and prepared for a long chase.

Having fed and filled their crops with reserve nourishment the contingent, half a dozen strong, set off into the night through the fury of the thunderstorm. The advance parties had not been able to find the escapers' scents in that fierce weather, but Fleet knew the way they had come and guessed that they must eventually seek out that same trail if they were to find their way home again. The party battled their way through the driving rain and crashing thunder, finding it no less daunting than did their quarry some way ahead of them.

By the time the storm had abated and a faint greyness silhouetting the huge shapes of the trees around them indicated that the dawn was not far off, he knew that his intuition had been right. One by one they had picked up the scents of the fleeing ants, until now they knew that all three had joined the trail separately and were somewhere ahead of them. Fleet, with that easy gait of his, set a pace that stretched his soldiers' endurance to the limit, and it was a weary force who, having travelled through the night without a rest, reached the spot where the spider's corpse had been hidden. Here, in the brightening light and the clean air of the storm-washed morning, Fleet called a brief halt while he scouted around the area with his feelers. The plundered maggots' nest and the jumbled trails told their own story. He knew now that the three smaller ants had come together at that place, had fed and had resumed their journey. Moreover, from the freshness of their scents, they could not now be so very far ahead.

He allowed his soldiers to consume what was left of the unfortunate maggots' nest, and then once more they took to the trail, decreasing with each long, powerful stride the distance between themselves and their quarry.

*   *   *

Some way ahead Snake's Tongue's little band was running in silence, Dreamer and Joker concentrating on keeping up with the fierce pace of their leader. The going was a little easier now as the rain began to dry off the sodden track, but this brought into sharper focus the steady vibration of the pursuing footfalls behind them. Dreamer, running last of the three, was desperately trying to remember how far they had to go to reach the little riverside mound, which might provide their first chance of sanctuary, and possibly— if any scouting parties were around—of help; and he was also trying to estimate how far behind them the following footsteps were and how fast they were catching up. His calculations did not increase his confidence. He wondered too whether there were any red ant parties ahead of them, but so far at least they had come across no signs.

Several times, as they ran, they passed junctions with other trails branching off amongst the trees. Snake's Tongue never seemed to hesitate at such points and the other two blithely trusted his judgement, hoping that they were still on the right track. There was certainly no time to stop and debate the matter. All three ants could now quite clearly feel the tremor caused by the enemy party behind and the realization that they were being gained on gave added impetus to their flight.

Snake's Tongue spoke for the first time, calling back over his shoulder, "Can you tell how many there are, Dreamer?"

"Six or seven, I think," panted the other. "And they're catching up fast."

"I'm done for, leader," gasped Joker, from the middle. "I can't keep up this pace much longer. You'll have to go on without me."

"Keep going," commanded Snake's Tongue in a firm voice. "When they get really close we'll split up. That will confuse them for a while. Then try and break your scent and find somewhere to hide. One of us *must* get through!"

The canopy of branches above their heads, the tangle of undergrowth and grasses through which the trail wove its way, all merged into a single blur in Dreamer's mind as he ran on, his heart pounding, his muscles aching. In his imagination the sound of the enemy's feet seemed to grow to a thunder as menacing as that of the storm, and the evil scent of their poison already seemed to taint the wind. It appeared now that there was little chance of their reaching their own territory in time and he felt a despairing anguish that they should have got so far, only to fail in the final stages of their journey. He thought that perhaps he and Joker should turn and fight there and then on the path, which might at least give Snake's Tongue, the fastest of them, the chance to get away. He tried to convey this to Joker, but the words would not come: merely a hoarse, gasping mutter which was lost in their pounding footfalls. He kept glancing back over his shoulder as he ran, until finally he caught the sight he was dreading—a distant blur of bobbing reddish-brown far back up the trail behind them.

This time he was able to get the words out. "I can see them, leader," he panted. "They're in sight!"

"Right," called back Snake's Tongue. "Split up when we've rounded the next bend. You two to that side, I'll go to this. Find some cover and climb if you can. Good luck."

Their chance came almost immediately. The trail took a curve round the big, grey root of a beech tree, and for a few precious moments they were out of sight of their pursuers. "Now!" called Snake's Tongue and he was away, veering off the path into the unmarked wilderness at the side. Joker followed his example, crashing clumsily through the dead leaves and humus of the forest floor on the other side. Dreamer ran on a few more paces to clear Joker's trail and then left the path at that side also, plunging into unknown territory.

The vegetation was thick and tangled here, new growths and shoots battling for space and light. It offered a great deal of cover but at the same time impeded progress considerably. As Dreamer ran, staggering and stumbling through the verdure, his heart pounding as if it would burst out of his body, he tried frantically to think of a way to use the ground to advantage over his pursuers. It occurred to him that to run blindly on, making the amount of noise that he was and leaving an obvious trail over the forest floor, was not the wisest tactic: the more powerful red ants would soon catch up with him. What was it Snake's Tongue had said? "Break your scent and hide. Climb if you can." Yes, that was it! Get up high, away from this jungle, to where one could be silent and use one's nimbleness and finer senses to advantage. But how to break the trail? How to make them lose his scent?

Dreamer forced himself, despite his fear of the creatures at his back, to stop for a moment, listen and think. He could hear Joker careering through the undergrowth off to one side and prayed that he would do the same. Then, behind him, he heard a gabble of red ant voices, of hurried consultation, of commands being issued, and he guessed that the enemy had reached the point where they had split up. A few moments later, as expected, there came a new crashing in the vegetation and he knew that they had dispersed into separate groups to follow the three different trails.

He scanned the air with his antennae, searching for a particular scent. Then he received a waft of what he was seeking, ahead of him and off to one side. He began to run again, this time more carefully, more discerningly, his senses alert to his surroundings. Yes, there it was—water! Clear running water, not the stagnant, earth-stained, after-rain variety. A tiny rivulet was meandering across the ground, draining a bank of moss at the foot of an old oak tree. It only ran a little way, scarcely out of the shadow of the oak itself, before sinking into oblivion beneath the soft earth, but it was enough for his purpose for in its final stages it reached the undergrowth beyond the tree's shade, and here the tangled stems of bramble, hawthorn and elder dipped into its shallow flow.

Dreamer overcame the natural distaste that all ants have for wetness of any kind and splashed straight into the water near its source, ignoring the cold, unpleasant effect on his legs. It was so shallow that it only came halfway up his limbs, but that was enough to hide his scent for those vital few strides, and he waded down the tiny stream's length towards the sanctuary of the entwined tendrils. On reaching the spot he threaded his way between them, selected a thick bramble stem which reared out of the water and disappeared into the general tangle above his head, and began to climb, weaving his way round the sharp thorns which protruded at intervals from its surface.

As he climbed higher into the thicket the sounds from the forest floor came more sharply into focus. He could hear the footfalls of the chasing ants—two, by the sound of it—quite clearly behind him. And some way off at a tangent was the noise of a further pursuit, presumably after Joker. The air was remarkably still after the storm and the sounds came in clear relief through the otherwise strangely silent forest. It was as if all other life was frozen, holding its breath to observe the outcome of this chase to the death. Sound, Dreamer realized, was the crucial factor in the contest. The air was too still for scent to carry far, but for the same reason every tiny noise was clearly audible through the echoing arches of the woodland. He climbed with greater stealth than ever, crossing to different stems whenever they came within reach in order to confuse his scent trail; listening all the while to the approaching footfalls.

The bramble was now heavily entwined with the stiff, straighter stems of an elder bush, whose pungent odour filled the air, and Dreamer transferred to one of these, partly to disguise his scent further, and partly because its larger, sprouting leaves would provide better cover.

The sounds behind and beneath him grew louder and more immediate, and he slipped onto the broad, curling surface of one of the leaves and crouched there motionless, trying to still his thumping heart, peering down over the edge at the scene below.

He did not have long to wait. Within moments the figures of two red soldiers come into view, partially glimpsed through the intervening screen of vegetation. He did not recognize either of them, but they were big, powerful beasts who did not seem much incapacitated by the rigours of the chase and they were following his trail at speed, if a little uncertainly. When they came to the tiny stream into which he had digressed, they ran backwards and forward beside it, having lost his scent. Then they held a muttered conversation together which Dreamer was unable to hear, being too far above them. One of them waved his antennae in the direction of the water's flow and they parted, each taking one side of the rivulet, and began to move down its length towards him, seeking for his scent.

Dreamer held his breath in an agony of suspense as the soldiers approached, scanning the ground and the stems of vegetation for the telltale spoor. He intermittently lost sight of one or other of them through the leaves and stalks between, but always they reappeared, coming nearer and nearer to the spot where he had climbed from the water. Was their sense of smell good enough, he wondered, to be able to track him up through that maze of interwoven growth?

He began to look about above him for further ways of escape in case they should pick up his scent. The tangle of elder and briar spread itself above in an ever-widening canopy. It seemed to offer plenty of scope for further progress, but the danger was that the higher he climbed the more likely he was to find himself trapped on a final stem that led nowhere but to the empty air. He turned his gaze back down below again, willing the two enemy ants to move on past the vital spot.

So intent was he on what was happening directly beneath him that he did not notice the sounds of a separate activity until the soldiers themselves halted in their search and turned their heads and feelers towards the distraction.

Then he too became aware of the noise of something approaching from that direction and turned to identify it. The sound of running feet and crashing undergrowth told its own tale and in a few moments he caught a glimpse of scurrying bodies through the leaves. With a surge of horror he realized that it was Joker who was approaching, the figures of two more red soldiers close on his heels.

The next few moments were a nightmare which was to haunt Dreamer for the rest of his life. He would awake from future dreams of the event with Joker's name a strangled gasp at the back of his throat, and then, such was the unreality of the occurrence in his mind, he would sigh with relief, thinking it only a dream, a product of his imagination—until memory returned, clutching his heart with the icy hand of truth.

Joker blundered on, staggering and gasping, blindly unaware that he was approaching Dreamer's hiding place. The latter tried to shout—to warn him, to cause a distraction—but no sound would come. The two red ants immediately beneath him crouched low and slipped stealthily towards the oncoming prey. They did not have to move far for Joker was moving on a line which would take him very close to where they were. In his blind desperation to escape from the ants at his rear he saw no sign of the others until he was almost upon them. Then, simultaneously they both leapt out in his path. Joker swerved wildly away to one side but it was too late. The bigger, faster ants were up with him in a few strides and pounced. He went down in a flurry of kicking, flailing limbs, his sting lunging wildly from side to side. One of the red ants staggered away momentarily, having received a stab in his side, but the second held on ferociously with claws and mandibles until the other two ran up and then all four set upon their unfortunate quarry.

It can only have taken a few moments to finish the business, but to the watching Dreamer, crouched in impotent paralysis on his elder leaf, it seemed an eternity. He could see Joker, buried under a mass of red-brown limbs and bodies, fighting and squirming like a creature possessed. Time and again one of his assailants had to leap clear of his lashing sting, but only to return with another snap of those powerful mandibles. The red ants did not appear to be using their own jets of poison—preferring to rely on their sheer superiority of force—and certainly there was no need for it. Joker's valiant struggles grew weaker and weaker as the big insects simply hung on, wearing him down through their solid combined weight.

Then Dreamer saw one of them shift his grip and get a purchase with his jaws on the vital joint between head and thorax and he knew that it was the end. Joker's efforts diminished to a feeble twitching, his head bent back to an unnatural angle, and then he gave a convulsive heave and lay still. The red soldiers relinquished their hold and stood back, contemplating the twisted body. Then two of them took hold of it again, one at each end, and together, dragging the corpse unceremoniously between them, all four set off back towards the trail.

Dreamer did not move for a long, long moment. The fact that his own pursuers seemed to have abandoned the chase, that the danger to himself had suddenly evaporated, did not occur to him for some time. All he was aware of was a huge, numbing ball of grief, crushing his soul, weighing down his heart. Joker was gone. The warm, trustworthy, irrepressible Joker, who had become the only real friend he had ever had in the world, was no more. And actually to have witnessed his terrible death without being able to do anything to help was an experience which changed Dreamer forever. Henceforth he was an infinitely more cynical, more hardened being, who knew never to take anything the world had to offer on trust. He knew now that he had no sway over anything but his own will—that destiny was an uncompromising master who had no truck with sentiment or mercy, respecting only logic and power and who bowed down only before the irresistible force of pragmatism. He cursed the Lord of the Stars for his ruthlessness; and deep down perhaps even began to doubt, for the first time, his very existence.

Finally he turned and, for the moment uncaring for his own safety, made his way openly along the elder stem, concerned only with the engulfing sense of sadness he carried with him. He did not retrace his steps—he could not bear to go near the awful place where his companion had died—but moved blindly on up the stem into the unknown tangle of greenery above his head. The elder bush grew side by side with a thick covert of hawthorn and their upper branches were heavily intertwined. He crossed easily to the thorny branches of the latter tree and made his way steadily above the ground, across the hawthorn, through a tangle of crawling bryony and eventually back to the earth again down a trailing spur of bindweed. The sun was high in the heavens as he set off over the ground, away from the place of death, away from the trail and the enemy ants, towards he knew not what.

But the day had not yet yielded up its full quota of drama for Dreamer. He travelled on for some time across the forest floor, making slow progress as there was now no trail to ease his path and neither mind nor body could be induced to strive for speed. The sun had moved some way across the sky and the woodland had to a great extent yielded up the excess moisture from the storm to the warm south breeze which had whispered in almost unnoticed. Dreamer, as he went, became almost subconsciously aware of a familiar sound filtering through from ahead. As he emerged from the shelter of a large patch of ground ivy the noise increased in volume and he stopped, consciously hearing it now, his antennae stretched in its direction. The scent of fresh water came to him and confirmed his eager suspicions. A stream!

He ran forward, hope once more blossoming inside. Through a patch of rye-grass overgrown with briar, across a bank of moss beneath a young aspen tree, and suddenly he was out under the open sky, familiar river-bank grasses were all around and the sound of running water was sweet

music in the air. He plunged eagerly through the grass and
came to a stop on the crest of a bank, looking down over
the swirling waters. It was a wonderful sight to eyes grown
so used to the gaunt shapes and shadows of the forest and
he was suddenly filled with a longing for his own bank,
and stream, and clearing, which he had kept held down
inside him throughout the trails and uncertainties of the
mission, but which now engulfed him in a flood of emotion and homesickness.

There was no way that he could tell whether this was the
same stream that flowed past his own home. The spot he
was at now was certainly unfamiliar, though the stream
itself was roughly the same width as his own. Its waters,
however, were swollen and turbulent after the storm and
the way they clutched at the bankside vegetation, dragging
the ends of grasses and reeds down towards their muddy
depths, indicated how much higher they were than usual;
and there was a considerable amount of flotsam riding
downstream upon them: twigs, leaves, stems of vegetation
and the occasional larger, storm-torn branch.

He turned downstream and headed along the bank, searching for some clue as to where the stream might lead and
whether its terrain was friendly or hostile to such as himself. And it was now that he so nearly blundered into
another of Nature's fatal traps.

He was vaguely aware of a low hillock ahead of him at
the edge of the bank, but he was too concerned with the
sights and scents of the water's edge itself to pay much
attention. The breeze was blowing roughly in the same
direction as the stream's flow, so he received no scent
from that direction and assumed the irregular-shaped mound
to be that of a stone or possibly an exposed tree root.
Then, as he approached, something about the hump's unusual shape and colour made him stop. He peered at it
curiously. He suddenly became aware that what he had
taken for a natural protuberance on its surface—a lump, or
a knot of wood perhaps—was actually a huge raised eye-

ball, which was staring at him, unblinking, unmoving. He froze, paralysed with terror.

Dreamer had never seen a toad before. But he had heard stories of these huge creatures with their insatiable appetites for all forms of insect life. He had been taught how they waited, still as death, merging in with their surrounding habitat, until some unfortunate mite came within reach; how they hypnotized their victims with that terrifying stare; and how their principal weapon—an immensely long, glutinous-surfaced tongue—could flick out faster than the mind could think and vanish inside that cavernous mouth again with the prey helplessly attached, before even a muscle could twitch in defence. The accounts had been so nightmarish that the beast had acquired an almost mythical status in his mind, as if it were the product of imagination and legend, not real at all; and yet here it was, comforting him with that unblinking stare, in all its vast, squat grossness just as it had always been described.

The moment seemed to last for an eternity, insect confronting amphibian in an expectant, frozen tableau. Then gradually Dreamer's petrified brain began to work again. He realized that he was still some distance from the creature, perhaps half a dozen ant-lengths, and probably just out of reach of the deadly tongue, which was why it had not yet struck. From all the accounts he had heard he could not have been far out of range and possibly another two paces would have meant the end for him. As it was it seemed he had a moment's grace. He thought frantically. He was not sure how fast the beast could move its huge body, but he knew that it could easily cover the distance between them with one leap. It was presumably waiting to see what he was going to do first.

He scanned his surroundings while keeping his head and feet motionless. To move back or sideways towards the trees offered little chance of escape; the creature would cover the grass far faster than he could traverse it. His only hope lay to the other side, where the stream bank fell away directly beneath him. He had no idea how to utilize this feature, for he had never before risked approaching really close to deep running water—and, moreover, he knew that the bank was the toad's natural habitat—but his instinct told him that he stood a better chance in that direction.

A few paces behind him the dead trunk of a stem of last year's meadowsweet leaned out at a dangerous angle over the water. By some freak of nature it had survived the gusts and floods of winter and was still clinging grimly to its precarious hold on the edge of the bank amidst the new young shoots of this year's growth. Dreamer sensed that if he could somehow get to the top of its tall, skeletal frame he would be out of reach of the monster's terrible tongue. The question was, could he get there faster than the toad could leap the intervening distance?

He had no time to ponder the matter. Instinctively he sensed a tautening of the muscles beneath the beast's gnarled skin as it prepared to leap. Panic unleashed Dreamer's own limbs from their paralysis and he sprinted for the stem, having first made a feint towards the forest side.

It was that feint which probably saved him. Instantly the toad responded to his movement, rising from its resting place and looming up, up into the air in a seemingly interminable uncoiling of its vast body. But, such was the speed of its reaction, that it was committed to its leap in the direction of Dreamer's feint before it realized that he was off the other way, running for his life back towards the river. The toad landed behind him with a thud that shook the ground beneath his feet. Then, furious at its mistake, it gathered itself for another leap.

Dreamer had reached the gaunt trunk of the meadowsweet and was scrambling frantically up its rough, brown surface, away from the ground and out over the swirling waters of the stream. Desperation lent strength to his limbs as he heard the crash of the toad's second landing right at the base of the stem and he felt the entire fragile structure shudder beneath him, threatening to fling him off into the water. He waited in suspense for that lethal tongue to strike and heard quite clearly the swish in the air as it whipped past his back, missing him by the merest fraction. Then he was up amongst the slender limbs of the meadow-sweet's crown, which spread their thin, bare tracery of dead wood in a forlorn memorial against the empty air.

He clung there and turned to look back. The toad's colossal bulk crouched at the base of the plant's trunk, staring after him with malevolent fury. Then it stretched out one of its forelegs and grasped the stem as if wondering whether it could climb after him. The whole flimsy structure trembled and bent towards the water, Dreamer holding desperately on. The toad sensed the fragility of the dead plant and gripped it harder, attempting to pull it towards itself. For a moment Dreamer thought that his end had come as his refuge reared up into the air again and threatened to topple over towards the bank; but then came a splintering crash as the dead wood at the base of the stem gave way, the entire plant shook in a final death spasm and plunged down towards the water.

Again he was almost shaken from his precarious perch as the meadowsweet hit the surface with a heavy splash. Then the sky was spinning about his head, the water roaring beneath his feet and the river bank, with its huge predator crouched upon it in frustrated fury, drifting away behind—like a nightmare that fades into the distance, only to be replaced by another, still more frightening one.

* 19 *

All the winds, tempests and torrents of the world were roaring about his head. He was spinning amongst the clouds in the grip of forces more powerful than any creature on earth could compete with. And in his exhaustion, and his terror, and his confusion, he gave himself up to those forces, saying, "Take me then where you will. I have had enough of searching, and fleeing and fighting. I no longer care what my purpose is. I no longer care what the world is about. I am too weary and too afraid. Let the Lord of the Stars take my body and swallow it up with the rest of the earth's refuse. I am happy to die."

But the Voice came out of the roar and murmured: "Who then will save your kin? Who will warn them of their danger? Because you wish to perish, must they perish also?"

And he replied: "Let others warn them. Let others be the heroes. I know now that I am not made to be a hero—as Black Sting or Snake's Tongue is. Let Snake's Tongue be the one to warn them."

And the Voice answered: "It is not always those built like heroes who must fulfil the deeds. The choice is not always ours to make."

He replied again: "I have no more strength. I have no more courage. Snake's Tongue is the one with the power and the speed. Let him be the one to warn them."

And the Voice said, "Look down. You shall see more of the ways of the world."

He looked down and saw through the raging whirlpools and the swirling clouds to the green canopy of the trees' foliage; and then still further, down through the dense mass of the undergrowth; and there he saw an ant running, running for his life amongst the fecundity of the forest floor. And he recognized the ant as Snake's Tongue. And close behind, pounding in Snake's Tongue's wake, ran several of the enemy spread out in a line on either side. And the first one, ahead of the line, running with swift, graceful strides, was the ant called Fleet.

Then he saw Snake's Tongue reach an open space and run out into it, looking around him for a way to escape as the enemy drew nearer. And at that moment, out from the greenery on the other side stepped a large, squat, bedraggled figure, whom he recognized instantly as Dew-Lover. And the two ants ran to each other and embraced antennae in welcome recognition. And then the enemy broke out into the open space and they turned to meet them. And they looked at each other and the look said, "Now I am not afraid to die. Now I have a friend beside me and together we shall make them buy our deaths so dearly that never again will they face any of our kind with contempt."

And back to back the two ants faced the encircling enemy. And they met them, fighting a battle such as he had never seen nor could ever imagine. They fought through the day, amongst the dust and the blood and the poison and the tumbled grasses, like two creatures with the strength of a whole army behind them. And when at last they finally lay still amongst the dead and wounded bodies of the enemy about them, the forest was hushed in reverence at their departure. And the ant called Fleet stood for a long while, staring at the corpses, utterly still, utterly silent— until finally he turned and made his way slowly back into the trees.

Then the Voice came again and murmured: "Now you have seen. Now you must decide. You are the only one left. Are they and Joker and yourself all to die in vain, or is there still a step to be taken, still a lesson to be learnt somewhere in all this that will even yet give it meaning?"

And the Voice was gone, and the roaring filled his head again, and the sky and the earth were spinning once more endlessly about him.

∗ 20 ∗

Consciousness gradually returned to him as the warmth of the afternoon sun bathed his aching body, eased his tired limbs, soothed his tormented brain. He realized that, although the roar was still sounding about and beneath him, the movement had ceased, only a gentle rocking motion now affecting his perch. He remembered dimly an interminable nightmare of deafening sound and plunging motion, of drenching spray and jarring shocks, of limbs aching with the strain of holding on and of a stomach heaving with the constant stirring of the movement. He remembered his desire only for it to end.

And now it seemed that, partially at any rate, it had. He looked about him, fearful of what new terror might confront his eyes. But there was only a gently waving blur of green, flecked with dancing spots of gold where the sun reflected off the water on to the flora of the river bank. There was only the great golden star of a celandine flower nodding smilingly above his head and a steady slithering sound as an earthworm disappeared with stately langour into a hole in the earthy slope beyond. There was only quiet sound and easy motion and friendly warmth.

He looked behind him and realized that he was still on the meadowsweet, wedged in a fork amongst the branches of its battered crown. Behind, the thick brown trunk sloped away into the water, which still rocked it up and down with each passing ripple, but up at this end the head was resting on a little beach of earth and pebbles, lodged against an exposed root of willow which had adventured away from the main tree some way off along the bank.

He stretched his limbs stiffly, explored the air with his antennae and, still wary, still not quite able to accept that his ordeal was for the moment ended, climbed gingerly down from his perch to solid ground. He stood looking up at the bank above him, half expecting to see the evil shape of the toad looming there, but there was only a waving fringe of grasses and the blue of the sky flecked with innocently hurrying young clouds.

He became aware of a raging thirst and drank deeply at a pool by the stream's edge, unafraid now of the nearby water's flow. Then he realized that he was also ravenously hungry and wondered what these parts might have to offer in the way of food. He began the stiff climb up the bank, looking out for suitable seeds, or even—miracle of miracles—a nest of larvae hidden in some recess on the way.

He reached the top of the bank and peered cautiously between the grass stems. The looming shadow of the forest edge was still there, filling the immediate eyeline. His antennae scanned back and forth, seeking some clue as to his whereabouts. There seemed something strangely familiar about the place. He could not define it, but something about the tree-line above him, something about the scent of the air and the lie of the vegetation around, brought a quickening to his heart and an eagerness to his eye. He ran forward through the grass away from the stream, his heart thumping expectantly. A little way on he broke out of the tangle of grassy undergrowth on to the clear, curving path of a trail; a trail he knew, he was sure of it! The trail that led along the bank from the riverside mound to his home.

He turned on to it in the downstream direction and with quickening pace and increasing certainty headed along it. He was not sure how far off he was but every pace brought renewed recognition and joyful anticipation. Tiredness and hunger were forgotten and the terror and the grief subsided to a distant ache in the excitement of seeing home again. As the trees to one side became more and more familiar, as the open sky of the clearing spread ahead of him, and as the river's sound gradually changed to that exact melodious harmony which had filled the background all his life, he was aware of how dear that beautiful place was to him and of how much he had missed it during the long days of his ordeal.

A scouting party met him on the trail before he reached the clearing itself. They stared in wonder, scarcely recognizing the gaunt, scarred, dishevelled figure before them. Then they surrounded him with cries of welcome, much embracing of feelers, questions and exclamations. They escorted him back towards the mound through the clearing, where the work parties stopped and stared, waved and cheered. They stood while he halted, staring in amazement at the change in the mound's shape and at the frantic rebuilding activity upon it, where workers and soldiers toiled side by side. They told him of the Tawny Killer-Bird's attack and of Black Sting's stupendous feat, which had saved the colony from almost certain destruction; of the worker-ants' revolt and the torture of Five Legs and Still One; of the banishment of Dew-Lover and of Black Sting's recanting; and of the new agreement granted to the workers. They told him of the stories that had filtered through of the tremendous happenings out in the forest and of the growing fear in the colony that none of his little party would ever be seen again. And then they took him into the mound and down to the Council chamber, with runners going before to tell Black Sting, Great Head, Five Legs and the other elders that he had come.

As the company was gathering in the Council chamber, Dreamer was given food, mixed with a little fresh honeydew to revive his exhausted body. Then he went before the assembly and told them his story. He told them everything, from the details of the expedition's journey outwards, their capture and their imprisonment in the huge mound; to their escape and pursuit, the death of Joker and his own miraculous, floating return. He told them all he knew about the red ants and their awesome leader, their living habits and their fighting methods. He told them about their extraordinary transient life cycle, their ruthless philosophy and their innate need to expand their territories. And finally, hesitatingly—for he was not sure how they would react—he told them of his strange dream while adrift on the water of Snake's Tongue's pursuit and the meeting with Dew-Lover and their final mighty battle out in the forest.

His listeners did not scoff at his dream or dismiss it. One and all listened with the same solemn attention with which they had heard the rest of his story. It seemed so much a part of the almost surreal circumstances of his return that they accepted it without question. And when he had ceased speaking there was a grave silence and a heavy feeling of sadness over the company, as if, although they did not quite understand how his vision had come about, they sensed that it fitted the facts so obviously that it could not be discounted as mere fantasy.

Then Black Sting praised Dreamer for his bravery and resourcefulness. He congratulated him on his extraordinary deliverance—for never before had an ant been known to use water as a means of transport—and on behalf of all the colony's members he thanked him for the great service he had done them. And Dreamer bowed his head to hide his awkwardness and the depth of his feelings.

Then finally Black Sting said, ''I have one more thing to tell you. Our Great Mother, the Queen of Queens, imparts her happiness at your safe return and wishes me to conduct you to her presence that she may convey her gratitude in person.''

There was a murmur in the Council and a general nodding of approval. Dreamer was struck dumb. Only on the rarest of occasions was a humble inhabitant such as himself granted the privilege of meeting the great personage to whose service his entire life was dedicated. He was overcome with humility and emotion and not a little apprehension at the prospect.

Black Sting murmured for a moment with Great Head and Noble and others of the senior councillors and then he turned again to Dreamer. ''Come,'' he said, ''Our Great Mother awaits us.'' And he led the way from the chamber.

With two of the Royal Guard as escort behind them, they descended to the very deepest areas of the earth beneath the mound. Here was a region which Dreamer had only visited in his imagination before: a region of wide, straight corridors and huge, silent brood chambers; of quietly scurrying household staff and motionless, rigid Royal Guards; of whisperings and secret movements in the dark; and of warm, heavy, scented air that spoke of birth and fecundity and the eternal heartbeat of growing life.

Finally they came to the deepest, innermost chamber of all, and, as the guards fell back behind them and they crossed the threshold with heads bowed and feelers curled respectfully, Dreamer was aware of a gigantic, serene, feminine presence, whose quality, simply by being there, seemed to confirm an instinct that had long lain dormant in his subconscious knowledge, and which seemed finally to complete all the disparate findings of his confused and searching mind into one revelatory, illuminating picture.

He stood there in wonder and veneration as Black Sting spoke.

''Great Mother, this is the soldier called Dreamer. He has survived great hardship and braved many dangers and has returned alone to bring us the much-needed knowledge for which we waited. I have brought him to you as you requested.''

There was a moment's silence; then came her voice—gentle, low, calm with the knowledge of incalculable age and wisdom—"Why do they call you Dreamer?"

He replied hesitantly, shyly, "I have dreams which I cannot always explain, Great Mother."

"Dreams of what?"

"Dreams of happenings, and searchings, and discoveries—and of a voice that answers my questions with strange answers."

"Ah yes, I know that voice. And have your dreams been of use to you?"

"I . . . I think so, Great Mother. But I'm never sure quite what they mean."

Here Black Sting broke in. "He has dreamed that Snake's Tongue and Dew-Lover together fought a band of the red ants and that both are dead. It seems possible that this may be true."

The Queen of Queens was silent for a moment. Then she went on, "That is a great gift that you have, brave Dreamer. Listen to your dreams and do not be afraid to trust them."

Then Dreamer said uncertainly, "You said you know the Voice, Great Mother. Whose is it?"

"Ah; that you must discover for yourself," she replied. "Listen hard and one day it may reveal itself. Now, tell me how you are after your long ordeal and what you have learned."

He hesitated. "What I have learned?"

"Not your information," she went on. "Black Sting will use that to the best advantage in our danger, I know that. I want to know what you have learned of yourself and of life. That is the real knowledge that will help us in the end."

Again he hesitated, flustered. The Queen of Queens waited with patient calm for him to collect his thoughts. Finally he said diffidently, haltingly, "I have learned that there is always something more to learn. I have learned that nothing is what it seems. I have learned that hope is never lost, even in death. I have learned . . ." He broke off, emotion suddenly halting his voice. "I have learned that there is something missing from our lives, without which we will never be safe."

"What is that?"

He searched for a way to explain. "It was something I found on our expedition that I felt I must have always been seeking. It was a closeness, a trust, a . . . an intimacy with the others with me that I had never felt before. It was a friendship with the soldier called Joker that, now he is dead, I cannot think I will find again."

Her voice was soft as the air. "Why do you think that?"

"I don't know, I . . ." Again he searched his mind. "Great Mother, why is it that the giant beasts have mates? Why do the birds and the animals in the forest and even the fish swimming in the stream, mate one with another and live together in twos or in families with their mates, and we do not? Why do only a few of us, the winged ones, mate, and then are banished from the colony, never to return on pain of death? And why are you and young Queens the only female ones amongst us?"

There was a long silence. He felt Black Sting stir uneasily behind him. Then the Queen of Queens spoke again.

"I will tell you a story. A story of something that it is said happened long ago. Long before our mound was built or I was born or even the trees that now live about us had grown. A story of when the world itself was young and ignorant and foolish, and the Lord of the Stars had little patience with its ways.

"It is said that then there was a madness over all the world—that it was a place of gigantic storms and upheavals and explosions, and that all the beasts upon it, the Giant Two-Legs, the fourlegged beasts, the serpents and the creatures of the air, all fought constantly with each other, causing the blood to run in rivers and the carrion to litter the whole surface of the earth, more than the scavengers could dispose of.

"And it is said that then the ants were the true leaders of

the world, for they were the most numerous, the most intelligent, the most organized and the most peaceable species of all. And they lived and progressed together, male and female in harmony, the females breeding and caring for the young, and the males doing the hunting and fighting and the heavy work. But then the males started to become arrogant, complacent and lazy in their ways. They felt superior in their lofty intelligence over the other species and they forgot the obligations and the responsibility that such a privilege brings. They began to tyrannize their females, their offspring and everyone else around them, to abuse their power, to usurp the forces of Nature and of justice, and to be even more ferocious than the other beasts, and they became greedy for ever more power in the world.

"So then the Lord of the Stars grew angry at their betrayal. He decreed that they should lose their privilege as the chosen species on the earth to others. He decreed that they should no longer be masters even over their own species; that they should retain only their duties as breeders and that their functions as rulers, soldiers, builders, hunters and even as ordinary workers, should be taken away and given to the females. And that the females should have command over all the workings of their colonies, and the males, once they had performed their mating duties, should be banished forever from their homes, to live alone as best they could, prey to all the beasts of the forest.

"And it is said that that is what happened—that the females divided themselves into different castes to take over the duties of the males; and the castes developed in their different ways to suit those duties—some remaining as females to do the breeding; some forsaking their sex and growing fierce and strong and quick to do the fighting; some becoming steady, efficient and resilient to do the heavy work. And they took their titles away from the males and became masculine even in name. And the pleasure of the companionship between the two sexes was lost forever to the ants.''

The Queen of Queens stopped talking and in the silence that followed Dreamer's brain was a whirl. Suddenly so many things seemed to make sense. And yet it was such a weird tale.

"Do you believe that story to be true, Great Mother?" he asked.

"Who knows?" she answered. "There can be truth in a story whether it happened or not, as I believe the ant they call Still One has shown. Many are the stories that have survived out of the mists of time for the truth that is in them, though it will never be known whether they happened as told." She paused a moment, and Dreamer sensed the passage through the air just over his head of a long, graceful, all-sensing antenna. "You have many fine qualities, my young Dreamer," she said. "Think on the story, and, whether it is true or not, learn what you will from it, as you have learned from all else that has happened to you. For that is the way of hope for us."

She sighed, and there was the faintest hint of weariness in the sigh. "Go now, Dreamer and my splendid Black Sting. You have much to do to save our beloved colony from the dangers that threaten it. Our safety is in your keeping."

So the two soldiers took their leave of the Queen of Queens, and made their way back through the Royal Quarters and up to the busy regions of the mound again, where the torn and battle-scarred bodies of Snake's Tongue and Dew-Lover had just been brought in, having been found by a scouting party far out in the wilds of the forest.

* 21 *

The colony knew now very clearly of the fearful danger that threatened it. The details of Dreamer's account were spread amongst the ants, from the most reclusive of the elders to the humblest of the workers, with astonishing speed and the fearsome nature of the wounds on the bodies of those two formidable fighters, Snake's Tongue and Dew-Lover, told their own tale. Dew-Lover had now to some extent redeemed himself through his heroic death and the whole adventure entered the annals of the community's history, to be related dramatically to future generations, should there be any. The rebuilding of the damaged part of the hillock went on with yet more urgent haste, though no one was quite certain how that was going to help them. There was just a general feeling now that, if they were all going to have to defend their mound to the death, then they wished it to be a complete mound they were going to die for.

The urgent discussion of what measures should be taken, the speculation as to how long it would be before The

Spider's hordes arrived, the wild conjecture as to what would be the fate of all in the settlement, went on in every corner, every chamber and every outside gathering place. Black Sting had ordered lookouts to be posted deep in the forest and upstream as far as the riverside mound, with a system of signalling to relay news of any movement back instantly; but beyond that there was little he could do. The spring days were lengthening and a long, dry warm spell was upon them after the ferocity of the storm—which had assailed their own region as well as that of the red ants—and the first of the new brood of larvae would soon be ready for hatching; but it would be some time before the young ants would be of any use as fighters. Even then, thought Black Sting hopelessly, of what use could they be against these huge, aggressive creatures that would soon be ranged against them?

He realized, deep in his heart, that the problem which confronted them was far more than just a matter of tactics. There were in fact no known battle methods which could be of any use against such an immensely superior force and the dilemma was therefore a philosophical one rather than a merely military one. Did one surrender and beg for mercy? Did one fight to the last dying soul? Did one abandon the mound, the established and deeply loved home of generations of ants and seek some new territory far off? Did one offer appeasement and subservience to the conquerors and condemn all future generations to a life of slavery in return for survival?

Had it been he alone who had to face these questions he knew that, as a fighting ant born and bred, he would not have hesitated but would have chosen to die, defiant to the last, as his two lieutenants had done. But there was not just himself to consider. There was the whole future of the colony. There were the old ants, incapable of fighting, and the young ones, yet to be born. There were the young Queens, gentle, unaggressive, whose only instinct was motherhood and devotion. And lastly there was the Queen of Queens herself, figurehead of creation, of wisdom, of hope, of the whole of life itself. She could never be abandoned to such an end, for that would be an end to everything. To Black Sting, as to everyone else, the problem seemed insoluble.

However, he realized that somehow or other a decision of some nature had to be arrived at. Therefore, on a day when the season had reached the summit of its glory, when life and warmth and greenness were affirming the miracle of creation everywhere outside, he called a select gathering of all the wisest minds in the colony in the darkness of the Council chamber within. Great Head was there and Mutterer and old One Feeler; and so was Noble and his closest aids; and Five Legs with Never-Rest as support; and various others of the elders; and Dreamer too, bringing his knowledge of the enemy at Black Sting's own request. And finally, at the suggestion of Five Legs, there was Still One, who came quietly, diffidently, and stayed in the background at the rear of the assembly.

Black Sting opened the proceedings by recounting his thoughts and explaining in broad terms the dilemma as he saw it. Then he left the floor free to whoever wished to speak. One after the other the elders took the centre in a motley procession of shuffling, gesticulating, mumbling, declaiming and generally concerned speakers. Occasionally one would turn to Dreamer with an enquiry. How big a force did he think the red ants would bring? How soon? What was the best way of fighting them?—and so on. Now and again, as the discussion went round and round in circles, always seeming to return to the same insoluble crux, Black Sting would intervene because one or other of the speakers was being unduly repetitious or was straying from the point at issue or seemed in danger of being overcome with emotion.

Dreamer, as he listened, was amazed at the divergent views and opinions, at the confusion of logic, and at the general lack of consensus within the assembly. He had always assumed, as a humble outsider, that Council meetings, by the very fact that they were a congregation of the oldest and wisest heads in the community, would be a model of lucid argument and communal decision; but now he began to realize that the more difficult and fundamental the problem, the more diverse and contentious were the attitudes it induced. He could almost hear his Voice whispering to him, "You see? Nothing is simple. No one is infallible. Listen only to your own conscience; that is the only advocate you can trust." And even then he felt like asking how, amongst all this gabble, he could possibly be expected to hear what his own conscience had to say.

Broadly speaking, opinion was divided into three main schools of thought. There were those headed by Noble and other officers of the Royal Guard, who felt that the survival of the Queens and their progeny was paramount, and that therefore they should persuade the Queen of Queens to abandon the mound and escort her and the young Queens—carrying as many of the larvae as was practicable—and establish a new home far beyond the range of the red ants. There were those headed by Mutterer and One Feeler and other elders, who felt that reason could always prevail in the end and that they should negotiate terms, however stringent, with The Spider. And there were those—mostly the younger and more militant ones—who saw a betrayal of all principle in any action that did not involve defending the mound to the last dying ant.

In the end it was left to Great Head to sum up all the impassioned arguments and define the enigma before them. He shuffled out into the middle of the floor and the buzz of argument and discussion faded away to a respectful silence. He coughed and fidgeted for a moment, nodded his enormous cranium and then looked round the chamber.

"It seems to me," he said, "that when all the talk of strategy and tactics, of diplomacy and intrigue, of rights and wrongs, is over, there are but two choices open to us. Either to die honourably in battle or to live dishonourably in slavery or exile." He paused a moment to let this sink in, then continued: "The question then is, which is more important, life or honour? That is what we have to decide.'' Again he paused. There was a hum of discussion. Then he said, ''There is someone here, I believe, who has not yet spoken, and who, I am told, often has remarkably pertinent things to say on such fundamental matters.'' He peered shortsightedly round in the dim light and everyone looked about them, wondering who it was he meant. ''Is the ant known as Still One present?'' Great Head asked, and there was an immediate ripple of interest.

Dreamer could see Old Five Legs, on the opposite side of the floor, turning and beckoning with his feelers. There was a pause and then a parting in the ranks and Still One stepped diffidently into the space. Great Head gestured to him to come to the centre.

''I have not been privileged to hear any of your famed stories,'' he said. ''Nor, I think, have many here. But if you have anything to say that may be of help to us now, then I'm sure we would all welcome it.''

Great Head stepped back to his place at the side of the floor and the slight figure was left alone, looking very small and insignificant in that eminent company. However, that extraordinary quality of calm stillness soon impressed itself on his audience, who waited with hushed expectancy for him to speak. When he did so his quiet voice filled the chamber with ease and soothed the charged atmosphere with its gentle serenity.

''I take no sides in this debate; I cannot persuade; I cannot advise; I cannot argue. I may only listen to the voices of this wise and distinguished gathering—and mourn with them that such a fate should threaten our home, which was built on peace, industry and fellowship—and state my own belief. And in the end each must decide for himself in the light of all that has been said and all that remains unsaid but whispers in the secret places of the heart.'' He paused and stared into the distance through the dim light, still as stone.

''I am a tender of an aphid-bug herd. I love my task. It is hard at times, for I work outside close to the wind and the rain and the cold—but I am also close to the warmth of the sun and the scents of the forest and the workings of the Lord of the Stars. It is dangerous at times, for I am easy prey to every passing beast and bird, but I am also in the company of my aphid-bugs, who are the kindest, gentlest, most peaceable of creatures. It is lonely at times, for I work alone above the paths of other ants, but that allows me to listen to the messages of the wind and the songs of the water and the thoughts of my own heart. I would like to tell you a story about a family of aphid-bugs, if you would hear it.''

No one spoke. There was no need of affirmation. He continued with little pause. ''This family lived on the branch of a spruce tree. It was a perfect home: wide, and green, and still; facing the sun and shielded from the wind by a hill; with plenty of food, yet high above the ways of most walking predators, and with many places to hide from winged ones. The family thrived, and multiplied, and had a good life.

''Then one day a party of fierce rove beetles arrived at the aphid-bugs' tree and climbed to the base of their branch, where their leader called out to the leader of the aphid-bugs and said, 'We are going to fight you.'

''And the leader of the aphid-bugs called back and said, 'But we cannot fight. We have never learnt to fight.'

''So the rove beetles' leader said, 'Then we shall kill you.'

''And the aphid-bugs' leader said, 'Why?'

''The rove beetles' leader said, 'Because we need your territory.'

''So the aphid-bugs' leader said, 'In that case, you may share it with us. There is room for all.'

''But the rove beetles' leader said, 'We shall still kill you—because we need food.'

''So the aphid-bugs' leader said, 'In that case, you may share ours with us. And we will provide you with our own eggs. There is enough for all.'

''But the rove beetles' leader said, 'We shall still kill you—because we need your honey-dew.'

"So the aphid bugs' leader said, 'We shall provide you with honey-dew. As much as you need.'

"But the rove beetles' leader said, 'We shall still kill you—because you have a different way of life to ours, which we do not know how to share.'

"So the aphid-bugs' leader said, 'Then we shall explain it to you. And perhaps you may learn some things of interest from us. And perhaps we may learn some things of interest from you.'

"Then the rove beetles' leader thought hard but he could think of no other reason to kill the aphid-bugs. So he said, 'We shall kill you anyway.'

"And the aphid-bugs' leader said, 'Why?'

"And the rove beetles' leader said, 'Because you are not of our kind—that is why.'

"So then the aphid-bugs' leader said, 'Ah, that is different. That is pure evil. In that case you shall have none of the things we have offered and we shall fight you after all.'

"And, as the rove beetles came along the branch, the aphid-bugs destroyed their honey-dew and their egg-clusters and their food supplies, laid waste the branch and turned to fight the rove beetles. And the rove beetles, led by their leader, slaughtered the aphid-bugs mercilessly until not one was left alive on the branch.

"But when the battle was over, the rove beetles looked about them and saw the devastated tree branch, the ruined egg-clusters and the massacred bodies of the aphid-bugs, and they felt strangely wretched and sick in their bowels. And they said, 'The aphid-bugs were right. This is pure evil.'

"And they turned on their leader and hurled him from the branch to his death below. And then they left the branch and went away and the sickness stayed with them so that they never killed again, not even when they were truly in hunger."

Still One paused and for a moment there was utter quiet

in the chamber. Then there was a movement in the front rank, and Noble stepped forward.

"Yes," he said, "that is a good story and I understand the moral it is making. But there is one factor which makes the situation of the aphid-bugs different from our own. They had nowhere to escape to from their branch. We do." He looked round the chamber and there was a buzz of discussion and bobbing of heads.

Then Still One said, "There is a part of the story that I have not yet told you," and immediately there was silence once more.

"A small group of the aphid-bugs had seen the rove beetles climbing the tree and had fled to a higher branch before the beetles arrived. And there they escaped the massacre of their kind, and although they were sad at the death of their kindred, they were relieved that they had been spared.

"But then they discovered that on this new branch there lived a tree-spider, who also threatened to kill them. So they made their escape to the next branch above. But there they discovered that on the branch lived a tree-snake, who also threatened to kill them. So they made their escape to the next branch above. But there they discovered that on the branch was a nest of finches, who also threatened to kill them. And so it was on every branch, until finally they reached the highest limb of the tree; and there at last they found that the branch was empty and, breathing sighs of relief, they settled down to make their new home there.

"But they soon discovered why there was no life on the topmost branch. During the night there came a high wind off the hill behind the spruce tree, and it caught the topmost branch in its full force and hurled all the aphid-bugs upon it to their death far below, where lay the bodies of all the rest of their kind."

He stopped speaking and stood, looking at Noble. The soldier was quiet and thoughtful. Then he nodded imperceptibly and stepped silently back to his place.

Dreamer was fascinated by the way Still One's story

crystallized the general opinion in a way that all the discussion, argument and persuasion had not managed to do. There were still a few voices of dissent, but from now on it was clear that the main body of feeling was for staying and facing the danger, however terrible the outcome might be. The moral imperatives had been illustrated in a way that no one could challenge and it was with a feeling of relief and determination that the colony now got on with the task of repairing the mound and preparing the defences.

Black Sting, his own deepest inclinations now confirmed, first consulted with the Queen of Queens, who agreed wholeheartedly with the decision. He then put body and soul into the business of organizing and inspiring every section of the community, and all his ingenuity into devising the best way of protecting the hillock and in particular the Royal Quarters and the brood chambers below ground. Most of the tunnels were blocked off at some distance within the mound, thus forming fake entrances into which the enemy might be decoyed and then trapped. The few that were left open were deliberately chosen for their devious and complex routes, which would, he hoped, confuse and scatter any intruders, and in these piles of earth were made ready at strategic spots with which to close them off at the last moment. All paths of communication between the upper mound and the Royal Quarters were severed completely except for one obscure passage and a generous store of food was collected in those regions so that their inhabitants could survive for a long time without contact with the outside world.

Outside in the clearing barriers of grass and twigs were made ready by the sides of all the main trails leading from the forest, and any bare space was filled with obstacles and debris to prevent the red ants from using their extra size and speed to advantage. The line along the forest edge to the river bank was barricaded and manned day and night by picked soldiers as the first line of defence. Every ant in the colony, from the lowly workers such as Bug-Rump to the elder Council members such as Great Head, was instructed in the best way of getting in close and fighting the red ants, and spent his spare time sharpening claws and mandibles and practising sting-thrusts.

And throughout all this activity, a constant watch was maintained far out in secret places in the forest for the first indications that the red ants were approaching.

There was, however, no sign of them for the moment. The days passed and lengthened and the foliage thickened on all sides, turning the clearing into a secret, enclosed island of light amidst the shadowed vaults of the woodland. It did not grow quite as fast as usual at that time of year, however, for there was passing an unusually long, hot, dry spell, which temporarily held back the hectic rush to fill up all available space with greenery and brought a dry, brittle feel to the grass and undergrowth which normally only came some months later at the height of summer.

Now that Black Sting was temporarily leader of the Council as well as of the soldiers, he reorganized his chain of command. New officers were appointed to positions of prominence and the system was modified to accommodate both the soldiers' participation in the physical work being carried out and the marshalling of the worker-ants in their new role as reserve soldiers.

Snake's Tongue and Dew-Lover having both departed the scene, Black Sting also appointed a new select contingent of personal aides—not this time chosen purely for their fighting capabilities—and, much to his surprise, Dreamer found himself enrolled in this capacity. It was not really so strange, for his achievement on the expedition had proved his worth. Moreover, he was no longer the somewhat naive, eager creature who had embarked on that adventure. The aura of awareness, of alert curiosity, was still there, but now there was also a self-confidence that had been missing before, as well as a tougher, more cynical realism in his approach to life. Physically too he was maturing. He would never be an intimidating physical specimen as soldiers go, but he had filled out, and his limbs had strengthened, giving his agile stride a weight and authority that it had not possessed before. His antennae were still his most distinctive feature and had continued to lengthen their sensitive curves. This, coupled with the fact that the outward signs of his dreams were becoming less and less nervously evident, brought about the frequent use of a new name for him, as is often the way with ants.

It was Old Five Legs, who had himself been rechristened after his injury long ago, who initiated the new name, although Dreamer was unaware of it as the old worker-ant had first used it out of his hearing. Conversing with some other workers he had referred to Dreamer in the third person as "our friend with the quick feelers," and from then on the name had stuck. Dreamer heard himself referred to as "Quick Feelers" with greater and greater frequency and, truth to tell, was secretly not displeased with his new title.

Many continued to use his old name, however, and although it was not so evident to observers, his dreams still visited him; not perhaps with the same urgency and vividness as before, but taking more complex, obscure forms and with his Voice still invariably present, challenging him with yet further unanswerable questions, presenting still more unfathomable enigmas. In fact this was merely a reflection of his conscious state, for he was finding as he grew more worldly, more experienced, that the mysteries of life, far from resolving themselves, simply multiplied and became more involved in proportion. Such is the eternal paradox of existence and Dreamer was now beginning to appreciate it.

The only ant who seemed never confounded by the illogicality of events, who always appeared able to put them into perspective and see the horizon beyond the tangle of the undergrowth, was the Story Teller, now accepted without question as a regular member of the Council. He still continued his solitary occupation as an aphid-bug tender but always came when summoned to a Council meeting. With his quiet, self-effacing presence and his uncanny knack of summing up and resolving a dispute with a simple, inoffensive parable, he became a highly potent influence on the assembly. Black Sting himself came to value his presence so highly that at times, when the strain of command became too onerous, he took to quietly visiting the gentle worker-ant on his birch sapling and snatching a few stolen moments of reflection and relaxation in his company. On several such occasions Dreamer was privileged to accompany his leader and he too came to value these visits as oases of calm sanity in the hectic routine of daily life.

It was on one such occasion, when the three ants were together amongst the quietly browsing aphid-bugs—high above the ground in the simmering midday heat that was quite unseasonable in its intensity—that Black Sting voiced the main concern now troubling him. His powerful figure reclined uncharacteristically at ease on the bark surface with Dreamer nearby and Still One working unhurriedly at his morning collection of honey-dew.

"What worries me now, Story Teller, is how to communicate with this formidable-sounding Spider."

"Communicate?" queried Still One, looking up from his task.

"Yes," said Black Sting. "You see, we have now done all we can with regard to the defences of the mound. We've organized everyone; we've planned our tactics; we're proceeding as fast as possible with the rebuilding and the fortifying. But all this is providing for the last eventuality, the final confrontation in battle, when all else has failed. What we are hoping is that we won't get that far; that reason will prevail first; that we can find some point of contact with these creatures and persuade them that such drastic action is not necessary. However, I am a soldier not a diplomat. I'm trained in the ways of battle not of psychology. And from what Quick Feelers here says, it sounds as if The Spider is not the most amenable personality with whom to negotiate. How do you suppose we should approach him?"

Still One left his work and came to join the two soldiers.

He contemplated Dreamer with his impassive eyes. "Tell me about this enormous Spider," he said, "Did you detect no pliancy in him at all; no hint of vulnerability anywhere?"

Dreamer thought back over his one brief meeting with the enemy leader, which culminated in that appalling act of cruelty to Snakes's Tongue.

"No," he replied. "Doubtless there must be some softness in him somewhere—there must be *something* that would touch him—but I saw no sign of it."

Still One nodded. "And his soldiers, what of them?"

Dreamer replied, "Well, the one called Fleet, as I have told you, showed signs of compassion, and indeed of wanting to communicate with us. Presumably there must be others like him. But if my dream was true—and it was he who led the hunting-down of Snake's Tongue, after having allowed us to escape—then it shows that his conditioning is still the most powerful factor in his make-up."

"Tell us more of your conversations with him," said Still One.

Dreamer told them as much as he could remember of those strange stolen discussions with Fleet; of his curiosity about their own lifestyle; of his surprise at the concept of a self-perpetuating, self-sufficient and non-aggressive colony; and of his emphatic rejection of that concept for his own species.

When he had finished, Still One was silent for a long moment. Finally he said quietly, "It sounds as if a reform of their philosophy might be possible, but that it would be a long and difficult process, which could probably only be undertaken from within."

"Within?" queried Black Sting.

"By living with them, integrating with their system, communicating one's own ideas slowly, by example." Still One turned his eyes to Black Sting. "Are we prepared to surrender everything and go into captivity to achieve that?"

"That would mean the certain death of all our Queens and probably of all the most prominent soldiers and elders," said Black Sting. "The Spider would never risk keeping them all alive within his mound. Therefore the answer must of course be no, as it was for the aphid-bugs in your story."

Still One nodded and gazed silently at the blue sky far beyond the gentle nodding fronds of his birch tree.

"I shall tell you another story with a different moral," he said. "Two ants were a little drunk on honey-dew and were debating the ways of life. And one said, 'I see an ugly world, where misery and pain and squalor exist, and only selfishness can survive.'

"And the other said, 'I see a beautiful world, where the seasons come, and contrast lives, and anticipation lightens the heart.'

"And the first said, 'I see a cruel world, where strength rules, where viciousness is rife and uncertainty fills the days.'

"And the second said, 'I see a brave world, where truth wins in the end, where justice prevails and knowledge grows with every deed.'

"And the first said, 'I feel anger and the strength of evil.'

"And the second said, 'I feel only love and the power of beauty.'

"And the first ant was so angry at the optimism of the second ant that he flung himself upon him, crying, 'Very well, let us see how your beauty and love can save itself from my anger and hatred!'

"And they fought a fierce battle.

"But, because the second ant was content in his heart, he was not afraid of death, for he had found the meaning of life. Therefore he fought fearlessly and coolly. And because the first ant was unhappy in his soul, he was afraid to die, for he still desired to see the light. Therefore he fought fearfully and frantically. And so the second ant defeated the first ant.

"But he did not kill him as the first ant would have

done in his place. He left him to creep away, and nurse his wounds, and ponder again about the eternal problem.''

Black Sting was quiet for a long time after that. Still One did not speak again but left him to contemplate his thoughts.

Dreamer too was thoughtful. Is it true for me? he wondered. Am I happy enough inside to be unafraid of death? Do I love the world enough to be able to forsake it willingly? He looked across at his leader. And what about you? he thought. Are you afraid? Not of the fight or the pain or the wounds; I know you are not afraid of those. But are you afraid of losing *life?*

Then Black Sting lifted his head and met Dreamer's gaze and Dreamer saw the glint in his eye and knew that he was not. And in fact the big ant confirmed it with his next words.

"Thank you, Story Teller. That has helped me a lot. I have been worrying on behalf of the colony because I saw it as my duty to protect it. But of course I am not on my own. We are all together in this crisis. And I think the colony is like your second ant. We may have to die in the end, but we are not afraid to. For I think that, despite everything, it has been a good life.'' He looked at Dreamer. "What do you say, Quick Feelers?''

Dreamer looked down through the foliage at the sunlit clearing; at the groups of workers busying about their tasks; at the old ones gossiping in a corner, where they thought no one could see them; at the soldiers confidently striding about their missions; he gazed at where the waters of the stream ran sparkling on their endless journey, and where the kingcups and the wood anemones nodded approvingly at all the goings-on from their vantage points upon the banks, and he felt a warmth deep inside.

"Yes, leader. I have not seen enough of it yet, but it has been a good life. I don't think we shall be too afraid to leave it.''

Black Sting nodded approvingly and then raised his antennae briskly. "However,'' he said, "we are not going to die unless we have to." He turned again to Still One. "I have a suggestion to make, Still One. It is not an order, merely an idea put forward for your consideration."

Still One cocked his antennae questioningly. Black Sting went on: "When the red ant army arrives, I imagine it will be led by The Spider himself. Now someone is going to have to speak with him directly. Someone is going to have to negotiate, and *attempt*, at any rate, to come to terms with him. And, as I have said, I am no diplomat. If I meet him, it will merely be a trial of strength between two military leaders, at which he will feel honour-bound to display his superiority. I suspect that would not be the clever way. We need someone who would be no threat to him; who could get beneath his skin; take him by surprise, psychologically." He gazed at the slim worker-ant steadily. "You are the only one I can imagine being able to do that."

Still One was quiet, motionless for a long moment. Then he said softly, "Yes, I will speak with him."

Black Sting said, "I know it is a frightening thing I am asking of you, and perhaps a very dangerous thing." A twinkle came into his eye. "But it seems to me that if you can persuade our Council of something, then you have a good chance of persuading The Spider."

Dreamer envisaged the bizarre picture of the diminutive Story Teller confronting the gigantic Spider—with the hopes of the entire colony resting on his fragile head—but in a strange way it did not seem such an unequal contest. A pure case of mind versus muscle; and he had seen enough of Still One now to know that, however much the muscle might rage and destroy, the mind would leave its mark somewhere.

✳ 22 ✳

As in a dream the days passed: sunny, benign, full of activity. By all outward observances the colony appeared a happy, thriving place, throbbing with industry and energy. Yet underneath lurked the ever-present shadow of fear; no longer that initial sharp sting of terrified expectancy, but lulled now to a dull ache of grim, patient suspense, like the throb of a deep bruise that will not heal.

Then, inevitably, events began to gather momentum. Yet still with that same unreal, dreamlike quality, for the first indications seemed to come from some other grotesque world, which bore no resemblance to the familiar domestic one. The first reports began to filter in, via the forest's own mysterious warning system which operated far beyond the colony's own lookout posts, of a huge ant army on the move, led by an insect so enormous that it was rumoured he was not an ant at all but a member of some new order never seen in the forest before. The army was said to be making slow progress, due to the problem of keeping such a great body of insects supplied, but nonetheless to be advancing inexorably through the woods from the direction of the red ant mound, devouring everything in its path. The ants in the clearing who heard the rumour looked at each other with grim faces and said little, for there was little to say.

Then a further strange report came in, which was even more nightmarish and confusing in its unreality. A party returned from a visit to another of the small satellite mounds—this one a night's journey in the opposite direction to the riverside mound—and reported that they had found its inhabitants buzzing with excitement at a weird tale told by two of their members who had been out on a scavenging expedition. It was said that these two had travelled as far as the bank of the river, which was some way off from that mound and which in that downstream direction broadened out to a wide, slow-running flood. And there they had witnessed a sight which had sent them fleeing back in a state of near hysteria to report to their elders. They claimed to have seen a gigantic beast standing leg-deep in the water, towering above even the bushes on the bankside, and actually *walking* on the riverbed upstream against the current! If the account could be believed and the garbled description correctly understood, the monster could have been none other than the legendary Giant Two-Legs.

Like all others who heard the tale Black Sting was highly sceptical and put it down to the effects of an overdose of honey-dew, but nevertheless it added to the general mood of nervous unease. Prudently Black Sting took the precaution of posting a lookout on the bank some distance downstream, for if there *was* a creature of some kind moving upriver, it must eventually, after negotiating the various twists and turns between the two colonies, arrive at their own stretch. That done, however, he turned his attention to the much more credible threat of the approaching red ant army.

Having checked that all the defences were ready and all sentinels posted, and having toured the entrances to the mound itself and inspected the almost completed repairs to the damaged section; he requested a last meeting with the Queen of Queens for himself and the leaders of the various sections of the community.

The afternoon sun was sinking beyond the gorse clump, sending its shadow stretching across the parched grass towards the trees, as Black Sting, Great Head, Noble and Five Legs met solemnly and respectfully in the Great Mother's deep chamber. Despite his having served her for so long, it was Five Legs' first actual meeting with the Queen of Queens—indeed it was the first time any worker-ant had met her on this official basis—and the old ant was quite overcome with emotion at the magnitude of the occasion. When Black Sting presented him in the darkness of the chamber and the Queen of Queens welcomed him with her quiet, regal courtesy, he was so overawed that he could only stammer and stutter and back away until he came up against the chamber wall, where he stayed throughout the meeting in a state of complete reverential trance.

Black Sting informed the Great Mother of their reason for believing that The Spider's army was now approaching and he explained his plan to cut off the Royal Quarters from the rest of the mound and to seal off all the entrances to the mound itself. He told her of his soldiers' determination to fight the red ants for every blade of grass before they could reach the hillock and then Noble assured her that the Royal Guard would take up the battle to the last dying ant to prevent the enemy's entry into the mound itself. Even if every soldier and every worker in the colony were to perish in the struggle, there was still the chance that she, the young Queens and all the precious larvae might survive to build the settlement again.

The Queen of Queens listened in calm silence and when they had finished she touched both their antennae with her own in a gesture of royal blessing and said, "I know I can trust you, my brave soldiers, to do all in your power. Do not fear for us here. If the Lord of the Stars wills that it must be so, we are not afraid to die."

Then, as they were about to leave the chamber, Black Sting, almost as an afterthought, stopped and asked, "Great Mother, what do you know of the Giant Two-Legs?"

"Why do you ask?" she said.

"There is a rumour from one of the outer mounds that a creature sounding like the traditional description of the Giant Two-Legs has been sighted. It is probably just a wild story, but is it possible? Does such a creature really exist?"

The Queen of Queens was silent for a moment before she answered. "They are supposed to exist. I have never seen one myself but in the far colony where my own Great Mother, the Queen of All Queens was born, it was said that many ants knew of their existence. She often told me tales about them."

"Would you tell us about them?" asked Black Sting.

The four ants listened with rapt attention as the Queen of Queens recounted what she knew.

"It is said that they are truly gigantic. They do not in fact have only two legs. They have four, like the other huge animals of the forest and the grassland, but they have learnt to walk upright on only two and this gives them a height that puts their heads up amongst the branches of the trees themselves, almost some say, to the sun. Because of this, it is said, they are able to steal some of the light from the sun and use it at night to make their own suns, which roar and flash and give them light and warmth. It is also said that they have made themselves masters of the other great beasts and keep them as slaves, doing their work for them; and that they have immensely long stings, which shoot their poison with a deafening sound and with which they can kill a creature such as the Tawny Killer-Bird from a whole tree-length away. All this, as I say, is just legend to me, but I have heard it told many times."

After a moment Black Sting asked, "And are these monsters said to be the enemies of ants?"

The Queen of Queens replied, "It is said that they are so big that they do not even notice the existence of such as we upon the ground, but that they can crush whole colonies beneath their feet as they come without realizing it. It is said that they are concerned with such gigantic works upon the face of the world that we are specks of dust to them.'' Her voice carried a hint of amusement in the darkness. ''If such things are true, my splendid Black Sting, and one of these astounding creatures is indeed in the vicinity, then the problem of the red ants will be as a mere gust of wind in the grass.''

Black Sting saluted his Queen, and the little group took its leave of her.

That night the colony was to experience things which added a hundredfold to the legend about the Giant Two-Legs and which provided the source of stories which were told thereafter to generation after generation of ants.

It was the first really dark night for a long while, the moon and stars hidden for the most part by a wide blanket of cloud, which parted only intermittently to show brief glimpses of their still glimmering presence. The air was still relatively warm and dry for the time of year though, and the darkness provided good cover for an approaching force, so a constant guard was maintained outside in the forest and upon the barricades.

Not long after the darkness had fallen the lookout, whom Black Sting had placed upon the river bank came rushing back in a state of terrified excitement to report that some creature of gigantic size was indeed approaching up the stream. He had heard the sounds of its limbs splashing in the water, had glimpsed the flash of white spray in the current, and even claimed to have seen the beast's vast shadow silhouetted against the last gleam of twilight in the sky. The news spread like wildfire around the colony and every eye and every antenna was turned in the direction of the stream as often as towards the woods, when the red ants were expected to come.

Black Sting immediately set out further scouting parties along the stream bank and reports came back at frequent intervals verifying the first account. Whatever it was, however, did not seem to be making urgent progress, for it appeared to remain at one spot in the water for long periods, exploring the current with strange sweeping motions, before moving upstream again. None of the witnesses could give a satisfactory account of the creature, for it was right out in the deepest regions of the stream and the night was too dark for a clear sight, but all confirmed that it seemed to be a monster of colossal proportions.

The night was well progressed when the being finally arrived at their own stretch of water and then all talk of rumour and hallucination ceased. Every ant in the colony could hear and see and smell for himself that something of a size beyond comprehension was out there in the swirling currents. As it drew level with the mound at some distance out in the centre of the stream every tunnel mouth and vantage point, every grass clump, thicket and plant frond hid a myriad peering eyes and tensed antennae. All could hear the swish of angry water and see the white gleam of foam as the current came up against its great limbs; they could scent the strange, heavy odour hanging in the night air; and, most awe-inspiring of all, they caught glimpses, as the moonlight pierced the thin veil of cloud from time to time, of the towering silhouette, which seemed to be indulging in some weird personal ritual, waving and bowing above the waters and brandishing some immense antenna of its own, which hissed through the air with a fierce rhythmic sound, as if challenging the Lord of the Stars' own sovereignty over the ether.

Then the beast was past the mound and progressing round the curve of the stream to the other end of the clearing. And here a still more terrifying development took place, for the ants on guard at the barricades by the river bank and on the trail heading for the riverside mound were forced to scatter and flee as the monster loomed out of the water and clambered up on to the bank itself. Every creature in the clearing could feel the heavy vibration in the earth, as the great thing stomped ponderously about; they could hear the tearing of the undergrowth and the crash of breaking timber as it foraged around at the forest's edge; and they could see the vast shadow—a mere intensity of the blackness—moving against the trees' own dark background.

Then the shadow returned to the far side of the sombre mass where the gorse clump grew and here it disappeared from the immediate gaze of those on the mound itself. Watchers out in the clearing reported that it appeared to be settling for a rest, for it had lowered itself to a crouching position, and was busying itself with some relatively tranquil business amongst the grasses on the other side of the gorse. Then came the sight which seemed to verify the Queen of Queens' own stories of the Giant Two-Legs and caused a wave of awe and astonishment across the clearing. There was a harsh, rasping sound, a sudden flare of light through the fronds of the gorse bush, and then a steady glow, such as of a flickering earthbound sun, which grew and multiplied until it was a raging, crackling inferno, against which the monster's shadow was an unwordly silhouette, crouched as if in divine worship of its own miraculous creation.

Dreamer, out near the forest edge where he was commanding one of the advance defence-posts, gazed at the astonishing sight with a mixture of curiosity and wonder. Strangely he felt little fear, for the extraordinary vision seemed merely a culmination of the remarkable sequence of events that had swept him forward in their inexorable progress that spring; and, despite the drama of the occasion, he felt for some reason that there was no real threat in the arrival of this strange god of the river with his magical power of light. Not at any rate the sort of tangible threat that could be comprehended, such as that of the red ants. This was something far beyond the experience of any ant and beyond their power to react or defend themselves in any way, and therefore there was nothing to do but behold, and wonder and abandon oneself to whatever developments fate was contriving. Time passed, the light continued to leap and blaze and a pungent, choking scent filled the air, while the giant maintained his solitary watch at his creation's side. His strange rituals went on, seeming to involve dabblings in the very heart of the light itself, and resulting in further weird sounds and smells, but there never appeared any direct threat to the ants themselves or to their mound lurking beneath the branches of its beech tree at the end of the clearing.

Later in the night Dreamer was relieved and left his post under the command of another. He wandered across to the birch sapling, where he knew that Still One was spending the night, keeping watch over his precious herd. He climbed to the Story Teller's branch to find the latter amongst his aphid-bugs, quietly watching the vision by the river bank, which was very clear from this lofty viewpoint. The two ants stayed side by side for a long moment, staring at the scene.

Eventually Dreamer asked, "What is it, Still One? This is no phenomenon of the real world. Is it some visitation sent to warn us or to help us or to tell us something?"

The other was silent for the habitual moment and then replied, "I do not know. I only know that we know very little of the workings of the world, yet if we were able to understand them there is always a way they can be used for good somehow." He paused and stared at the light, its reflection flickering in his limpid eyes. "And if one fails to understand them, then it can mean destruction."

Dreamer pondered this for awhile. Then: "How can this be of advantage to us? Perhaps to frighten off The Spider, do you think?"

"I know no more than you do, Quick Feelers," replied the other. "But you can be sure the way is there and you can be sure the brain can find it if used well enough." He turned his calm gaze to Dreamer. "There is one thing I have discovered. The power of thought is the greatest power there is. There is nothing it cannot achieve, ultimately." He gazed back towards the light, and sighed.

"The trouble is, that word 'ultimately' is such a long, long time."

It was the first time Dreamer had ever seen a sign of uncertainty from Still One. He felt a great feeling of warmth for the gentle worker and touched his nearest antenna momentarily with his own. "Are you afraid of meeting The Spider, Still One?" he asked. "Do you wish it had not been you whom Black Sting chose?"

"Yes, I am afraid," said Still One simply.

"What will you say to him?"

The pause. "I do not know. The power of thought has not served me yet on that subject." A further silence. Then, in a still quieter tone: "The trouble is, I fear it might indeed be pure aggressive evil that we are up against—as in the story of the aphid-bugs and the rove beetles. And in that case my reason and my stories will be of no use against The Spider." Again he turned his look towards Dreamer. "Then it will be up to you soldiers to use your brains. It will require a different kind of thought power to mine."

Dreamer thought a little longer. "The power of thought," he murmured, savouring the phrase. "Is it greater than the power of the Lord of the Stars then, do you think?"

Still One did not answer. Dreamer went on: "Do you believe in the Lord of the Stars, Still One?"

Pause. "Why do you ask?"

"There is a red ant called Fleet, whom we got to know quite well whilst in captivity. Deep down one felt he is not unlike us. In different circumstances he could perhaps be a friend. There must be others like him. If the Lord of the Stars is really such a force for justice, how can he allow creatures like us to fight and wound and destroy each other?"

"Perhaps he wishes us to discover the futility of these things for ourselves."

"Ah," replied Dreamer, "but if we are to discover them for ourselves, what need have we of him at all?" He looked at Still One.

The other was regarding him with a hint of amusement in his eyes, as if to say, "You are learning. You are finding out."

Dreamer looked back towards the light. "There is a voice I hear in my dreams sometimes. A voice I seem to recognize, that constantly challenges and questions me. The Queen of Queens said she knew it. Do you know it, Still One? Is it the Lord of the Stars' voice?"

After a long moment Still One answered, "I will tell you one last story." He paused, as if remembering something from a long while ago. Then he went on:

"There was an ant who was plagued all his life by the Voice. It challenged him and worried him and questioned him, waking and sleeping. And at the end of his life, when he finally lay dying, he cried out to the Voice, 'Tell me before I die: are you the voice of the Lord of the Stars? I must know before I go.'

"And the Voice replied, 'If you believe it, then that is what I am.'

"And the ant cried, 'Can you prove it? Can you show yourself to me?'

"The Voice said, 'I can, but only if you believe in me.'

"The ant cried, 'Then show me! Reveal yourself!'

"The Voice said, 'I can only reveal myself if you truly believe. Look into your heart and ask yourself if you truly know that I am the Lord of the Stars, or if you doubt it.'

"So the ant did this. He looked into his heart and asked himself whether he truly believed. And when he had the answer he shouted, 'Yes! Yes, I know that you are the Lord of the Stars!'

"And the Voice came back, 'That is good. In that case there is no *need* for me to show myself, is there?'

"And the ant replied, 'No, there is no need.' And he died, content at last."

Silence, and the stillness of the forest, and the crackle of the dancing, magic light. Then Dreamer said, "And if he had not truly believed?"

"Then the answer would still have to be found."

Dreamer nodded and was silent. Then he said, "If we survive this night of the Giant Two-Legs, Still One—and if we still have to face the red ants—then I shall ask Black Sting if I may take you to meet The Spider. You should not have to go on your own and I am the only one who has met him."

"Thank you, Quick Feelers," said the other quietly. "I should be glad of that."

They said no more as the night blackened around the island of light and the myriad watching eyes.

* 23 *

He was alone in the centre of the clearing, alone except for a little group of larvae huddled beneath a dandelion leaf, the last survivors of all his kin. He knew he had to save them, or all was finished. Yet he was assailed from all sides by the most terrible of dangers. On one side loomed a huge, seething mass of red ants, with the gigantic figure of The Spider at their head; on another side leaped and crackled the angry, dazzling light, with the even more gigantic shadow of the Giant Two-Legs in its midst; on another side roared and tumbled the waters of an endless, bottomless flood; and on the fourth side advanced an army of terrible monsters: spiders and toads and Tawny Killer-Birds and many others, all fighting and clawing to be the first to get at him. Every way he turned one of the dangers reared to destroy him.

As they came closer and closer, he shouted above the horrendous din: "Have you left me then? Have you abandoned me at the last? What can I do now? Are we to perish after all?"

And the Voice came to him, rumbling through the tumult: "It is up to you. Think. Are they all truly your enemies? Is there no way out? Think. Remember what was said: 'The power of thought is the greatest power there is.' Think!"

And the Voice faded away as the monstrous forces approached.

* 24 *

He awoke in a terror to find himself still on the birch branch and the dawn edging up, the palest glow behind the trees, and with Still One resting nearby, watching him with his calm, humorous gaze. He shook the awful images from his mind and turned to look towards the gorse clump. There was no sign of the giant or of the leaping light, but instead there was a strange red glow lying along the ground, to show that that part at least had not been just a figment of the night's dreams. He looked back at Still One, his antennae cocked curiously.

"The Giant Two-Legs left while you were asleep," said Still One. "He simply rose and went back along the river bank and disappeared into the forest. But he left his light—which as you can see is dying without him."

Dreamer stared back at the strange glow. Though still weird and unearthly, there was a comforting warmth about it, which did not seem too threatening from this distance at any rate.

Still One was speaking again. "Did you have a very frightening dream?"

Dreamer looked back at him. "Yes," he answered. "The most frightening of all."

"I heard your Voice advising you. Was it of help?"

Dreamer was curious. "You heard?"

"Yes," said the other.

"Did you recognize the Voice?" asked Dreamer eagerly.

"Oh yes."

"Whose was it? Was it the Lord of the Stars?"

Still One gazed back with amusement. "The only voice I heard was yours," he said.

There was silence for a long while on the branch.

Then gradually Dreamer became aware that there was considerable activity going on beneath him on the ground, much scurrying hither and thither and a general feeling of urgency. "What is happening?" he asked.

"Messengers have come through, saying that the red ants are approaching," answered Still One. "They will probably be here by sun-up."

Dreamer came instantly alert. "I must go down," he said. "Are you coming?"

"I shall follow shortly," was the reply. "You go ahead, Quick Feelers. You will be needed."

Dreamer touched the smaller ant's feelers briefly with his own and an unspoken message passed between them as their eyes met. Then he turned, threaded his way through the grazing aphid-bugs and descended the tree.

Amongst the grasses on the ground, in the dim light of the approaching dawn, all was alertness and tension. The piles of twigs and debris had already been heaved into place across the trails and the front line of defence, some way back from the actual forest edge, was ready with soldiers and workers side by side behind the barricades. Dreamer strode along it checking that all was well, that every ant knew his task. In the distance he could see Black Sting's lofty form, with several officers in attendance, moving briskly from position to position, inspecting, questioning, encouraging.

Dreamer did not go to join them immediately, however. First, out of sheer curiosity, he went across the clearing towards the stream and the gorse clump, where the strange red light gleamed between the grass stems and a peculiar wisp of grey spiralled up towards the fading stars like some concentrated stream of the dawn mist itself.

As he approached he noticed that the air appeared to be getting miraculously warmer, until eventually the heat was almost oppressive in its force. The choking scent too was increasing in strength, blotting out all others with its pungency. He finally broke out of the grasses altogether to find himself in a wide, clear space at the gorse's side, where the grass stems had been trampled and flattened into the dust and in the centre of which loomed the wide, glowing mound of red light, perhaps half the height and twice the width of their own hillock. Around its circumference were scattered groups of curious ants like himself, staring with wonderment into the heart of the living light, yet held back from approaching closely by fear and the intense all-enveloping heat.

Dreamer noticed a group of the older worker-ants nearby, with Five-Legs, Never-Rest, and Wind-Blow amongst them and he went to join them.

"What do you make of it, Five Legs?" he asked as he came up.

The old ant turned towards him. "I have never seen the like. It is extraordinary," he responded. "Even the sun cannot give such warmth as this. It is so powerful that one can only approach so far. If one went any closer I'm sure one would perish." He gazed back at the light. "And yet the strange thing is that it does not seem to threaten us, provided we keep our distance."

There was a sudden flare of whiter light and a crackle from the centre of the mound.

"There goes another one!" cried Wind-Blow excitedly.

"That is an oak twig—look! It is vanishing into the light, just like the others."

"The others?" asked Dreamer, staring at the white flare.

"The light appears to consume things," said Five Legs. "We noticed that the Giant Two-Legs fed it with things from out of the woods—huge branches, dead bushes and leaves and grasses from the ground—and it consumed them all. And the more he put into the light, the fiercer it grew. But now he is not here to feed it, it is dying."

Dreamer studied the surroundings of the glowing mound and indeed it seemed that for many ant-lengths all around the ground was bare. All the grass and the plants and even the humus from the previous year had been devoured by the raging beast of light and nothing was left but an odd grey-black dust, lying deathlike about the living centre. He noticed a tall stem of sedge-grass standing nearby, withered and browned by the heat, leaning in towards it and swaying, as if drawn towards the supernatural power despite itself. He shuddered to think what such a force would do to a living body that came within its grasp.

Then he remembered his dream. What was it the Voice had said? "Think. Are they all truly your enemies? Think." He thought, staring into the mysterious golden glow, but nothing came to him. He turned towards Five Legs.

"What will you do when the red ants come, old one?" he asked.

Five Legs stared over towards the forest edge.

"Oh, we shall be here," he said. "We may not be much good for fighting, but we can help to hold up the barricades, swell the numbers, encourage the young ones." He looked at Dreamer, his eyes challenging. "Don't you worry, young Quick Feelers, we can be of use."

Dreamer nodded, admiring the old ant's fighting spirit. Then he looked once more at the great vapour-emitting mound of light, turned his back on its heat and went to join Black Sting.

*   *   *

The red ants came just as the sun was clearing the far trees on the other side of the stream and the usual morning breeze had sprung up, blowing across the clearing from the direction of the water and rustling the undergrowth out of which they appeared. The advance lookouts had come rushing back some time before, warning of their approach, so all were ready and silent, the sickening sense of apprehension mounting inside them.

None, however, except perhaps Dreamer, could have anticipated the fearful effect of that first appearance of the enemy army. One moment there was nothing except for a faint vibration and rustle amongst the undergrowth and the hint of a strange, thick scent in the air, the next there were rank upon rank of huge, long-legged, russet-bodied insects, materialized as if by magic out of the trees and standing silent, motionless, staring back at the defenders with scarcely the flicker of an antenna to indicate that they were alive.

There was a murmur and an uneasy stirring amongst the smaller ants, gathered behind their barricades. A long moment passed as the two armies faced each other and then there came a movement and a breaking of ranks in the centre of the first line of the red ants. Another gasp of incredulity rippled through the defenders as a stupendous figure loomed behind the line, broke through the gap and stood before it, breath hissing, huge head swaying from side to side, eyes gleaming with malevolent triumph as it surveyed the scene. At the monster's side, dwarfed by the towering body, stood Fleet and several other senior red soldiers. It was evident that, from where they stood, they were unaware of the slumbering mound of light through the grasses on their flank, for none looked in that direction, and none seemed to observe the strange scent in the air.

Having seen what he wished to see, The Spider lifted his head and roared, "Who speaks for you puny creatures?"

Almost opposite him, in the centre of the defenders' line of barricades, Dreamer and Still One stood with Black

Sting and his small band of officers. Dreamer looked at his leader and Black Sting nodded imperceptibly. He touched both the smaller ants' antennae briefly with his own, then they passed him and squeezed through a narrow gap in the barrier of twigs and grass and stood looking through the grass stems towards the line of red ants ahead.

Dreamer looked at the other. "Here we go, Story Teller," he said softly.

"I am with you, my friend," answered Still One.

Dreamer led the way through the grass towards the huge figure. He came to within three ordinary ant-lengths and stopped. He was standing on the very edge of the Spider's shadow which spread over the ground before him. Dreamer looked towards Fleet—their eyes met briefly—then the red ant turned his away and stared ahead without expression. Dreamer looked back at The Spider, aware of Still One's presence at his side.

The enemy leader nodded with a flicker of ironical amusement, the weird bronchial hiss of his breathing grating harshly upon the hearing organs of the two ants facing him.

"So, you managed to escape back to your colony after all," he growled. "You were indeed lucky."

Dreamer said nothing, merely waited, trying to appear as calm and confident as possible.

"Not that it makes any difference in the end," went on The Spider. "For here we are, as I promised."

"Here you are," replied Dreamer.

The Spider lowered his head aggressively. "However, I have no wish to see *you* again. Where is your leader? Who is your spokesman? I wish to speak with someone of importance."

Dreamer half turned and indicated Still One at his side with a feeler. "This is our spokesman," he said. "You may speak with him."

The Spider stared at the insignificant, fragile figure with incredulity. "This?" he rasped. "This pathetic thing is your leader?"

"Our leader is back there with the soldiers," replied Dreamer. "This is the one he wishes you to talk with. His name is Still One."

The Spider stared again at Still One's immobile form, the incomprehension still showing in his eyes. "Why?" he roared. "Why should I speak with this feeble creature? Is your leader afraid to meet me?"

"Black Sting is afraid of nothing on this earth," said Dreamer, "as you will discover if we have to fight you. However, he is hoping that will not be necessary. He believes that is the foolish way. That is why he has sent Still One to talk with you. We call him the Story Teller. He has a wisdom far beyond his size."

"Has he indeed?" rasped The Spider derisively. "The Story Teller, eh? Well, I can tell you now there are no stories that can save you from what I have in mind. Only miracles." He glowered down at Still One from his great height. "Do you have any miracles that you can perform, friend Teller-of-Stories?"

"No," answered Still One simply.

"Then come forward and tell me what you have to tell. And you'd better make it short because I get impatient with timewasters."

Still One stepped forward from Dreamer's side, right into the shadow of the great beast before him. He looked up the immense head and waited, in that powerful, quiescent way of his. A long moment passed, the other growing more and more impatient as he looked into the all-seeing eyes.

Finally The Spider roared, "Well?"

"What is it you want from us?" asked Still One quietly.

The malicious gleam in The Spider's eyes hardened. "What is it I want?" he repeated. "I want everything."

"What do you mean by everything?"

"What do you think I mean?" bellowed The Spider angrily. "Everything means everything!"

Still One's voice rose not a fraction. "If you want food we can give it. If you want space, we can give it. If you want knowledge, we can give it. If you want friendship, we can give it." He paused. The Spider was silent, staring down at him, a vague puzzlement on his face. "If you want our freedom, our souls, our lives—those we will not give. Those you must take."

The Spider growled deep in his throat. "And why should I not take them?"

"You may of course take them. You are more powerful in strength than we are. But the cost will be terrible."

The Spider snorted derisively. "The cost? A few dead soldiers. What of that? They are prepared to die. They are trained for death."

"How strange," replied Still One. "Ours are trained for life." He paused and glanced along the line of red soldiers. "That is what I mean by the cost."

The Spider glowered at him with incomprehension. "I do not understand you," he said.

"Have you looked at our home?" answered Still One. He turned his head and gazed around the clearing, his antennae raised. "Have you ever seen such a beautiful place? Can you smell the sweetness in its air? Can you sense the industry and the energy that has gone into creating it? Can you feel the contentment of the generations of ants who have lived here?" He looked back at The Spider. "All this we would share with you, if you wished it. All this will vanish, leaving only bareness and waste, if you abuse us."

The Spider nodded his huge head, his confidence returned. "It is indeed a pleasant spot," he said. "That is why we want it for ourselves. It is not the place itself we wish to destroy, friend Teller-of-Stories, only the vermin who inhabit it." He lowered his head until it was on a level with Still One's, like an oak tree bending to a dandelion. "It is no use. You cannot snare me with clever morals as your friend Tongue-of-the-Snake tried to do. I do not give way to talks."

"To what do you give way?" asked Still One softly.

The Spider lifted his head again and shouted at the

heavens: "To nothing! I give way to nothing, except to eventual death! That is the only way to prove that one is alive."

There was a hush across the whole clearing. Even the breeze seemed stilled for a moment. Then Still One said, "Will you hear one of my stories then?"

The Spider looked at him with incredulity on his face. Then he broke into a great shaking bellow of amusement. "Very well, let me hear one of these remarkable stories. It will be the last you will ever tell, so make it a good one. Make it a story to end all stories!"

Silence. The Story Teller stood still, tranquil as the moon. Then he spoke.

"Once there lived a huge beast in the forest. Larger than all the other creatures, larger than the four-legged ones, larger even than the Giant Two-Legs. So large that the trees seemed as blades of grass to him and the rocks as mere pebbles on the ground. And this creature looked about him and thought to himself, 'There is no other creature upon the earth greater than I. I am the Lord of all.' And any creature who dared to disagree with him, or who hindered him, or who crossed him in any way at all, he crushed to death with a single blow of his huge claws, or a single bite of his immense jaws.

"But because he was so vast and so powerful, there were none whom he could call friends. All the other beasts were too afraid of him, or too small even to speak with him. So the giant was extremely lonely and grew more and more angry in his loneliness. And the angrier he became, the more ferocious he became; and the more ferocious he became, the more the other beasts feared him, and so the more lonely still he became, until he was a towering pillar of anger. And he went on the rampage through the forest, killing every living thing in his fury, until there was nothing left alive. Then he sat down upon the ground, utterly sick in his heart, so alone was he in his loneliness.

"But then, as he sat there, he noticed upon a leaf a single tiny aphid-bug, that was so small he had missed it in his rampage of death. So he picked the leaf and held it up to his face and roared at the aphid-bug, 'So, you have escaped my wrath! Now you and I are the only creatures alive in the forest. What do you say to that?'

"And the aphid-bug replied, 'There is nothing to say to that.'

"And the giant said to the aphid-bug, 'Am I not huge? Am I not splendid? Am I not the most powerful creature you have ever seen?'

"And the aphid-bug replied, 'Indeed you are.'

"And the giant said, 'Do you not wish that you were me?'

"And the aphid-bug replied, 'No, certainly not. I would much rather be me.'

"Then the giant was amazed and demanded to know why. So the aphid-bug said, 'Because I have known peace which you have never known. I have seen the beauty of the pimpernel flower, which is too small for you to notice. I have felt the warmth of the sun, which you have been too hot in your fury to feel. I have enjoyed the company of friends, who have had nothing to fear from me. I have known the pleasure of sharing my honey-dew, which you have always been in too much hurry to taste. . . . Because I have known happiness in my smallness and you have known only anger in your greatness.'

"And at these words the giant was so furious that, without thinking, he hurled the leaf with the aphid-bug upon it up, up into the sky, over the trees and out of the world itself.

"And then, his anger cooled, he looked about him and realized that instead of being lord of everything, he was now suddenly lord of nothing. For there was nothing left of which to be the lord."

Still One stood looking up at the lowering head above him and for a moment time was stilled. Dreamer could sense The Spider fighting a terrible battle within himself. Then the huge ant gave a deafening bellow of rage and he knew that he had lost.

Before anyone could make a move The Spider had grasped Still One about the thorax, easily encircling the slender body with his mandibles. He lifted him high into the air, snapped him in two like a dry straw, and with a toss of the head flung the broken body far away from him, over Dreamer's antennae towards the defending lines. It fell amongst the brittle grasses and lay there like some shrivelled autumn leaf, brown, dust-covered, already part of the earth from which it had sprung.

Dreamer did not move, so great was the shock. He stood transfixed, staring at the crumpled object, his senses numbed, scarcely aware even of the universal sigh of horror that had gone up from the ranks of his own kind. Then, slowly reality returned, and awareness. He turned his head and looked back at The Spider. The latter was regarding him with an anger such as he had never seen in his eyes, an anger that challenged him to show a flicker of reproach. But Dreamer felt no fear. Now nothing mattered any more. If such an act could take place upon the earth, then it would be no sacrifice to leave it.

The words of one of Still One's stories came into his mind, as if spoken with the Story Teller's own gentle inflections: "Because he was content in his heart he was not afraid of death, for he had found the meaning of life." And he did not feel sadness for the murdered ant, or fear for himself, or regret for his colony. He felt only a great calm. He looked up at The Spider, then across at Fleet, who was staring at the corpse with a dazed expression on his face, then round at the immobile ranks of the red ants. Finally he looked back at their leader and said quietly, "So, you have made the story come true."

Without waiting for the reaction, he turned and started back towards his own lines. As he went he heard a snort and a movement behind, but with utter coolness he half turned and almost matter-of-factly evaded The Spider's clumsy lunge toward him. He danced back out of range and then turned again and sped back, leaving the monster raging and hissing in his rear.

He reached the first barricade and squeezed through the gap. Black Sting was there and the two exchanged a glance that said all there was to say. The same look was in the eyes of all the defenders as Dreamer passed them on his way to his own spot further down the line.

The red ants attacked almost instantly. They waited until their leader had retreated back behind the front lines and then, at some signal that was not apparent to the onlookers, they launched themselves forward with phenomenal speed across the intervening ground.

It was as well that Black Sting had thought out his tactics and prepared the barricades, for there was no way that his forces would ordinarily have halted such an onrush. As it was the larger ants came up against the barriers of tangled matter and for a while were vulnerable as they clawed and struggled to surmount them. The defenders were able to wait and pick them off as they tumbled down the other side in ones and twos, or clambered clumsily through the centre. In such a position they were not easily able to bring their lethal sprays of poison to bear as they were set upon by swarming parties of brown ants, and the advance ranks suffered fearful damage. However, their great size and strength, and the apparently endless reinforcement of their numbers began to tell eventually. The barriers began to crumble and break down in places and here and there small groups of the enemy broke through and came skirmishing along behind the lines, diverting the defence. The line began to disintegrate.

Dreamer, commanding one of the major barricades across a main trail, took little part in the actual fighting at this stage. He conserved strength and poison, knowing that his turn would come in time, and he concentrated his energies on commanding his force, striding back and forth behind the barrier, encouraging here, exhorting there, ordering extra defenders to one spot or a team of workers with materials to reinforce another. Over towards the centre of the line he was aware of Black Sting doing the same, marching up and down at the back of his forces with calm, calculated authority, holding the precarious line by sheer force of will.

Behind the first barriers was a further line, and behind that more still, but these were not of the same size and strength as the first and would only serve as temporary delaying points. Then there was only Noble and his Royal Guard, waiting patiently on the flanks of the mound itself—surveying the battle from afar—between the red hordes and the royal brood chambers, and the Queen of Queens herself. The thought did not bear considering and Dreamer shook it from his head and bent himself to his task with renewed energy.

A fresh wave of the enemy was assaulting his barricade, shaking its structure, tumbling clumsily down from its height, and for the first time he took a part in the actual fighting, leaping upon a big red soldier who looked as if he might be getting the better of the two defenders, hanging on to his limbs and biting viciously at the vulnerable joint between head and thorax with his mandibles. Still he did not employ his sting, for his supply of poison was limited and he knew he would have all too great a need of it in time. The red soldier quickly succumbed under the combined attack of all three defenders and Dreamer returned to his task of command, but the incident was indicative of the general way the battle was going and he was forced to add his own strength and speed to the defence with greater and greater frequency.

Then there came a series of shouts and a commotion from nearby on the flank and he saw that the barrier across the trail next to his own had given way completely, the enemy soldiers swarming through in large numbers, fanning out to right and left and sweeping along behind the line in a destructive wave. Defenders from that barrier and from the grass forest in between were rushing back towards the next line in a panic and scrambling to get over, while the lofty figures of the red soldiers ran amok amongst them, picking them off and felling them with great snaps of their mandibles. Dreamer saw that the time had come to retreat himself and he ordered his contingent back to the second line. They sprinted back along the trail and scrambled over or round through the grass stems, with attackers hot on their heels. And there the fight began again: the same onslaught on the barriers, the same temporary stemming of the tide, the same gradual breaking through and overwhelming with size and numbers.

As the defenders retreated bit by bit towards their mound, they left the relinquished ground littered with the bodies of their soldiers. Increasingly the lines had to be reinforced with workers, resolute and prepared to give their all but smaller and inexperienced in battle. The ranks were condensing now as they converged towards the hillock—they were perhaps halfway back across the clearing—and the battle became fiercer and more concentrated as the numbers compressed. The commanders, Dreamer included, were fully involved now, with all pretence at an ordered defence gone. It was every ant for himself, biting, clinging, stinging, while the blood ran and the grasses shuddered, the reeking scent of poison clogged the air and the dust rose in clouds to obscure the sunlight.

Once more Dreamer felt as if it was all a part of one of his dreams. His mind became detached like some outside observer, aware of the pain and the exhaustion of his struggling body, yet somehow uninvolved, unaffected by the torment. It noted the fury and the madness all around; it beheld the weird, writhing shapes upon the ground, the giant figures of the enemy looming out of the dust; it was aware of his own moves, lunging, clawing, retreating; yet it remained totally cool, unmoved, objective, as if waiting for some signal that it knew would come to put an end to all this; some indication from an outside power which would show him the simple gesture that was needed to still the insanity at an instant.

As he fought he was aware of the general course of events around him. He caught glimpses of the gigantic shadow of The Spider towering behind his forces, roaring and goading but rarely participating directly in the fight; he

was conscious of a sudden rally amongst his own side as
Noble and many of the Royal Guard, unable to stand by
and observe any longer, came charging into the fray; he
recognized the figure of Fleet, bespattered with blood and
dust yet still swift and graceful as ever, swooping upon
that other personification of strength and agility, Black
Sting; and he watched the two superbly matched individuals embark on a private battle in the midst of the war,
which could well determine the outcome of both.

And, in a way, it did. Dreamer only caught movements
of that stupendous personal contest—quick flashes in the
midst of his own desperate encounters—but he was aware,
as were all in the vicinity, that the crucial hub of the whole
conflict was here between these two champions. As if in
recognition of this a space was cleared around them and no
attempt made to interfere with their single combat. And
when, after a seemingly interminable struggle in which the
speed of the movements, the ferocity of the grapples,
the raised flurries of dust and debris, all served to confuse the eye and even to prevent individual identification
of the two opponents—when at last both lay still, entwined
as if in a loving embrace, with Fleet's jaws locked about
Black Sting's throat and Black Sting's pointed sting embedded deep in Fleet's underbelly—when the two ants who
perhaps most of all should have been friends and accom-
plices in achievement, had finally succeeded in bringing
about each other's death—then Dreamer knew that all
hope for a just outcome to the day was gone, all attempts
at a natural solution doomed, and that the only thing that
could avert the final cataclysm was some supernatural
stroke beyond the imagination of ordinary ants.

He broke away from the battle which still continued—
the defenders, now under Noble's leadership, determined
to fight on to the death. He staggered, injured in a dozen
places and so exhausted that his legs could scarcely support him, in a daze towards the only nearby landmark that
he could recognize: the uneven outline of the gorse clump.
He scarcely knew why—he was beyond rational thought—

but some instinct directed his wavering steps, and as he went, evading the struggling bodies, scrambling over the trampled grasses, brief flashes of broken sentences drifted through his brain; voices speaking to him from out of the entangled mists of his experience.

There was Still One's voice, saying: "You can be sure there is a way, and you can be sure the brain can find it if used well enough. . . ."

There was the Voice of his dreams, saying: "At the last, in the midst of the great endeavour of all, you may find your purpose. . . ."

There was Black Sting: "We may have to die in the end, but we are not afraid to. For it has been a good life. . . ."

There was the Queen of Queens: "If one of these astounding creatures is indeed in the vicinity, then the problem of the red ants will be as a mere gust of wind in the grass. . . ."

There was Still One again: "The power of thought is the greatest power there is. . . ."

There was his own Voice again: "Think! Are they all truly your enemies? Is there no way out? Think!"

And suddenly, out of the confusion of his mind, he knew. He knew what it was he had to do. He knew the terrible deed that was necessary to save the last vestiges of his world from the total destruction that threatened it. The knowledge did not come as some new, blinding revelation. Like all great ideas, once realized it seemed so simple, so obvious, it was as if it had always been there, always a part of his understanding—it was simply that it was too enormous a concept to grasp under ordinary circumstances.

With calm determination now he increased his pace towards the gorse clump. There Old Five Legs, Never-Rest, Wind-Blow and several others of the older worker-ants had made their headquarters and were tending wounded and dying ants beneath the gorse fronds, while waiting calmly for the battle to engulf them. They stared as the bloody, dust-covered figure staggered out of the ferment towards them.

"Come with me, old ones," said Dreamer and there was no disobeying the authority in his voice. Blankly, accepting of whatever it was fate might now have in store for them, they followed.

He led the way beneath the gorse bush and out at the side, where the line of the river bank could be seen some little way off and the low mound of the Giant Two-Legs' mystical creation still glowed faintly, a dull, angry, red glimmer amongst the flaky grey dust that was all that remained of the vegetation it had consumed. Here the battle was sparse and intermittent—only the occasional isolated pursuit and skirmish—for the place was out of the direct line between the forest and the base-mound, and the still considerable heat emitted by the strange hill kept most of the fighting ants at a distance.

Without hesitation Dreamer led his little band towards the tall landmark of the isolated sedge grass stem which he had noticed on his earlier visit, standing beside the mound. Browned and withered by the Giant Two-Legs' heat, as well as by the unseasonal drought, it leaned precariously in towards the light, as if wishing too to be consumed like its brothers. Ignoring the blistering temperature, Dreamer went up to it and examined the stem. It was twice as thick as the body of an ant but the outer casing was brittle and fragile.

He turned and gestured to the following ants with his feelers. "Cut this down!" he ordered.

The old workers came forward, hunched against the barrage of heat, and without questioning the command they began to gnaw at the trunk with their mandibles. Dreamer glanced round for signs of any red ants who might interfere, but all seemed preoccupied with the victorious onrush towards the base-mound.

He commanded the two or three remaining worker-ants who could not find room at the grass stem: "Bring straw, grass, dead leaves—anything!"—and, as they hurried to obey, turned himself to do likewise. Grasping at bits of dry grass, twigs, anything that could be moved, he toiled with the last remains of his strength to pile them at the base of the sedge-grass stem, and from there in a jumbled line projecting into the forest of grass itself.

As he worked two red ants suddenly appeared out of the grasses in pursuit of a stumbling brown soldier and hesitated at the sight of the little group toiling before the weird, glowing hill; but Dreamer came at them with such a display of ferocity that they turned from his wild, threatening figure—approaching as if out of the very source of the heat itself—and continued their chase towards safer parts.

Then Five Legs called to Dreamer, "It's about to go!"

Dreamer turned back as the stem creaked and leaned in still further from the partly severed base of its trunk. Old Five Legs was looking at him with a questioning expression in his eyes and the other old ants too were hanging back as if waiting for his final command. Dreamer gazed at Five Legs with a calm reassurance.

"This is the only way, Five Legs," he said. "I don't know what will happen, but the Giant Two-Legs' power was sent to help us, I'm sure of that. We may all have to die together in his light, but I think Our Great Mother may be saved."

Five Legs nodded and touched Dreamer's feelers with his own in the briefest of salutes, then turned back to the grass stem. The others joined him and together, heaving and biting, they completed their work. The stem shuddered and tottered—its heavy, feathered head outlined against the sky—and then tumbled in towards the red glow.

There was a crash as it landed and a cloud of grey dust, a momentary, trembling pause and then a flare of whiter light, bursting out with an angry hiss. The flare grew, dazzling in its intensity, seeming to envelop the entire head of the plant. The ants drew back as it ran towards them along the stem with ferocious speed, bringing an increase in the heat with it. It stuck the little pile of collected debris at the base and blazed up again, white and yellow, dancing and crackling like a living thing. It leapt along the line of dead matter, sending minor tentacles of light skirmishing out amongst the living grasses. The prevailing breeze from the river urged it on away from the bank and Dreamer and his band of workers fled instinctively round the outskirts of the mound towards the water to escape the spreading menace.

They watched, trapped between the water and the light, as the latter ran wild amongst the grass, leapt and spread with exultant abandon, rushed at every clump and thicket like an invading army, mad with victory. An arm reached the gorse clump, jumped across empty air from the grass to the hanging fronds, hung there for a moment as if securing its grasp, and then flared jubilantly and sped along the branches towards the centre. There came a tremendous *woomph!*—the very air shuddered as it was sucked in from all around—and the entire bush exploded in a great blaze of light and sound, while rolling clouds of the grey mist swirled skywards, signalling the eruption to the world.

The ants across the clearing ceased in the midst of their struggles and stared in wonder at the awe-inspiring beacon. They hesitated, wondering what it signified, until the shouts and screams of those nearest the phenomenon made them aware that a wide wall of the magical light was racing across the grass towards them. The blazing sun that had been the gorse clump leapt and roared behind, exhorting the wall forward as The Spider had done in the wake of his own forces. All turned and began to race away: towards the trees, towards the mound, towards anywhere that seemed to offer sanctuary.

But there was no escape. Faster than any attacking wave of red ants could travel, the leaping bulwark of light swept ahead of the breeze, consuming grass, plants, ants— everything that stood in its path. The fleeing insects were overtaken, engulfed and melted like so many drops of honey-dew; the entwined bodies of Black Sting and Fleet and the crumpled corpse of Still One evaporated as though they had never been; the barriers, the trails, the nodding spring flowers, were eradicated like rain from a smooth rock surface; Noble and his Royal Guard, racing for the mound, were overtaken and consumed in an instant; and The Spider, stumbling and bellowing before his shattered army back towards the forest, was seized by huge, greedy mandibles of light, devoured, digested and vomited skywards as so many tiny particles of dust.

The blazing wall traversed the clearing in less time than it takes an ant to climb a stem of willow-herb, and then it thundered into the forest, crackling and dwindling amongst the trees. . . .

* 25 *

He was the centre of a whirling sun. He was at the very heart of the leaping, living light. The light blinded his eyes with its whiteness and the heat scoured his body with its agony. But he was not afraid.

And he called out: "Are you there? Are you there in the light? Speak to me!"

But there was nothing. Only the roaring of the light, and the dazzling whiteness, and the searing, cleansing heat. And then it was that he knew.

And he rose up in the midst of the light; and stood triumphantly; and called out: "I have thought the thoughts. I have ridden the waters. I have harnessed the light. I have defeated our enemies. And, in the midst of life and of death, for good or for evil, I am the Voice!"

And his words echoed and re-echoed around the wild pillars of light: "I am the Voice . . . I am the Voice . . . I am the Voice. . . ."

Then the blazing heat of the light merged with the swirling cool of the waters and there was nothing. . . .

* **26** *

It had been a mild winter and the Long Sleep ended early that year. The big mound by the marshes came to bustling life with a large proportion of its population having survived the dark months. It was therefore well equipped to send out exploration parties and extend its boundaries. The season was well advanced when a small expeditionary party, travelling further afield than most, came upon a strange region within the forest. The undergrowth was dead and blackened, twisted into gaunt shapes; the ground was charred and dormant; the very trees themselves were scorched and seared about their trunks, and their lower branches withered, as if they had been assailed by some giant, unearthly force.

The small party of ants picked their way wonderingly over the black earth between the sparse new shoots of greenery that were struggling to rise in that blighted place. Eventually they came to an open clearing in the trees, where the sound and scent of water drifted as a cleansing strain from the far side. Like the wooded region the space was a ravaged spot, blackened and charred by some fearful holocaust, but the grasses were struggling to reassert themselves, the occasional hardy shoot of bracken or hesitant cowslip rising above the desolation, and on the farther side the barren skeleton of what had once been a gorse bush was showing flashes of green around its base.

Strangely there was a considerable amount of activity in the area. A scattering of ants of their own species was busy about the place: scavenging, digging, clearing. Their base was evidently a large blackened mound at the far end of the clearing and it was towards this that the newcomers directed their steps. As they went they noticed with curiosity that the ants about them were almost all youngsters, few being more than a summer old. Just here and there was an occasional older ant, supervising operations.

The party arrived at the mound and enquired where they might find someone in authority. They were directed towards a run up the flank of the hillock and, climbing it, arrived at the entrance to a tunnel about halfway up, where an ant sat warming himself in the pale spring sunshine. He was of uncertain age, for his skin was withered and scorched like that of the trees they had passed and his antennae were shrivelled to mere stumps upon his head, but he was evidently considerably older than the majority. He turned his head towards the newcomers as they approached, straining to pick up their scent with his impaired feelers, and then it was that they realized he could not see.

The leader came up to him and enquired as to whether he was the chief.

"We have no chief," replied the sightless one.

"No chief?" was the puzzled answer. "But who then is leader of your colony?"

"We have no need of a leader," came the reply. "We make our decisions in Council together." His clouded eyes showed a twinkle of amusement. "But I have some influence. You may speak with me."

The other explained his party's presence there and the older ant bade them welcome. Then the first ant turned and indicated the surroundings with his feelers, forgetting that his gesture could not be seen. "This is a strange place," he said.

The older ant replied, "Perhaps—to you." He turned his sightless gaze towards the tall line of trees on the far side. "Believe it or not this used to be the most beautiful spot you could imagine. One day it will be so again, though probably I am too old to witness that."

"Why do you stay here?" asked the visitors' leader.

"Because it is our home," answered the other simply.

"What happened to make it like this?"

"Ah, that is a long story. A story which you may find hard to believe."

The visitor then looked across the clearing. "Why are most of your ants young ones?" he asked.

"The old ones are all gone. All perished. Only myself and a few lucky ones left."

The others looked at him curiously. "What do they call you?"

The sparkle of humour showed again through the opaqueness of the older ant's eyes. "They still call me Quick Feelers," he replied, "out of kindness I suspect." He anticipated the other's puzzled glance at his withered stumps and added, "You may call me Dreamer if you prefer."

The visitor nodded. "Well, Dreamer, if there is anything our colony can do to help . . ."

"Thank you," was the reply, "but I think we can manage. We have survived this far; I think the future is bright now."

The small group exchanged perplexed glances at the thought of anyone considering the future bright amongst such desolation.

"How many Queens have you?" asked one. "Have they survived?"

There was a look of calm satisfaction on the disfigured ant's face. "We have several Queens, all as healthy as could be. And we have a Queen of Queens who is older than you or I could imagine, and who has the wisdom of the world in her head, and who is as the shining moon to us.''

Again they stared. Their leader hesitated and then said, ''Won't you tell us what happened? We would like to hear.''

The ant called Dreamer pondered a moment, scratched one of his feeler stumps with a forefoot and peered up at the sun. ''Well,'' he said eventually, ''if you have plenty of time . . .''

''Oh yes,'' said the others together, ''we are in no hurry.''

He gazed into the distance. ''Then I will tell you a story.'' He paused, deep in thought. There was a strange, still quality about him, which they did not think to interrupt. He began: ''There was once a thriving colony of ants, who lived in a great mound beside the singing waters of a stream . . .''

BESTSELLING BOOKS FROM TOR

THE BEST IN FANTASY

☐ 53954-0 SPIRAL OF FIRE by Deborah Turner Harris $3.95
    53955-9   Canada $4.95

☐ 53401-8 NEMESIS by Louise Cooper (U.S. only) $3.95

☐ 53382-8 SHADOW GAMES by Glen Cook $3.95
    53381-X   Canada $4.95

☐ 53815-5 CASTING FORTUNE by John M. Ford $3.95
    53826-1   Canada $4.95

☐ 53351-8 HART'S HOPE by Orson Scott Card $3.95
    53352-6   Canada $4.95

☐ 53397-6 MIRAGE by Louise Cooper (U.S. only) $3.95

☐ 53671-1 THE DOOR INTO FIRE by Diane Duane $2.95
    53672-X   Canada $3.50

☐ 54902-3 A GATHERING OF GARGOYLES by Meredith Ann Pierce $2.95
    54903-1   Canada $3.50

☐ 55614-3 JINIAN STAR-EYE by Sheri S. Tepper $2.95
    55615-1   Canada $3.75